HE STARTED IT

HE STARTED IT

SAMANTHA DOWNING

THORNDIKE PRESS
A part of Gale, a Cengage Company

GALE
A Cengage Company

LIBRARY OF CONGRESS CIP DATA ON FILE.
CATALOGUING IN PUBLICATION FOR THIS BOOK
IS AVAILABLE FROM THE LIBRARY OF CONGRESS

ISBN-13: 978-1-4328-7866-5 (hardcover alk. paper)

Published in 2020 by arrangement with Berkley, an imprint of Penguin Publishing Group, a division of Penguin Random House LLC

Printed in Mexico
Print Number: 01   Print Year: 2020

HE STARTED IT

PART 1

PART 1

14 Days Left

You want a heroine. Someone to root for, to identify with. She can't be perfect, though, because that'll just make you feel bad about yourself. A flawed heroine, then. Someone who may break the rules to protect her family but doesn't kill anyone unless it's self-defense. Not murder, though, at least not the cold-blooded kind. That's the first deal breaker.

The second is cheating. Men can get away with that and still be the hero, but a cheating wife is unforgivable.

Which means I can't be your heroine.

I still have a story to tell.

It begins in a car. Rather, an SUV. We sit according to our rank, the oldest in the driver's seat. That's Eddie. His wife sits next to him, but I'll get to her.

The middle seat is for the middle child, and that's me. Beth. Not Elizabeth, just

Beth. I'm two years younger than Eddie and he never lets me forget it. I'm okay to look at, though not as young or thin as I used to be. My husband sits next to me. Again, later for that, because our spouses weren't supposed to be here.

One seat left, way in the back, and that's Portia. The surprise baby. She's six years younger than me and sometimes it feels like a hundred. With no spouse or significant other, she has the whole seat to herself.

In the very back, our luggage. Stacked side by side in a neat single row because that's the only way it fits. I told Eddie that the first time. Our handbags and computers bags go on top of the roller bags. You don't have to be a flight attendant to figure that out.

Under the bags, there's the trunk compartment. One side has the spare tire. In the other, a locked wooden box with brass fittings. This special little box in this special little place, all by itself with nothing else around, is to hold our grandfather. He's been cremated.

We aren't talking about him. We aren't really talking at all. The sun beams through the windows, landing on my leg and making it burn. The A/C dries out my eyes. Eddie plays music that is wordless and jazzy.

I look back at Portia. Her eyes are closed and she has headphones on, probably listening to music that is neither wordless nor jazzy. Her black hair is long and has fallen over one eye. It's dyed. We all have pale skin, and we were all born with blond hair and either blue or green eyes. My hair is even lighter now because I highlight it. Eddie's is darker because he doesn't. Portia's hair has been black for a while now. It matches her nails. She's not goth, though. Not anymore.

The music change is abrupt. I didn't even see Krista move. That's Eddie's wife. Krista, the one with olive skin, dark hair, and brown eyes with gold flecks. Krista, the one he married four months after meeting her. She used to be the receptionist at his office.

Pop music blares out of the speakers, a dance song from five years ago. It was bad then, too.

"The jazz was putting me to sleep," Krista says.

My husband's eyes flick up from his laptop. He probably didn't notice the change in music, but he heard Krista's voice.

Maybe she's the heroine.

"It's fine," Eddie says. I can hear the smile on his face.

I continue to stare out the window. Atlanta

is long gone. We aren't even in Georgia. This is northern Alabama, past Birmingham, where the population is sparse and skeptical. If we were trying to rush, we'd be farther along by now. Rushing isn't part of the equation.

"Food?"

That's Portia, her voice groggy from her nap. She's sitting up, headphones off, wide-eyed like a child.

She's been milking that baby-of-the-family shit for a long time.

"You want to stop?" Eddie says, turning down the music.

"Let's stop," Krista says.

My husband shrugs.

"Yes," Portia says.

Eddie looks at me in the rearview mirror, like I get a say in the matter. I'm already outnumbered.

"Great," I say. "Food is great."

We stop at a place called the Roundabout, which looks just as you imagine. Rustic in a fake way, with the lasso and goat on the sign, but naturally run-down with age. Authentic but not — like most of us.

We all climb out and Portia is first to the door; Krista isn't far behind. Eddie is the one who takes the most time. He stands outside the car, staring at the back. Hesitating.

It's our grandfather. This is our first stop of the trip, meaning it's the first time we have to leave him alone.

"You okay?" I say, tapping Eddie's arm.

He doesn't look at me, doesn't take his eyes off the back of the car because Grandpa's ashes are everything to us. Not for emotional reasons.

"You want to stay out here? I can bring you a doggie bag," I say. Sarcasm drips.

Eddie turns to me, his eyes wide. Oh, the shock. Like if I had just told him I was leaving my longtime partner for someone I met two months ago.

Oh wait, he did that. Eddie left his live-in girlfriend for the receptionist.

"I'm fine," he says. "You don't have to be so bitchy about it."

Yes. I'm the villain.

Inside the Roundabout, everyone is sitting in a semicircle booth. It's twice as big as it needs to be. The seats are wine-colored pleather. Krista and Portia have scooted all the way to the center of the booth, leaving Felix on one side. That's my husband, Felix, the pale one with the strong jaw and white-blond hair with matching eyebrows and lashes. In a certain light, he disappears.

"No," Portia says. "There's nothing vegan."

She isn't vegan but checks anyway. Portia also looks for wheelchair access and won't go in anywhere that doesn't have it because fairness is important.

"Should we leave?" I say.

No one answers. I sit.

The burgers are chargrilled, the fries are crisp, and the bacon is greasy. A fair deal, if you ask me. The only thing missing is decent coffee, but I drink their bitter version of it without complaint. I can be a good sport.

"We probably should get something settled," Eddie says. He looks like our father. "We're going to be driving for a while. A lot of gas, food, and motel rooms. I propose we take turns covering the expenses. More than anything else, let's not argue about it. The last thing we need to do is fight over a gas bill."

Before I can say a word, my husband does.

"Makes sense," Felix says. "Beth and I will pay our fair share."

Only a spouse can betray you like that. Or a sibling.

That leaves Portia. Given that she's doesn't really have a career, the deal isn't fair.

Oh, the irony.

She yawns. Nods. In Portia-speak, she's agreeing for now but reserves the right to disagree later.

"Great," Eddie says. "I'll get this one."

He takes the check up to the register, because that's the kind of place this is. Felix goes to the restroom and Portia steps out front to make a call. That leaves Krista and me, finishing those last sips of lukewarm coffee.

"I know this must be terrible for all of you," she says, placing her hand on mine. "But I hope we can have some good times, too. I'm sure your grandfather would've wanted that."

It's a nice enough thing for Krista to say, if a little generic. Given the circumstances, I expect nothing less and nothing more.

Still. If everything falls apart and we all start killing one another, she goes first.

You think I said that for shock value. I didn't.

No, I'm not a psychopath. That's always a convenient excuse, though. Someone who has no empathy and has to fake human emotions. Why do they do bad things? Shrug. Who knows? That's a psychopath for you. Or is it the word *sociopath*? You know what I'm saying.

15

This isn't that kind of story. This is about family. I love my siblings, all of them, I really do. I also hate them. That's how it goes — love, hate, love, hate, back and forth like a seesaw.

That's the thing about family. Despite what they say, it's not a single unit with a single goal. What *they* never tell us is that, more often than not, every member of the family has their own agenda. I know I do.

ALABAMA

STATE MOTTO: WE DARE TO DEFEND OUR RIGHTS

We've been on this road trip before. Twenty years ago it was Grandpa's trip for us, the grandkids, and it was because our parents hadn't been getting along. Lots of yelling, lots of slammed doors, and too many silent meals. Dad slept on the couch but pretended he didn't, and Mom pretended not to be mad. Not easy for her, given that she was always slamming cabinets, doors, and whatever else got in her way.

Eddie and I were the closest in age and we talked about it a lot, preparing ourselves for an inevitable divorce. We even picked a date: New Year's Eve. Eddie marked it on his Nine Inch Nails calendar, filling in December 31 with a big X. We bet that by next year our parents would no longer be

17

together.

That was in the summer, when the fighting made the hot days seem even longer. We all lived in Atlanta then, including Grandpa. He showed up at our door in August and he was alone. Grandma had died six months earlier.

Grandpa gathered us all up, sat us down on the couch, and said, "Your parents need some time alone. They need to figure out grown-up things."

"Are they getting divorced?" Eddie said.

"No, they are not. They just need to be alone, so we're going on an adventure."

"What kind of adventure?" I said.

"An amazing one." Grandpa said it strong and loud, trying hard to convince us it was true.

I was ready for anything other than another day at home. The summer had been long, hot, and miserable. When Grandpa said an adventure would make things better with our parents, I couldn't get out the door fast enough.

Grandpa drove a minivan. Always had, as far as I could remember, and it was that same greyish-green color as every other minivan. A lot of my friends' parents had them and I'd been in them a million times. The upside was we had plenty of room to move around if we wanted. There were enough seats for at least six people, so we all piled in and off we went.

First stop: Tuscumbia, Alabama. North of everything, almost into Tennessee. In 1880, Helen Keller was born in a house called Ivy Green and now it's a tourist site. That was where Grandpa brought us first.

The house itself isn't large; it's a simple, white, one-floor building. We went on the tour and learned all about Helen's silent, dark world and how Anne Sullivan had saved her. The original well pump is still there, the place where Helen first learned the word *water* and started her long climb out of the abyss.

Outside the house, we walked around the grounds. Grandpa kept going on and on about how amazing Helen Keller was. I can't remember if I knew who she was before we went there or not. It feels like I should have, but maybe that's me hoping I knew more than I did.

What I also remember is when we were done and heading back to the car. Eddie walked on top of a short brick wall lining the street. Portia ran from one side of the sidewalk to the other, trying to find the best-smelling flower. I chased after her, giving my own opinion on them. She didn't ask.

Grandpa stopped and looked at each one of us. He shook his head. "It's a lucky thing you have all of your senses."

"But you heard the guide," I said. "She went deaf and blind after being sick. We can't get the same disease now."

"Yeah," Eddie said. "It's been cured."

Grandpa shook his head again, like he was disappointed by our reactions. "Lucky indeed," he said again. "Maybe we can try it sometime. I'll cover your eyes and ears and see how you do."

I laughed because he was being so silly. We all were, because we were on a grand adventure across the country. Our goal, Grandpa said, was California, and that's where we would see the Pacific Ocean for the first time.

Today we go to the same house, except this time we already know the story. We've all seen *The Miracle Worker* and we've all read about Helen Keller in school. The only surprise is how small the house is, along with the cottage where Helen lived with Anne Sullivan. It seemed much larger when I was a kid.

As we leave, Felix claps his hands together. "What an amazing piece of history."

"Isn't it?" Krista says. "I love uplifting

stories. I wish there was a cable station that only played inspiring movies and TV shows."

"They already have religious stations," Portia says. Sarcasm intended.

"Oh, not like that. Like Helen Keller," Krista says.

"So, a station about kids who overcome physical challenges?"

Krista gives up and steps away from Portia, realizing she is being made fun of.

We all get back into the car to leave, and no one says anything else about Helen Keller. The drive continues along an empty road, heading neither north nor south. Sometime after dark, Eddie pulls up to a roadside motel called the Stardust.

"What do you think?" he says.

It looks like a shithole with Wi-Fi and cable. Perfect.

"It's so early," Portia says. She has a slight childish twang in her tone. "I can drive if you're tired."

"I'll keep that in mind," Eddie says. He drives up to the front office and jumps out of the car.

It's no surprise Eddie insists on driving and choosing our motel rooms, because that's who he is. Who he always has been. It doesn't seem to bother Krista, who sits in the front, smiling and bobbing her head to the music. Portia rolls her eyes and lies down in the back.

I sigh and pick up my phone, scrolling through Instagram to check up on everyone back at home. To check up on him.

Tonight, Portia will stay with Eddie and Krista. She'll stay with one of the couples each night to save money on motels. Portia doesn't get a night by herself, because she's single so she's alone all the time. That's how Krista says it. I think it's payback for Portia making fun of her back at the Helen Keller house.

As soon as Felix and I get into our room, we use quick-drying disinfectant and anti-bacterial spray on the bedsheets, the towels, and the tops of all the furniture. Even the hangers. There are two.

Not that we're germophobes, but who wouldn't do this in a roadside motel? That's like not using an antibacterial wipe on the pull-down tray when you're on a plane.

When we're done, I flop down on one of the beds.

"I'll take a shower first," Felix says.

"Okay."

I watch him walk into the bathroom and I wonder, not for the first time, if our children would have his white-blond hair. We've been married for six years, together for almost nine, and I still haven't decided what our kids would look like. Haven't gotten pregnant, either.

We met during our senior year of college. Career day. He stood in line for Global Com, Inc., while I stood in line for Williams Kane Ltd. Both were international conglomerates with jobs for every major imaginable. Felix and I ended up next to each other as we waited. It seemed rude not to acknowledge each other, so we exchanged recommendations about where to apply and warnings about who to stay away from. It was the most normal conversation. At that stage in my life, normal was what I needed.

At one point he said, "We're lucky to be born when we were."

"Why's that?"

"We don't have to stay at the same company forever. Five years, max. If it's really terrible, it's perfectly acceptable to leave after two. Anything less than that . . ." Felix shrugged, as if to say you were screwed. Spending less than two years at a job might mean you're a flake. Or you're trouble.

"That's true," I said. "We are lucky."

Neither of us got jobs that day. Instead, we both ended up at the largest conglomerate of all, International United, but in different departments, of course. No corporation would allow married couples to work side by side, not if they want to stay in business.

Felix emerges from the bathroom already dried off, wearing boxers and a Miami Dolphins T-shirt. We're not big on football but we don't hate it.

"Your turn," he says.

Not much hot water, if there was ever any. When I come out of the bathroom, Felix is sprawled out on one of the beds. Not the one I was lying on.

"My legs hurt from being in the car all day," he says. "You mind if we each take a bed?"

"That's fine. They're small anyway."

"Yeah, compared to ours."

I sit down on my bed and pull up the alarm on my phone. "Should we walk in the morning?" I say.

"Definitely."

I set it for seven.

"How are you feeling?" Felix says.

"Fine."

"I mean about seeing Eddie and Portia. Been a while."

It has. None of us live in the same area. Eddie and Krista live on Dauphin Island, Alabama, just south of Mobile — the other side of the state from our current location. Felix and I live in Woodview, Florida, while Portia went to Tulane in New Orleans and still lives there. None of us live in Atlanta, but we grew up there. It's where our last trip started.

For the Morgan siblings, separation is the best form of togetherness.

The last time we were all together was a few years ago, when Portia graduated from college. Two days in the same city and we spent about eight hours together, all of it intoxicated. Portia insisted we try the hurricane, the mint julep, and the Pimm's cup. Dangerous on their own, lethal together.

Grandpa wasn't there. None of us had seen him in years.

This was back when Eddie was still with Tracy, the girlfriend he used to live with. He hadn't met Krista yet. I liked Tracy. She was smarter than my brother and told him that a lot. He even seemed to like it.

I remember being at a bar uptown, near the university, on the night before graduation. It was hot as hell and I wore a tank top with a print skirt. Tracy wore a fancy sundress that showed off her arms. They were ridiculously toned.

"You know the thing about your brother," she said. A gentle slur, not sloppy. "He can be an asshole but he's a lovable asshole, you know?"

I do. You know the type, you've met him. He's the guy who gets away with mouthing off in class, the one who can convince teachers to give him a makeup exam, the one everyone wants to be around even when he screws up. Especially when he screws up.

That's Eddie.

I never got a chance to ask Tracy what she thought about the woman Eddie went out with right out of college. Bet that woman wouldn't call him lovable. She said Eddie slapped her, and she even reported him, but nothing came of it. Eddie said she was the crazy one and he never hit her, not in a million years.

I believed him. I believed her. Back and forth, back and forth, just like that seesaw. Still haven't decided who's right, if he's a lovable asshole or just the latter.

This is what I'm thinking about in bed, at the Stardust, when Felix asks me how I'm doing. I'm trying to keep my balance.

"It's fine," I say. "I'm doing fine."

"I'm glad. Good night."

"Good night."

I wait for his breathing to slow. Doesn't take long. Felix has always been able to fall asleep instantly, no matter where he is.

I get up, get dressed, and leave the room.

Outside, I glance around looking for any movement, any form of life. It's not even ten thirty at night and I know Portia isn't lying in bed, listening to Eddie and Krista breathe. The options are the diner across the street or the liquor store behind the motel. I go that way first.

The parking lot is empty enough to hear footsteps, and I think I hear someone behind me. Twice I stop to check. Once I kneel down to look for feet on the other side of that broken-down truck. This place is so empty, so quiet, I am convinced someone else must be out here.

I don't see anyone until I get to the liquor store. The parking lot is full, and there are living, breathing people everywhere. Dan's Drip-Drop Liquors is the closest thing to a bar for at least a mile or two.

Portia is inside the store, waiting her turn at the register. She is one of two females around; the other is sitting in the passenger seat of a car smoking a cigarette. Busy night at the Drip-Drop.

Portia doesn't see me until I'm right beside her. "Get enough for two," I say.

She smiles and holds up a six-pack of Coke and a bottle of rum. I nod. A stack of plastic cups sits on the counter. The price — five cents each — is handwritten in red marker on the back of a lottery ticket. We get two cups.

"Let's go back to the car," Portia says. "I've got Eddie's keys."

She never did get enough credit for being smart. Maybe there were too many years between us.

Minutes later, we're in the back seat of the car and I'm drinking my first rum and Coke in years. Maybe since college. We don't have ice but the Coke is cold and this seems perfect, given where we are at the moment. Environment is everything.

"This is weird," Portia says.

"Which part?"

"Did you know about the will?" she says.

"No. I found out when Grandpa's lawyer read it." I look toward the back of the car, where his ashes are stored.

"Eddie brought them to his room," Portia says.

"Oh. Of course."

We take another gulp of our drinks. Goes down easier after a few sips.

"This is what we drink at work," she says. "Because it looks like soda. The whole waitstaff does it."

Lie.

Portia claims to be a waitress in a bar. She's a stripper, and she has been through most of her college years and now beyond. I may not see my siblings very often, but I know what they're up to.

"You must get sick of being around drunk people all the time," I say.

"Yeah, it got old a while ago. Just can't make the same money in an entry-level job."

"I bet not."

"I mean, I'm not going to do it forever," she says, pausing to finish off her first drink. "Just until I find a good starter job."

"Grandpa's money will pay for your student loans," I say.

Portia nods. "Thank God."

We're the only ones left to inherit his estate. Grandma passed away long before he did, and our parents are not in the picture.

"What do you think you'll do?" I say.

She shrugs, refilling her glass and topping off mine. "I'd like to get into the medical

31

field. Maybe be a physician's assistant or something. One day maybe I'll go to nursing school."

"You'd be good at that."

She smiles. There's just enough light for me to see her eyes. Clear blue, just like Grandpa had. Mine are murky, like dark water, and Eddie's look like blue marbles.

"How do you think this trip will go?" she says.

Funny she asks this now, when we're already on our way. This is the question we all should have asked about, pondered over, and discussed before we got on the road.

We all heard about this trip at the same time, on the conference call with Grandpa's lawyer.

"No funeral, no memorial service. He specifically notes this," the man said. He spoke with a deep Georgian drawl. Grandpa didn't have that. "Your grandfather requested just a brief obituary in the local paper. He has provided the wording that should be used."

It's odd how silent we all were. Like we were having a staring contest through the phone.

"Your grandfather asked that his body be cremated. The next part I will read exactly as he stated it," the lawyer said. A paper shuffled. The sound was strange, like Grandpa had found the one lawyer who didn't use a computer. " 'Go on the road trip. Scatter my ashes at the end. Once I'm in my final resting place, my estate will be equally divided between you.' There's also a provision for a rental car. Any questions?"

The road trip, not *a* road trip. There had been only one.

No, we had no questions.

"As for the estate, your grandfather's assets include his house, a car, a retirement fund, and an investment account. Everything is to be divided equally between the three of you." The lawyer paused. "While the house, car, and furnishings still have to be valued, the total in liquid assets is $3,453,000. By the time his remains have been delivered to their designated place, we'll have the total."

The amount seemed staggering, at least to me, and that was just the cash.

"There a few final conditions to receive your inheritance," the lawyer said. "Your grandfather stipulated that anyone who ends up in jail, who does not complete the trip, or who deviates from the original trip in any way will get nothing."

This is how it must go. First the trip, then the money. Grandpa didn't even work for it

33

— he inherited it from Grandma's sister, who had no kids of her own, and he'd kept it all to himself ever since.

When the call ended, Eddie sent an e-mail to Portia and me asking about logistics. He did not question what Grandpa said or if we would do it. No one did.

We deserved that money. Our payment had been a long time coming.

Twenty years ago, when we first went on this road trip, Grandpa wanted to show us the world, starting with as many states as possible. Instead, it turned into one of those things we don't mention, don't talk about. It stays in our heads, swimming around in denial, in disbelief, even in delusion.

So how do I think this second trip will go? It's going to be the trip of a lifetime. And when it's over, everything is going to be different. Just like the first time.

"It'll be fine," I say to Portia. "It will all be just fine."

She rolls her eyes. I don't argue with her.

I also don't tell her about the journal. No one knows I have it. The paper has yellowed, the stickers on the front faded, but the fancy title is still readable.

Your Feelings: A Guide
Thoughtful Questions for Thoughtful Girls

August 12, 1999

Which Three Women Do You Most Admire?

First, I was never going to use this journal for anything. It was a birthday present, a lame one, and it's been under my bed until today. I saw it when I pulled out my suitcase to use for the trip. I brought it in case I got bored and here we are. So there's that.

Second, I don't admire anyone. This is a trick question, because I'd basically be saying "I'm not these three women, I'll never be these three women, but I admire them more than I admire myself."

That's screwed up, if you ask me. Like girls don't have enough self-esteem problems already.

On the upside, my therapist would probably be crazy proud of me for recognizing such an unhealthy question. I'm going to tell him about it when we get back. Dr. Lang isn't a real doc-

35

tor, he's just a therapist, but I call him Dr. Lang to remind him of what he's not.

Our sessions are like being on one of those spinning things on the playground — the metal kind with the bars on them. Why can't adults see how stupid and dangerous those things are?

I ask the same question about my therapy sessions.

13 Days Left

Felix doesn't know a lot about the first road trip. He knows it happened, yes, but not everything about it. I know, it's terrible of me to keep such big things from my husband, but I stand by my decision, even now. Couples who think they need to tell each other every little thing they do or did are destined to fail. All those details build up to a heaping pile of crap and you can't stay married to that.

But I'm in no condition to go on a walk, so I don't hide my late night with Portia.

"Good for you," he says. "I'm glad you spent some time with your sister."

I want to hit him. It's probably the hangover.

Even when I get to the diner for breakfast, the rum is still seeping out of my pores. Portia is young, so she still looks good without makeup, and her hair is tied up in a knot on top of her head. Just looking at it makes mine hurt more.

"You guys went out last night?" Eddie says. He looks crisp and ironed, even in a T-shirt and khakis.

Krista is beside him and she's pouting. I bet she didn't realize what kind of motels we'd be staying in.

"We didn't go *out,*" I say. "We just drank."

"Yeah, we didn't go anywhere," Portia says.

Eddie's eyes narrow, like he's about to say something fatherly: *We should be careful. We're not here to party. We have no business drinking alone in a strange town.*

But he doesn't say that. Instead, he smiles. It lights up his eyes and shows off his dimples. Eddie morphs from asshole to lovable asshole just like that.

"You should have asked me to join," he says. "We need to have some fun on this trip."

Portia nods. "*You* need to have some fun. You're starting to be a boring old man."

"Thanks."

"If I don't tell you, who will?" Portia asks.

"That's what little sisters are for," I say.

Eddie is still smiling as he looks over at Felix. "They're ganging up on me."

"Looks like it," Felix says.

38

"Any advice?"

"Head down, mouth shut?"

"Solid."

They bump fists.

We return to the motel to get our things. On the first trip, I took an ashtray from every motel room. Twenty years ago, motels like this had ashtrays and matchbooks. All the rooms were smoking rooms. Every ashtray was the same, too, like they were all bought them from the same company: square, with indents at each corner for the cigarettes. Made of glass, I think. They felt heavy and solid and I liked that, so I took them.

I wrapped them up in my T-shirts so they didn't clink together. When I had five, Grandpa noticed how heavy my bag was.

"Books," I said.

He gave me a funny look, like it was weird that I'd have books.

A few nights later, my bag was even heavier. Grandpa emptied it that time. He unwrapped ashtray after ashtray, eight in total. "But Beth," he said, "why?"

I shrugged. "Because I can."

Grandpa hemmed and hawed, saying what we should do is take them back. If we were honest people, that is. Grandpa wasn't.

"Keep one," he finally said. "We'll drop the rest off at a Salvation Army or something."

I kept two. Never settle. Even at the age of twelve, I knew better.

Today, there are no ashtrays in the motel room. There's nothing solid or heavy at all. The room has nothing except some threadbare towels and scratchy linens. No Bibles. The TV is bolted down and the remote is attached to a wire.

This is an unexpected letdown. I leave the motel with nothing other than a drunken night of sleep. As we drive away, I look back at the Stardust sign and think about taking a picture. I don't, because I don't want to remember that rat hole.

My husband is one of those picture people. If anything interesting happens, Felix takes out his phone. He's that guy in the middle of a parade who also records the parade. He recorded us loading our luggage into the SUV, driving away from the car rental place in Atlanta, and he took pictures of the Roundabout. Probably of the Stardust, too. I didn't ask.

Sometimes he posts the videos on social media, other times he reviews and deletes. Doesn't bother me. I never watch them. Does anyone? Bet not. Bet you don't, at least not more than once. Not until someone dies, and then you watch and replay every little thing they did because it's all you have. I've done that.

One day, those pictures and videos may be all that's left of someone. Pick and choose with care.

But if Felix wants to spend his time recording life, that's his choice.

As soon as we're on the highway, I curl up on my side of the seat and lean against the window. Sleep. It's the only real way out of a hangover. Time and sleep and a lot of wishing I was Portia's age.

I drift off with ease, and wake up to the sound of laughter. Above it all, I hear Felix.

". . . and then they had a baby named Pop Tart," he says.

"Strawberry Pop Tart!" Krista yells.

"And then they went back into space," Eddie says. "To find their lost loves."

"Wait," Portia says from the back seat. "Did that hedgehog have sex with the alien?"

"And the mutant!" Felix yells.

The story game. We played it as kids, in the car, but not like this. I pretend to still be asleep as I listen to the sexual exploits of a hedgehog named Bonnie. She's an equal opportunity fornicator, Portia says.

41

On the first trip, we had an ongoing story about another hedgehog. His name was Chester and he did not fornicate with anyone. Not once. He did, however, like a girl hedgehog named Paulina and he used to give her worms and crickets to eat. Mostly, he hung out with his friends and they went on quests like the kind in video games.

Grandpa loved the stories. He compared the adventures to the comics he used to read as a kid. I always knew when he was giggling because his whole body would shake. I used to watch from the back seat.

I listen to the Bonnie story until I can't anymore, then I sit up.

"Well, if it isn't Sleeping Beauty," Eddie says.

"Are you guys seriously talking about hedgehog sex?" I say.

Krista wags her finger at me. "Not strictly hedgehog sex. Hedgehogs with other animals, too."

"But not exactly animals," Portia says.

Felix shakes his head at me. "More like creatures?"

"Alien creatures!"

"Mutant creatures!"

"Mythological creatures!"

"Gods, even. The Greek ones. And the

Norse gods."

"Bestiality," I say. "This is bestiality of the worst kind."

"Look out!"

Krista's voice is drowned out by the squeal of tires, followed by a bang.

We are halfway off the two-lane road and facing the wrong direction.

"Is everyone okay? Is everyone okay?" Eddie keeps saying this the same way, like a recording.

"Yes," Felix says.

"I'm alive," Portia says.

I'm fine, too. No broken bones, just a pain in my arm where I slammed it against the door. Krista is crying. Well, she's sniffling. She has a bright red spot on her forehead where she hit her head. Eddie grabs her and looks at the wound.

"It's fine," he says. "No broken skin."

I take a look too, because you never can tell with head wounds, but he's right. It doesn't look bad at all, not even swollen.

Felix stares out the window. "What happened?" he says.

"A truck came right toward us. You didn't see it?" Eddie says.

"Did we hit it?"

No one answers.

I open my door and get out. There are no other cars around, although down the road I see a pickup truck driving away from us. "It's gone," I say. "They just left us here."

"Asshole," Eddie says.

Felix gets out of the car as well, and he walks around the car. "We've got a flat," he says.

"For the love of God," Portia says, climbing out of the back. "Please tell me someone knows how to fix it."

We all stare at the flat. The back tire looks like it went full speed into a rock that was sharp enough to cut glass.

Eddie maneuvers the car off the road, just in case another comes along. Not likely. The road is empty, lined with cornfields on both sides and farmhouses behind them. That's it. Nowhere to go, nothing to see.

"I can change it," Felix says.

Eddie gets out of the car. "So can I."

I'm watching Portia, who's leaning against the car and standing on one foot. "What's wrong?" I say.

"It's my ankle. I had my feet up when we crashed."

"Let me look."

She brushes me off. "I'm fine, *Mom.* It's

nothing."

At the back of the car, Felix and Eddie unload the luggage to get to the spare tire. Felix is really good with cars. No one expects that, because he's the kind of guy who's always staring at his laptop, but he knows cars. He claims it's because engines are interesting.

Lie.

It's because he grew up poor and his family always had old run-down cars.

I overhear Felix say, "We're going to need to stop and get a real tire. Can't drive across the country on this."

"Of course we can't," Eddie says.

Like he knows. My brother is a call-Triple-A kind of guy.

I take great pleasure in watching Felix tell Eddie what to do, essentially making him a helper. Felix likes it, Eddie doesn't. Maybe it's weird I'm enjoying this, or maybe everyone feels this way about their siblings. A little competitive. A little vindictive.

One day I might analyze these feelings instead of cleaning the house or something.

"Take off your shoe," I say to Portia. "Let me see if it's swollen."

She does and it is. We'll need to get ice and some kind of wrap, and I give her some ibuprofen for the pain. I'm so absorbed in making this mental list — and trying to forget my hands are still shaking a little from the accident — that I don't hear the other car. Not until I see it drive up and stop.

A black pickup truck. Just like the one driving away from us a minute ago.

"You guys all right? Need any help?" the driver says. A young guy with yellow hair, a baseball cap, and a cigarette. The man in the passenger seat is older and heavyset with a full, greying beard. The truck is huge, with an extended cab, and a woman sits on the far side in the back. All I can see is her long auburn hair.

"It's just a flat tire," Felix says.

Eddie steps forward, his shoulders squared up. "We're fine," he says.

"You sure about that?" the older man says. He smiles at Eddie. "Because we're pretty good with cars." Although he offers to help, no one in the truck moves to get out of it.

"We're good," Eddie says.

"Was it you?"

Portia.

Up until this moment, she had been sitting in our car and resting her foot. Now she's up and out, hobbling on one foot and giving the newcomers her best evil eye. "Were you the ones who ran us off the road?"

"Was it us?" the older man says. He laughs. The other two join in. "Honey, we were just passing by and stopped to see if we could help."

"That's not very hospitable," the driver says. "We stop to help and you accuse us of trying to run you off the road."

"Not very hospitable at all," the older man says.

Krista's out of the car now, hands on hips and her back arched, which can't be a good sign. She's one of those suburban women who have never seen real trouble and think it only happens on the Internet.

Eddie takes another step forward, his eyes never leaving the men in the truck.

Part of me wants to watch this play out, if only for my own amusement. The other part of me steps in front of Eddie. "Thanks," I say to the older man. "We appreciate the offer, but we're fine. The tire is almost changed." I motion to Felix, who waves with the wrench in his hand.

Forget the villain. I'm the peacemaker.

The older man stares at me a bit too long. I smile and nod, smile and nod.

"All right, then," he says. "Glad everyone's okay."

The truck moves forward and then turns around, driving back in the direction it came from.

"They turned around and came back," Portia says. "It *was* them."

No one confirms or denies that.

"The Godfather," Portia says. "I swear that guy was like the Alabama Godfather."

"Pretty much," Eddie says. "I'll drink to that."

We all laugh. We all drink.

A few hours have passed since our on-the-road incident. The rental has a new tire, the spare is back in place, and Krista has put makeup on her forehead. Portia's ankle is wrapped and she's wearing a new cheap pair of flip-flops.

The initial horror of the event has passed, dulled by time, by alcohol, by laughter. Same as anything else. You can't stay that tense for too long, otherwise someone is going to get hurt.

Now that it's over, and we're safe, I find myself happy that Felix is here. So far, I haven't been. He's not supposed to be here, neither is Krista. It should've been just the siblings.

Not long after our conference with Grandpa's lawyer, Eddie called and said Krista was coming with us. "We've been married six months," he said. "I can't just leave her to go on a road trip with you guys."

"She can't take care of herself?" I said.

Eddie sighed. A big, frustrated sigh like this was all my problem. "Look, I know you haven't met her —"

"Whose fault is that?"

Silence. I had never met Krista because Eddie didn't invite any of us to the wedding. He claimed it was a last-minute decision to go to city hall right before they took a trip to the mountains, but I suspect he didn't want us there. Maybe because he cheated on his girlfriend and married the receptionist.

But I didn't say any of that and he changed the subject.

"Bring Felix," he said.

"That's not the point."

"We aren't kids anymore, Beth. I'm a married man and I'm going to bring my wife."

This is why I brought my husband. Because I'm a married woman and I should bring him with me. It also occurred to me that our spouses would keep things copacetic. Neutral. How bad can you really be when your spouse is around?

So far, I'm right and wrong. Today would have been much worse without Felix around to fix the car. Then again, if neither Krista nor Felix were with us, would Eddie have been as distracted while driving? No. Yes. Doesn't matter now. You can only do mental gymnastics for so long before you go insane.

LOUISIANA

STATE MOTTO: UNION, JUSTICE, AND CONFIDENCE

Mississippi? No. We cross diagonally through that state and into Louisiana. Everyone breathes a sigh of relief to be so far from the accident and from that pickup truck. The event was weird enough to put everyone on edge for a while.

They're not why we crossed through Mississippi, though. We did it because it's the same route we took the first time. Next stop: Gibsland, Louisiana. Of all the places to visit, Grandpa chose the place where the FBI caught Bonnie and Clyde — if dying in a hail of bullets can be considered getting caught.

On the way there, Grandpa told us the story of Bonnie and Clyde. He had a great voice, a deep baritone with no hint of an accent. It was the kind that should've been on the radio back when stories were told with voices.

"Bonnie and Clyde are one of the great love stories of the twentieth century," he said. "They were young and wild and robbed banks in the middle of the Depression."

He made me believe they were on a big romantic adventure, and that their exploits were harmless enough, given the time period. What did I care about banks and their money? I didn't. And I had no reason to doubt what he said about Bonnie and Clyde. We didn't have smartphones back then, so we couldn't fact-check anything he said.

That night we stayed in a cabin at Black Lake, where Bonnie and Clyde had a little get-together two days before they died.

"Tomorrow," Grandpa said, "we're going to the Bonnie and Clyde museum."

I fell asleep imagining what it would be like to be so famous they made a whole museum just for you, about you, to memorialize all that is you. I wondered if there was anything I could do, other than robbing banks, to get a museum of my own. Cure cancer, maybe. It was the only thing I could come up with.

Grandpa had talked so much about Bonnie and Clyde, I felt like I knew everything before we even got to the museum. I knew how they met, how many banks they robbed, not to mention the grocery stores and gas stations. A whole slew of robberies were attributed to them, or to their gang. Bonnie and Clyde had their own gang.

"We should have a gang," I said. We were at breakfast, eating eggs and bacon and grits. Everything was drenched in butter and syrup.

Grandpa laughed. "You don't need a gang, you're already in a pack. A pack of coyotes."

"It's a band of coyotes," I said. "Not a pack."

"See? You sounded like a yapping coyote when you said that. You're a band of little coyotes, and you're the toughest, meanest bunch this side of the Mississippi."

"We're on the west side, you know," Eddie said. "We crossed the Mississippi."

"So?" I said.

"I'm just pointing it out."

Like that mattered. We were little coyotes and we were going to have our own museum. Who cared what side of the Mississippi it was on?

On the way to the museum, we got lost. It

was down some windy roads, away from the highway, and nestled between two other stores. Out front, there was an old car riddled with bullets. It wasn't *the* car, but it was like the one they drove and then died in. Eddie thought it was the coolest thing ever until we went inside the museum.

It wasn't what I'd imagined. Whatever I had conjured up in my head from all those stories Grandpa told, it was wrong. In my mental museum, there wasn't any blood. No dead bodies, either.

Since we were close to where Bonnie and Clyde died, that's what the museum commemorated. The ambush. The walls were covered with black-and-white pictures of their bodies, the men who shot them, and the real car. A glass case of guns was in the center of the room, and it was there I saw what Clyde's favorite gun looked like. The Browning automatic rifle was big and heavy and not romantic at all.

"Isn't this fantastic?" Grandpa said. "All these resources just to bring down one couple."

Sure. Fantastic.

Especially in the back, where they had re-created the aftermath of the shootout, complete with dummies of Bonnie and Clyde. Bloodied dummies. They were slumped over each other in the shot-up car. She was twenty-three. He was twenty-five.

If that was love, it looked like an awful thing.

We weren't the only ones in the museum. Two couples were there, on their way to Savannah, and they had stopped in to see the museum just as we had. Both of the men were police officers, so their interest was in how Bonnie and Clyde were captured. They didn't care about love.

"He was shot seventeen times," one said. "She was shot over twenty."

Grandpa also left out the fact that Bonnie and Clyde weren't just bank robbers; they were murderers. Killed at least thirteen people, according to the records.

That's when I'd had enough. I went outside and sat down on a bench, feeling like I was the one who got swindled. I no longer wanted my own museum.

Grandpa came out to find me. "You okay?"

I shrugged.

"They weren't good," I said.

"Ah." He sat down beside me. "You know, sometimes your grandmother wore awful clothes. It's terrible to say, but she did. She had this one blouse with pineapples on it." He sighed. "I hated that blouse."

56

"So?" I said.

"Do you think I told her how much I hated that blouse?"

I shrugged. "Why not?"

"Because it would've hurt her feelings."

Yet he hurt her in so many other ways. Later for that.

But I knew what he was doing. I was twelve, for God's sake, not four. "You lied to Grandma," I said. "So you wouldn't upset her."

"That's right. I always told your grandmother she was beautiful. And she was, even in ugly clothes."

I stared at him. "People do bad things. I know that."

"People do bad things for the people they love. There's a difference."

"That's what Bonnie and Clyde did? Kill because they loved each other?"

He nodded. "I think so. Yes."

I didn't. In fact, I thought he was a little bit crazy for comparing pineapple blouses to shooting people.

"Who's up for the Bonnie and Clyde museum?" Eddie says.

This time we aren't lost, and won't get lost, because we have GPS.

"Good God," Portia says. She lying in the

57

back, her foot raised and still wrapped.

"You're joking," Krista says. "There's no such thing."

"Oh yes there is," I say.

"Are you serious?" Felix asks.

"Of course I'm serious. Bonnie and Clyde are one of the greatest love stories of the twentieth century. Don't you know that?" I say.

Krista turns around in her seat to face me. Her eyes are wide, the gold flecks shining. "I saw the movie," she says. "*So* romantic."

I smile at her, nodding my head. Maybe she'll be shocked when she sees the truth, just as I had been. Or maybe her belief in them is already so ingrained, so fully believed, that nothing will change it.

That's how Grandpa was. You can do bad things if it's for love.

It didn't make sense then, but it does now.

August 13, 1999

What Is Your Biggest Accomplishment?

I've beat my whole family at Risk and I've done it more than once. And that's no joke. Dad makes us play at least once a week. Always after dinner, always together, and no one is exempt.

The night I first beat everyone, I was accused of cheating. It's not a win if you cheat, just like in life. Dad's always saying stuff like that. He says people are all wrong about chess, because that game isn't the "pinnacle of strategy." The best strategic game is Risk. Especially Secret Mission Risk, because that's when everyone has their own mission but no one knows what it is.

That's why we play, Dad says. The game is about making allies and keeping your word right up until you can't. In other words, it's about life. He says that, not me. I'd never use those words. I'd say you have to screw them before they screw you, but if I did, Mom would give me a look and Dad would try to punish me, so I just keep my mouth shut. Sort of.

Still. I did win, and I've done it more than once. That's skill, not luck.

Sometimes I forget Grandpa's ashes are in the back. I've pushed them deep into a corner of my mind, and when they creep out, I push them back in. Ignore the ashes. Ignore him. Start talking.

"Isn't this fantastic?" I say.

We're in the Bonnie and Clyde Ambush Museum, which looks as I remembered it except it doesn't feel as scary.

Portia refuses to come in. She's outside on her phone, supposedly calling someone in New Orleans who may or may not be a boyfriend. Even when she was six years old, Portia wasn't impressed by Bonnie and Clyde or by the museum. Everything about them was too *old-fashioned.*

"I can't believe you've been here before," Felix says. We hold hands as we walk through, which feels as odd as it sounds. "You never told me about this."

"Slipped my mind, I guess."

61

Felix stops when he sees the car with the bloody dummies inside. "Whoa."

Krista gasps, which makes Eddie laugh.

"I knew you would freak out," he says. "They probably didn't show this in the movie."

Krista shakes her head. Her dark hair is pulled back into a ponytail and it swings back and forth, reminding me of a cheer-leader. "I don't remember that part," she says.

Eddie looks at me and winks. I roll my eyes, because I know where we're going next.

Down the road a bit from the museum is the place where Bonnie and Clyde died. There's a marker for it and everything. Grandpa thought it was great.

"This is crazy," Felix says. The memorial looks like a tombstone, and it marks the exact place where Bonnie and Clyde's bullet-ridden car rolled to a stop.

"People are crazy," I say.

"You're right."

That includes us. When we go to lunch, we eat fried bologna sandwiches in honor of Bonnie and Clyde. It was their last meal, some said. Bonnie died with half a sandwich still in her hand.

Portia is the only one who refuses. She

orders soup. "You guys are sick," she says.

"I have to admit, I'm starting to wonder what I married into." Krista side-eyes Eddie, who shrugs.

"This is a totally normal American thing to do," he says. "If it wasn't, would there be so many Bonnie and Clyde attractions?"

"No," I say.

"Exactly."

Eddie holds up his iced tea and we clink glasses.

Of all the things I've learned since the last trip, the most important is this: You can't fight every battle. Otherwise you end up bloodied, drained of energy, and unable to go on. Sometimes it's better to agree and keep your mouth shut. That's what I've decided to do on this trip. Otherwise we'll never make it to the end.

"You guys are so weird," Portia says. But she's smiling. "And fried bologna is gross."

Not a lie.

"So are we moving on to Texas?" Felix says.

"Texas?" Portia says.

"Not yet. We're going north," I say.

Felix starts to protest and I put up my hand, stopping him.

"North," I say. "We're going to Arkansas."

Grandpa called Arkansas the most underrated state because there were so many weird things to see: the place where Elvis got his hair cut before going into the army, the birthplace of Walmart, multiple historical sites devoted to Bill Clinton, not to mention a monument marking the state's first legal human dissection. All of these are in Arkansas, along with the Henry Humphrey memorial.

We don't tell Felix and Krista about it.

"It's a surprise," I say. "Just wait."

"Is there blood?" Krista says.

"Probably not."

"I don't know how you guys remember everywhere we stopped," Portia says. "Most of it's a blur."

I think of the book in my bag. It's the only one I brought with me.

"You were too young," Eddie says.

Portia sticks out her tongue like she's six years old. When we get back into the car, she puts on her headphones and disappears, lying down in the back seat.

Felix takes out his phone and I know he's going to look up tourist attractions in Arkansas. He can't stand not knowing.

I grab it. "No googling."

"I wasn't."

"You were."

We all retreat to our corners, metaphorically, and the car goes silent.

The same thing happened when we were kids. Grandpa didn't ever tell us where we were going next and it drove us crazy. We whined, begged, and pleaded, finally all three in unison. Grandpa laughed until he didn't.

"Shut up," he said.

It was the first sign of his temper.

We ignored it and we kept right on going. The Grandpa we knew wasn't an angry man. He was nice and funny and he loved to play games. Most of the time, he wasn't even a bad sport if he lost.

Plus, we were on a road trip, a grand adventure, a quest! Who got mad when they're adventuring?

Grandpa did.

I had never seen his temper before the road trip, and I wasn't prepared when it got even worse. He lowered his voice, speaking each word as if it were his last.

"Shut. The. Hell. Up!"

He banged his fist against the dashboard, making all of us jump. That's what really got me. The fist. None of us wanted that flying in our direction. Grandpa sounded like something right out of the TV, almost like Mom when she got mad, except

Grandpa was a lot bigger.

Even Eddie looked scared, and that didn't happen often. Somehow Portia managed to keep her mouth shut for a while. Not easy for a six-year-old. Not easy for any of us.

When Grandpa spoke again, his voice was normal.

"You guys must be getting hungry. Who wants McDonald's?"

We were. We did. And when we were alone, we vowed not to pester him like that again.

That's always the way, isn't it? The threat of physical violence eclipses everything. As a child, you know it, and as a woman, it's always in the back of your mind. The slam of a fist can change everything.

It even changed me. I didn't know it then, when I was twelve. Later, as I started dating in high school and having relationships in college, it became clear. Men who raised their voices, who showed any kind of violence, repulsed me. I wanted the quiet guy in the corner, the one on his laptop or reading a book, or just standing around being awkward.

Felix is like that. Doesn't scream, doesn't yell. He either walks out or goes for a drive and he's never slammed his fist into anything. That's part of why I married him.

I'm never afraid when I'm with Felix.

And he's so easy to manipulate. He still doesn't know the real reason we moved from Miami to Central Florida.

ARKANSAS

STATE MOTTO: THE PEOPLE RULE

We arrive after dark. Small town, quiet streets, and one very special monument. The Henry Humphrey memorial stands in front of the Alma, Arkansas, police department.

"This is it," Eddie says. He takes out his cell phone and turns on the flashlight. The rest of us do the same, lighting up the etched memorial on the lawn.

"Jesus Christ," Felix says. "*More* Bonnie and Clyde?"

True. Henry Humphrey was an unfortunate victim of the gang. They forced him into the local bank and stole the safe. Henry was left alive, which seems like a lucky thing, but it turned out he wasn't lucky at all. The next day, he got into a shootout with the gang and lost.

I still remember standing here with Grandpa, listening to him tell the story of yet another Bonnie and Clyde victim.

"Don't be so quick to think something's good," he said.

"Because you might get shot the next day?" I said.

Grandpa smiled. "Hopefully it won't be that dramatic."

"You're so stupid," Eddie whispered in my ear.

When Krista hears the story of Henry Humphrey, she covers her face with both hands. Her voice is muffled when she speaks. "Please tell me this whole trip isn't about Bonnie and Clyde."

"I thought you said they were romantic," Eddie says.

"Only in the movie."

Felix nudges my arm. In the dark, his pale eyes stand out like headlights. "It's not, right? This isn't a Bonnie and Clyde road trip?"

Eddie faces us, holding up both arms. "Relax. This is the last Bonnie and Clyde stop on the road trip. I *promise.* Cross my cold black heart and hope to die."

Krista smacks him on the arm. This marks the end of our visit to Henry Humphrey's memorial.

Less than twenty minutes later, we're settling into our crappy motel for the night. The Red Barn Inn is neither a barn, nor is it red, but there is a picture of one on the sign. The rooms are the same as the previous nights, right down to the scratchy towels. Tomorrow we'll need to pick up more insta-dry disinfectant.

Felix is in the shower when I get a text from Eddie.

Meet me outside in five?

I answer:

Vending machines.

Not for the first time, I imagine how different the first trip would've been if we'd had cell phones.

I yell to Felix that I need to get some snacks, then slip out the door with cash in my pocket. The machines are at the end of the motel, past all fifteen or so rooms. A quiet walk, just like the other night, and if someone is watching, I can't see them.

The only one I see is Eddie; he's pacing and staring at his phone. The glow from the screen lights up his face.

70

He looks up as I approach and says "Hey" in a low voice.

"Hey," I say. "Are you whispering?"

"Almost."

"Why?"

He opens his mouth and shuts it. The vending machines are on the left, one for drinks and another for snacks. I walk over and try to decide between Doritos and Ho Hos. Both, it has to be both.

"So what's up?" I say, dropping coins in the machine. The plinking sound is hollow, like they're the only coins inside.

"How are you doing?" he says.

I shrug. "How are *you* doing?"

"Krista doesn't know any details. Nothing important, at least."

"So I gathered." The Ho Hos hit the bin, followed by the Doritos. I move on to the soda machine. "Neither does Felix."

"At all?"

I shake my head. "No."

"Maybe that's better," he says. "It's weird enough as it is."

I turn to face him. "You're the one who insisted we bring them."

"I know. Not my best decision."

It's been forever since I've spent this much time with Eddie, but I can still read him. He doesn't want to admit how bothered he

71

is by the road trip. Neither do I.

"Why do you think Grandpa wanted us to do this again?" I say.

"He was an old man. This is one last sick game," he says. "He probably wants us to be paranoid. To think there's more to it." He pauses. "Portia thinks there is."

"She does?" I answer too quick, unable to hide my shock.

He sighs and leans against a wooden post. "She was just too young. She hated the first trip."

More than anyone else, she did. At six, she didn't understand half of what we saw or what happened, and she never understood why Grandpa would get so upset. Most of the time she thought it was something she did.

"I talked to the lawyer about getting out of this," Eddie says.

I did, too. "And?"

"And he said this is the only way. It's in the will."

Same answer I got. "Felix and I could really use that money."

"So could we. Over a million each is a lot."

It is. I already spoke to an accountant and figured out exactly how much we'd get. The answer: quite a bit. Yes, we'd have to pay income taxes on it, but federal inheritance taxes don't kick in unless it's over $5 million. We could pay off our house, keep the rest for retirement. Maybe take a real vacation. Or create a college fund for our future child. If we have one.

Those were my first thoughts. The next ones were not quite as practical. That kind of money meant I could look for a new job, maybe take a new career path — one that doesn't put me in the same office building as my husband. It would mean a pay cut. Worth it.

My last idea was the least practical. The inheritance would give me more than enough money to divorce Felix and get settled somewhere else. By then everything will be different anyway. The road trip will be over and everything will be back the way it should be. The way it always should've been.

Sometimes it feels terrible to think about life without Felix. It's wrong, and I know that.

It also felt wrong to cheat on him.

Even worse, I knew it would and did it anyway.

But that's the thing about being handed a small fortune: You start to rethink everything. Money gives you options, and the more options you have, the freer you feel.

73

"We have to keep going," I say to Eddie. "We don't have a choice."

He nods and starts to walk away, but I have one more question. "Did you tell Krista about our parents?"

"I told her they're both dead," he says.

Good. I told Felix the same thing.

August 14, 1999
What's Your Ideal Day?
No school, that's the first thing. The second would be a text or even a call from Cooper, but that may be asking too much. Depends on his mood, because he can be a real asshole. That's why we aren't together right now.

I'd spend the day out of the house, away from my family. I'd rather be with my best friends, Meghan and Sara, maybe out at Crater Lake, as long as it's not too humid and the mosquitos aren't out yet, because who wants those ugly bites all over their legs? Not me.

We'd spend the day swimming and gossiping and then go back to Meghan's, because she's rich and her house is so big her parents barely know when I'm over there. We'd do our makeup and then go down to the mall and buy some new clothes. Well, Meghan would buy hers because she can. I'd steal mine because I can.

I wouldn't go home until dinner. That's when I'd find out Cooper did call because he realized — finally — that we're obviously meant to be together forever. But I wouldn't call him back right away. I'd make him wait.

Dinner would be my favorite, chicken parmesan, and I wouldn't even scrape the cheese off the top. I'd eat it all, plus dessert, even if it meant not eating for a week.

Mom and Dad wouldn't fight at all. They wouldn't even give each other dirty looks. We'd all have a great time and after dinner we'd play Risk. Of course I'd win, because this is MY ideal day and not someone else's.

Oh, and Grandma would be there. I miss her so much. Maybe I'd even let her win Risk.

12 Days Left

If you've ever been on a long road trip, you know how it goes. On the first day, everyone is excited to get going, happy about leaving their everyday life behind. Everyone is nice to one another, even family members. That excitement flows into the second day. Not as intense, but still there.

The third day, fatigue sets in. There's a happiness hangover from the first day, plus the realization that you're stuck with these people for a while. You're too tired to pretend anymore, so you become who you really are because you can only hide it for so long.

Even Krista.

You know her. She's the one who's happy to organize the office Christmas party, the one who circulates the get-well cards for signatures, and when homemade goodies show up in the break room, you know she brought them because she does it once a week.

In Arkansas, we meet the other Krista. The one who is late to breakfast and looks like she's only slept for an hour. No makeup, under-eye circles darker than her eyebrows, and her sleek hair now looks dull, like she used a dry shampoo.

She plops down next to Eddie, who has already ordered the Southern special and is piling butter on top of his grits. Krista snarls at his food. Literally. Snarls. "I guess you don't plan on living long enough to see your kids graduate from high school," she says.

I freeze. My fork hangs in midair, and Portia's stops cutting the crust off her bread. Not sure what to think about the bomb Krista just threw on the table. Eddie doesn't have kids. He's smart enough to not point that out.

"I don't think a few weeks of bad food will kill me," Eddie says.

"Maybe tonight we can eat at a healthier place," Felix says.

"I'm in," Portia says. "Thank God."

Krista lifts her hands, waving at the waitress until the woman comes over. She's in her forties and has the varicose veins of someone who has worked on her feet for a while.

78

"Fruit," Krista says. "Whatever you have that looks good, I don't care what kind. One slice of wheat toast, no butter."

The woman nods. Waits. "Anything else?"

Krista glances at our coffee cups. Plain coffee, nothing fancy at this place. "Coffee. I guess."

"Thank you," Eddie says to the waitress. He adds a wink.

The waitress smiles at him as she walks away. Krista goes back to her snarling.

I try to remember what we were talking about before Krista walked in. Something about where we're headed next.

"So," I say. "Oklahoma."

Eddie nods and starts to speak. Krista doesn't let him. "We're not going to see another Bonnie and Clyde thing, right?"

"I told you we weren't," Eddie says.

"But sometimes you lie."

Boom.

Bomb number two releases a lot more information, and it tells me Krista is not just tired from a lack of sleep and bad food. Eddie has been an asshole again.

"The first stop is actually the Three Corners, so we're sort of going into Missouri first," I say.

"The Three Corners," Krista says.

"It's where Kansas, Missouri, and Oklahoma meet. You can stand in three states at one time."

Krista looks like she wants to say something about that, but the waitress appears and saves all of us.

The fruit is melon and pineapple, the toast is plain, and it all looks edible enough. Even the coffee is hot enough for me to see the steam. Still, Krista turns up her nose as soon as the waitress turns her back. She spears a piece of fruit with a fork with a bit too much force.

"Anyone see the game last night?" Eddie said, nudging Felix's elbow. "The Cowboys aren't half bad this year."

Krista stabs another piece of fruit.

Portia, never one for unsaid bullshit, rolls her eyes so hard I can almost hear them rotate in their sockets. "I'm done. I'm going to go outside and get some air."

She gets up and walks out, not mentioning the fact that this is her turn to pay. No one else mentions it, either. I nudge Felix, who I know is keeping track of these things, and he barely nods.

"So what's after the corners thing?" Krista says. "The Oklahoma bombing site?"

"No," Eddie says.

I'm done eating and get up to use the restroom. I stay long enough to check Instagram and see what he's up to, but he hasn't posted yet today. Still too early for anything interesting to happen, I suppose.

When I return to the table, everyone has cleared out and the table is empty. Felix waves to me from the cash register.

"We have a flat," he says.

A flat tire doesn't describe the whole situation. What we have is a flat *new* tire, the one we just bought yesterday. Several thoughts run through my mind, none of them good.

"Defective," Eddie says. "Must've been defective."

Felix nods.

Krista sulks.

Portia stares at her phone. "There's a place two miles down," she says. "Says they're open."

Two miles. We'll have to change the tire again to drive it. Or Felix will have to, since he's the fastest. He knows this, is proud of it, and goes to the back of the car to dig out the spare again.

"Hey."

Portia. She's next to me, walking, leading me back toward the diner and away from everyone else.

"Let's see if they have coffee to go," she says.

"Sure."

The cashier helps us this time. He's an older man who is wearing a button-up shirt and khakis instead of a uniform. His name tag says "Manager" and nothing else. We get coffee for everyone, even Krista. Today, we're damned if we do and damned if we don't with her.

As soon as we're alone, Portia says, "I saw that truck. The black one."

The third bomb this morning.

"Where?" I say. "Here? This morning?"

"No, on the road. Not all the time, just on and off."

"You're sure it was the same one? There's a lot of pickups around here."

"I'm sure," she says. "I saw the driver."

"So you think they're following us to slash our tire every day or so? Why would anyone do that?"

She shrugs. "I'm just telling you what I saw."

This time, Portia pays. She pulls out an impressive wad of cash and tips him well. Not broke after all, it seems, or maybe that's all the money she has for the trip. Hard to tell with Portia because I'm never sure what's up with her. She's sneaky like that.

Once again, Felix puts the spare tire on our car and we finally get to the auto repair shop. It doesn't take long for the mechanic to figure out what happened.

"Nails," he says.

"Nails?" Felix repeats.

"Yep, two of them. Probably happened yesterday. Went flat overnight."

We all stare at the mechanic. He's a young guy who looks like he'd rather be doing anything other than dealing with a flat tire.

"I put on the spare," Felix says. "I didn't find any nails in the flat."

"Here." The mechanic picks up the flat tire like it's a tissue and points to the nails. They are small. Easy to miss.

"Wow, didn't even see them," Felix says.

The mechanic doesn't look surprised. When he finds out we're on a long road trip, he tells us to replace it. "Don't want a blowout, do you?"

"Absolutely not," Felix says.

He goes with the mechanic to pick a new tire. Portia is off in a corner of the parking lot, drinking her coffee and talking on her phone. She does that a lot, like all of her calls are so important we aren't allowed to listen.

Eddie and Krista are in another corner of the lot, not talking. Sulking, maybe.

I send Eddie a text.

Did you see that black pickup following us?

I watch him take out his phone and read it. His back stiffens. Maybe surprise, maybe recognition.

From Alabama? Seriously?

Just asking.

No, I did not see them follow us through three states.

When Portia is off the phone, she comes over and says exactly what I know she's going to say.

"It's hard to believe this was an accident."

I sip my coffee, wondering how far into

this I want to get. Krista and Eddie are already in a fight and that's a lot of drama for one morning. "You think?" I say.

"If we randomly hit nails on the road, why are they only in that tire? Why not the front one?"

Because we were turning. Because we were changing lanes. Because Eddie was fiddling with the radio and swerved a little. A million other reasons I can't think of because this coffee is too weak.

Portia stands in front of me, her eyes unwavering, and I believe that she believes the truck is following us. In a movie, this would end with hillbilly cannibals, but we aren't in a movie.

"You've seen too many movies," I say.

She stares at me, unsure. "Maybe. Still seems weird to me."

"It is weird, I'll give you that."

"I should have taken a picture of them," she says.

Again I agree and nod my head. It feels a bit like when we were younger and Portia screwed up but tried to convince everyone she didn't. No one really believed her, though sometimes we pretended to because it was easier. She knows that now, and I bet she knows I'm doing it again.

"It's too bad none of us became cops,"

Portia says. "It would be easy to get this asshole's identity."

Our movie is now a TV show. A police procedural. "Right," I say. "Too bad."

"Or a hacker. A hacker would work, too."

We are, thankfully, interrupted by Eddie and Krista. She is pouting, he looks fine. No surprise there. Eddie asks if we know how much longer it will take and Portia opens her big conspiracy-laden mouth.

"You saw it, too, right?" she says.

"Saw what?" he says.

"The pickup. It's been following us."

Krista's head snaps up, the sulk gone.

Eddie turns to me, his eyes wide. I give him nothing.

"I didn't see it," he says.

Portia looks like she's about to stamp her foot on the asphalt. Before she can, Felix appears. I didn't even see him come out of the garage.

He starts talking about the tire, about the mechanic, about all the cool car things in the garage. Halfway through a detailed explanation for why he didn't find the nails in the tire, he stops talking. No one is listening and he finally realizes it.

"What?" he says.

"Portia has a theory," Eddie says.

"It's not a theory, it's a fact." She turns

her back to Eddie and faces Felix. "I've seen that truck. It's been following us ever since Alabama."

Felix looks at her, then at everyone else. "Well, yeah. I figured everyone saw it."

Portia smiles. Triumphant again.

"Wait," Eddie says to Felix. "You've seen it?"

"Yeah. I mean, not every minute of every day, but I've seen it. Honestly, I didn't know it was *following* us, not at first. I just thought they were headed the same direction."

"Zigzagging through three states?" I say. "And you didn't think to tell me?"

"I said, *at first* I didn't know." Felix's tone is the condescending one, the one I hate. "And now the tire," he says, with a shrug for emphasis.

Eddie puts up his hand. "Whoa. You think these people followed us through three states to put nails in our new tire?"

"Exactly. Who follows people through three states?" I say.

"Psychos?" Portia says.

We all stare at one another, almost like we're in a contest, and we don't break until the mechanic interrupts us.

"Car's ready!" he yells out from the front of his garage.

Portia walks off first, damn near stomping

87

her feet. Eddie and Felix continue to discuss — or argue, or whatever — about the pickup, the tire, the nails, the impossibility of it all.

Krista is the one who grabs my sleeve. The sun makes the gold in her eyes flash like blinking lights.

"Beth," she whispers.

I whisper back, because who wouldn't? "What?"

"They're right. That truck has been following us."

She is so serious, so convinced. "How do you know it's them?" I say.

"Last night, in the parking lot. Eddie was asleep and I heard something. When I looked outside, I saw him. The older guy."

I shake my head, which is filling up with questions. Did she tell Eddie? Did he tell her she was crazy? Is this what they were arguing about? Maybe this is why she called him a liar.

"What do you mean you saw him?" I ask. "He was just standing around the parking lot?"

"Not *just*," she says. "He was sitting on the hood of our car."

I Don't Even Care What Day It Is.
What Does "Living Authentically" Mean to You? Are You Accomplishing It?
This journal is worse than I thought it would be, but I'm still stuck on this trip, so here it goes.

If living authentically means not lying on a daily basis, I'm not doing that. I wouldn't even try because lying makes it so much easier to get through life. Should I tell Mom and Dad when I'm not where I say I am? Should I have told them the first time I tried alcohol or weed or anything else? Should I tell them about that time I went out with a guy who was way too old for me?

Nope. No one my age lives authentically, and if they say they do they're lying.

Just today, I've told so many lies I can't count them, starting this morning when I said "I'm fine" to anyone that asked how I was doing. That was a lie.

After eating one piece of toast and nothing else for breakfast, I said I was full. That was a lie. I was starving because I'm always starving but no way am I gaining weight on this trip.

When I said I was excited about seeing the Three Corners, it was a half lie. I don't care about standing in three states at the same time, but I am sick of Bonnie and Clyde crap. Especially when Grandpa starts going on and on about how much he loved Grandma. It's all I can do to keep from throwing up all over him. Instead, I just nodded and lied and nodded and lied.

As much as I hated it, that time lying was easier because you've got to pick your battles. That's a Risk thing. You can't fight everyone all the time, you'll just lose your whole army.

Now that I think about it, maybe I am living pretty authentically. It's just the Risk version.

MISSOURI

STATE MOTTO: THE WELFARE OF THE PEOPLE IS THE HIGHEST LAW

We're back on the road now, headed toward the Three Corners. Everyone is looking out the windows, searching for that truck.

"If you see it again, call the police," Felix says.

It's strange how adamant they are about that truck following us. I swear I haven't seen it. This makes me wonder if there's anything else I'm missing.

And I'm not the only one. Eddie hasn't seen the truck, either. Of all the things he and I don't agree on, this is the one thing we do.

I catch Eddie's attention in the rearview mirror. Raise my eyebrow. He rolls his eyes.

Eddie and I have to communicate silently, just as we did on the first trip. There were

91

times we couldn't talk out loud then, either.

That very first night, we stopped in North Alabama and stayed at a roadside motel that looked a lot like the Stardust. Grandpa got one room with two beds, and he let us kids have them. He slept on a foldout cot he had brought with him.

"No sense in getting two rooms," he said. "I'm not going to leave you guys alone in a motel."

"We're old enough," I said. But really, I didn't want to be alone in one of those rooms.

"Too bad," Grandpa said.

On our second night, he called our parents from a pay phone. "No cell phones for me," he said, although they weren't too common back then. "Too invasive."

I'm not sure I knew what that word meant, but I knew it was bad.

We stood outside the motel, at a bank of pay phones, and as far away as possible from the other man using one of the phones. He may or may not have been staying at the motel, just as he may or may not have been up to no good.

One by one, Grandpa passed the phone to us.

"Hi, baby," Mom said. Her voice was

tight, the way it was when she tried not to yell. She and Dad had to be fighting again. "How are you? Everything okay?" she said.

"Yeah, everything's fine."

"Where are you now?"

"Ummm . . . Louisiana? Yeah, we're in —"

Grandpa took the receiver out of my hand. "Let your brother talk now."

A few more days passed until I started figuring out what was going on.

We were in Texas. Grandpa had driven north of it and then back down because he said, "That damn state is so big, it'll swallow us if we try to go through it." For the most part we went up and around it, then crossed into the Texas panhandle, near Amarillo. Grandpa wanted to see the row of Cadillacs half buried in the ground.

Right after we crossed the border, we stopped for gas. Grandpa got out of the van and I was sitting right behind the driver's seat. Something fell out of his pocket and slipped down a crack between the seat and center console. I reached for it and found a cell phone.

I showed it to Eddie, and we opened the flip phone to see a long list of missed calls. They all came from our home number.

Hundreds of them.

They started the day we left on the trip.

Portia is with us tonight, although she has gone out for some air. I can't blame her, because it's a little weird having all of us cooped up in a single space. Sure, we could start pre-spending our inheritance on an additional room at a crappy motel, but there's no guarantee we're going to get that money. We haven't made it to the end yet.

Felix and I are in the room alone. He sits at the table next to the window, pretending to work, but he's really keeping an eye out for the pickup.

I sit on one of the beds and turn on the TV. The reception is sketchy and the channels are limited, forcing me to choose a sitcom episode I've already seen. It wasn't good the first time.

Felix manages to stay quiet for 1.2 seconds.

"Did you see the truck?" he says.

"Personally, no. I haven't seen it."

"I guess you and Eddie weren't looking," he says, turning back to the window. "The rest of us saw it."

"I guess you would make a better detective than me," I say.

"I didn't say that." He sounds offended. Yes, really.

Am I messing with him? Maybe a little.

I turn up the TV.

Despite all the togetherness, the close quarters, and being in a car with the same people every day, Felix and I have been getting along pretty well. Better than I expected, considering I never wanted him on this trip in the first place.

Things hadn't been going well before the trip — you may have guessed that. You also may have guessed that Felix wants kids, and soon. I'm not convinced. I'm not sure I want kids at all, actually. Not with him or anyone else. This has been the root of our recent arguments.

The latest was a few days before we left. We went out to dinner with two other couples. Both have small kids and love to talk about them. Felix gobbled up every story, anecdote, and picture, almost swooning at one kid's new dinosaur sheets and another's discovery of reading. Yes, swooning. No exaggeration.

When I placed my hand on my glass of wine to take a sip, Felix put his hand on top of mine. Everyone could see it. "We can't wait to get started on our own family."

The comment surprised everyone, including me.

"Wonderful!" said one of the women at

the table. We weren't close. She was a dinners-only friend. "Congratulations."

I pinched Felix's palm. He withdrew his hand from mine, his smile tight.

He knew I was going to say something about this later, which was why he disappeared as soon as we got home. The argument never happened. It's still there, simmering under the surface, waiting for us to pick it back up again. Maybe we will or maybe not. There's nothing like an old-fashioned road trip to make or break a relationship. Each day, sometimes each hour, I find myself shifting between sides.

"Don't be pissed," he says. Still staring out the window, looking for that truck. Looking to prove me wrong.

"I'm not." I turn off the TV and the lamp on the nightstand. "I'm just tired."

I pick up my phone to set the alarm and notice a missed text. It came in half an hour ago.

From Krista.

Eddie is lying to you. He saw that truck following us.

11 Days Left

Before this trip, I never met Krista and have no reason to trust her — or distrust her. She has my phone number because we all exchanged them on the first day, just in case. I don't answer her text, but it keeps me awake for a while. It's one thing for me to lie to Eddie, but it's totally different when he lies to me.

At breakfast, everyone reports in. No one saw the black pickup or its occupants. No one even *thought* they saw the pickup, which makes this more interesting.

I keep my mouth shut about Krista's text. It's left unanswered on my phone, and I don't mention it to Eddie or Felix or anyone else. Let her mind race for a while. It'll be good for her.

We're driving west today, straight to Dodge City, Kansas. It was hard to forget Grandpa saying we were "going to Dodge so we can get the hell out of Dodge." He must have repeated that a hundred times.

No one says it today. Everyone is quiet until Portia opens her mouth.

"So last night I calculated how long it would take if we just drove straight through," she says. Her voice booms out from the back seat, instantly filling the car. "If we take turns driving and stop only for gas and food, we'll be there in less than two days."

It sounds like a challenge, or perhaps it's a dare. We used to dare her a lot when she was young and maybe she's getting us back.

"Can't," Eddie says. "I mean, physically we could do it but that's not the deal."

"You really think the lawyer would refuse to give us the money?" Portia asks.

"He has to," Felix says. "As executor, he has to follow your grandfather's wishes."

Portia rolls her eyes. "But how would he *know*?"

The car is a rental, paid for by the estate, and it has a built-in GPS. Easy enough to check where we've been, when the car was in use, and when it wasn't.

I point to the GPS screen in the center of the dashboard. "It's being recorded. Everywhere we travel is on that thing."

Portia slumps back in her seat. "One of us

should've gone into computers."

I can't argue with her.

Regardless, there is no chance we are deviating from the original trip. None. I won't let it happen.

No one else says anything, so Portia gives up and puts on her headphones. We return to a silence that doesn't end until we stop for gas. Eddie randomly asks if anyone remembers full-service gas stations, and only Felix answers yes.

Krista opens her passenger door. "I'm going in to get some water. Anyone want some?" She raises an eyebrow toward me.

"I'll come with you," I say. "I want to get some snacks."

Alone in the Stop-Start Mart, Krista asks if I got her text.

"Just saw it this morning. I must've been asleep when you sent it."

She nods once, curt and quick. Her voice is a whisper. "I think Eddie doesn't want everyone to freak out, that's why he's lying. But he saw that pickup."

"How do you know?" I ask. Also a whisper.

"Because when I told him, he said he already knew they were in the parking lot. He had *seen* them."

I take this in while trying to decide between the salt-and-vinegar chips and the low-sodium popcorn. I grab both and decide Eddie may have lied to me. He's lied before and no doubt he'll lie again. Maybe this time it's for a good reason.

"He's probably trying to calm everyone down," I say. "Makes sense to me." I move on to a row of coffee machines. These are the newer ones that spit out dollops of flavored sauce and I pick the one with the most sugar. Krista is right on my heels.

"But that's weird, right?" she says.

"Weird that Eddie lied to protect us? No."

"Not that," she says, grabbing a few waters from the refrigerated shelves. "Isn't it weird that you're the only one who *hasn't* seen the truck?"

When she puts it that way, yes. It's a little weird, but I haven't seen it.

Maybe because I'm too busy looking for someone else.

"I've probably been sleeping at the wrong times," I say to her. "That's why I've missed it."

"Maybe."

As soon as I have a chance, I send Eddie a text.

How well do you know your wife?

Is that mean? Maybe a little.

That's the thing about siblings. There's always a payback for something they did, no matter how old it may be. And Eddie has done a few things.

We get back on the road and Eddie glares at me in the rearview mirror. I ignore him. If he lied to me, he deserved that text. If his wife lied, he needs that text. Either way, I'm right.

He knows I was right last time, too. I was right about Grandpa.

It came to me all at once, like lightning had struck my brain. Not long after we saw Grandpa's cell phone and all those missed calls from our parents, I turned to Eddie and said, "We aren't supposed to be here."

It was late at night. We were all crammed into another motel room and everyone was asleep except Eddie and me.

"We aren't supposed to be where?" Eddie said.

"On this trip. With Grandpa."

"Why wouldn't we be?"

I leaned in close and whispered faster. "Why else is he lying about having a phone? Why are Mom and Dad calling so much?"

"Because they worry about everything."

"And," I said, "he never leaves us alone.

101

Never." I pointed to Grandpa's cot. He always set it up in front of the door.

"That's so no one can get in," he said.

"Or out."

"You're crazy. You sound just like —"

"Haven't you heard the way Mom sounds like she's about to scream every time we talk to her?" I asked.

He shrugged. "I guess."

I didn't convince Eddie that night. It took a while for him to even consider that our grandfather had just taken us. To be honest, I never would've considered it if it hadn't been for Grandma.

She died about six months before the trip. Ever since then, we saw Grandpa all the time. Sometimes he was at our house when we got home from school. He stayed late into the night, to the point where Mom and Dad started whispering about who would tell him to leave. Once in a while he slept in the attic room above mine. I'd hear him scream in the middle of the night, but they weren't scary screams. It didn't sound like he was screaming *at* someone; it sounded like he was having nightmares. A couple of times I heard him yell our grandma's name. He wasn't taking her death well.

Every time I think about that, I have to force myself to stop. So I pick up my phone, open Instagram, and check up on him. He keeps me focused on what I really want, and why I'm really here. The rest is just noise. It always has been.

KANSAS

STATE MOTTO: TO THE STARS
THROUGH ADVERSITY

Kansas is big and flat, or at least it feels
that way. The hills are few and far between,
so are the towns and the people, and it feels
like we're driving in a loop.

"Did you know Dodge City is called the
Queen of Cowtowns?" Felix says, reading
from his phone.

"I did not," Eddie says.

"Why would I know that?" Krista says.

"This says it's the quintessential Old West
town," Felix says.

In the back seat, Portia is turned away
from us. She's staring out the back window,
phone in hand, waiting to catch that truck.
"The only thing I remember is the museum," she says.

That's where we're headed. The museum.

"The Boot Hill Museum?" Felix says, still reading off the site.

Not that one.

I tap Felix on the arm, nodding to his phone. "Don't. Just don't."

He doesn't look happy as he puts it away.

"Krista," I say.

She turns, her face half-covered by one of Eddie's baseball caps. The sun is strong in Kansas. "Yeah?"

"I just realized you're the newest one to the family and we haven't played the Twelve with you."

"Oh my God, I forgot about that," Portia says. She's still facing backward, watching the road.

Eddie says, "Oh shit, Beth's right. Everyone has to play."

"Oh shit?" Krista says.

"It's just a question game," Felix says.

I nod and smile. "So we can get to know you."

Krista's shoulders sink a little as she relaxes. "Oh. Okay."

Felix opens his laptop and pulls up a Word document. Answers to the twelve questions are documented, preserved for all time, just in case they come back to bite you. That usually happens during the holidays.

The first five questions are easy. Where

were you born? Brothers and sisters? Do you have any kids? Where did you go to school? What do you do for a living? Krista answers them without hesitation.

The next five aren't as simple.

"Three words to describe your personality," I say.

"Outgoing," Krista says, stating the obvious. "Kindhearted aaaand . . . fun. I'm pretty fun."

"You are," Eddie says.

"I'm gagging back here," Portia yells.

"Next," I say. "Three words to describe your mother's personality."

Krista looks surprised. The question surprises everyone, and it's a hundred times more revealing than the previous one.

"Okay . . ." she says. "My mom is sweet, complicated, and a deep thinker."

"Now your father."

"Funny, successful, a big softie."

That tells us a lot.

"Next, what job would you hate to have?" I say.

"Ummm . . . I'd hate to be a fisherman. I don't want to smell like fish all the time."

"Good answer," Eddie says.

"If you could change one thing about yourself, what would it be?" I say.

"I'd like to be more patient. I'm not very

good at waiting."

Eddie laughs and then shuts up quick. We aren't supposed to comment on the answers because the Twelve is a serious game. Grandpa taught it to us.

We learned it before the road trip. Uncle Stephen, our father's brother, got engaged to a woman named Ella and they both came to our house for dinner. Grandpa was there and we learned about the game.

Ella was very pretty. She had shiny red hair and wore a black velvet jacket that looked so soft I wanted to lie on top of it. One by one, she answered Grandpa's questions. Ella didn't get upset, didn't look shocked. She kept her cool the whole time. That's how it seemed to me, though perhaps I'm remembering it wrong. What I do remember is that Grandpa didn't like her.

"Won't last," he said later.

He was wrong for five years, then he was right.

On the road trip, he made all of us play. We already knew the questions, even Portia, so none were a surprise. I still have the spiral notebook with all of our answers, though I haven't looked at it in a long time.

As an adult, I learned Grandpa didn't invent the game. One day I was doing something random on the Internet, and there it was. The same questions in the same order, with one difference: The real game was called the Ten. Grandpa had added the last two.

"Question eleven," I say to Krista. "If you could kill one person, who would it be?"

She gasps. "Are you *serious*?"

"It's just a question."

This one takes her longer to answer than the first ten combined.

"Okay," she says. "In high school, there was this guy. Jeff Skilling. A real asshole, like, the king of all the other assholes. He went out with this girl for a few months and when they broke up, he put these embarrassing pictures of her on the Internet. The worst kind of embarrassing. Sexual things." Krista pauses, then nods her head once. "Him. I'd kill Jeff Skilling."

No one says anything. I would bet my entire inheritance that we're all thinking the same thing: Krista has to be the girl in the story.

"Last question," I say. "*How* would you kill him?"

"I'd shoot him." No hesitation.

We all stare at her, a little stunned.

"Well, that's violent," Eddie says.

Krista smiles. "My dad taught me and I wouldn't miss."

"Okay," I say. "Those are the twelve questions."

"That's it?"

"That's it."

"Did I pass?"

Eddie smiles at her. "Of course."

Felix closes the file called *Krista: The Twelve.* Honestly, it's only necessary for the first ten questions. Everyone remembers the answers to the last two. I still remember ours.

Our first road trip was in August, and the heat was stifling inside and out — much hotter than it is now, in September. By the time we got to the questions, I was paranoid about my own grandfather, who still alternated between adventurous and angry. Portia had been cooped up too long and was driving everyone crazy. When Grandpa got to the question about who we would kill, Eddie answered first.

He wanted to kill a friend of his who was rich and had all the new gadgets and bragged about it. Andy Fastow had everything and made fun of people who didn't.

"I'd shoot him," Eddie said.

Portia wanted to kill her teacher, who made her first-grade class do all sorts of boring things and they never got to have any fun.

"I guess I'd shoot her, too. Like Eddie," she said.

When it was my turn, I said I'd kill the guy who shot up the school in the next county over. He was just a kid like me, but he deserved to die.

"I'd give him a bunch of sleeping pills," I said. "He'd just die in his sleep, never knowing he wouldn't wake up."

I still think that's the best way to kill someone. No sense in making a bloody mess.

Monday, No Idea What the Date Is.
Doesn't Matter.
What Is Your Favorite Memory?
Before Grandma got sick, we used to go out
to lunch on her birthday. All the girls, Mom
would say. We all got dressed up and wore
big hats, like church hats, and even lacy
gloves. I hated it at first, because all we did
was sit around in the sun and eat tiny sandwiches while Grandma talked. It was her day,
Mom used to say. After a few years, I started
saying the same thing.

I don't know when that changed. I just
remember that her stories were actually pretty
interesting so I stopped pretending they
weren't.

The last birthday we had was over a year
ago, right before the doctor said she was sick.
I wore this light green dress with a giant
matching hat. It was a costume, just like
Grandma wore. Now I know that. Back then I

thought we were just dressing up. Grandma wasn't. She was playing a part.

I didn't know that. Not until I learned that all those great things Grandma used to say about Grandpa were lies. When the truth came out, she wasn't all dressed up in a hat and fancy clothes.

She was lying in bed, too thin, too pale, and too sick to worry about what she was wearing or how she looked. Cancer was making her waste away, and it was like whatever energy she had left all went to telling the truth about Grandpa.

"No way," Felix says.

Eddie smiles. "Way."

We're at the Gunfighters Wax Museum in Dodge City, which is conveniently located in the same building as the Kansas Teachers Hall of Fame. The building, the sign, everything about it screams the 1960s.

"This is where your grandfather brought you?" Felix says.

Krista is so annoyed. "What was *wrong* with him? Why would he *do* that?"

"Same reason they're here," I say, nodding to the people coming out of the museum. More than one family and lots of children are here today. "Everybody loves death."

"And teachers," Eddie says.

Portia waves at us from the car. "I'll stay out here and rest my ankle."

That ankle has become an excuse for Portia to skip anything she doesn't want to do. Either that or the damn thing is really broken. I don't call her on it, though. Arguing about every little thing is what makes people hate you, especially when it comes to family. They're the least forgiving of all.

Inside the museum, a helpful woman sells us two-for-one tickets to both museums, beginning with the Teachers Hall of Fame. Grandpa had skipped that. He said we could learn about school when we were *in* school, but not when we were on vacation.

"School's overrated anyway," he said.

"Did you even graduate?" I said. Rude? Sure, but I was a kid. This kind of brutal honesty is supposed to be funny.

Grandpa didn't think so. He pounded his fist against the hood of the van. "How did you turn out to be such a little shit?"

I stepped back, away from his hands, and I shrugged. Probably would answer the same way today.

This time we walk through the teachers museum before heading upstairs to see the gunslingers. None of us have any kids, let alone any old enough to be in school, but we do it anyway.

Upstairs we find Buffalo Bill, Wyatt Earp, Doc Holliday, Calamity Jane — they're all preserved here in Dodge City, staged in vignettes of the Old West. The old wax figures look more like mannequins than people. They scared the hell out of me when I was twelve.

So did the head of someone I'd never heard of. That's the display: a severed head still bloody at the neck. Now it's not scary at all.

"Okay," Felix says, snapping a picture on his phone. "This is pretty cool."

"You mean, this is pretty creepy," Krista says. "Your grandfather was obsessed with violence, wasn't he?"

Eddie and I exchange a look.

"Maybe," he says.

I shrug. "Possibly."

Definitely.

The most bizarre part of the museum is Dracula, Frankenstein, and the Wolfman, who appear without explanation. Twenty years ago, they made Portia cry. I can still see her running away, sobbing, and Grandpa chasing after her. Too bad we didn't have camera phones then.

No one cries today. We only laugh at how crazy it all is, but I have to admit it's entertaining.

When we're finally done and go back outside, Portia is leaning against the back of our car, scrolling through her phone with one hand and holding a gigantic soda cup in the other.

"Anything?" Krista says.

"Nope."

Neither of them mentions the truck everyone is looking for but hasn't seen. Not today.

Dinner is at a barbecue joint, because barbecue is the only appropriate food to eat when you're in the Queen of Cowtowns. We go to a hokey place with a plastic cow hanging from the ceiling and faded gingham curtains. Our waitress wears a Betty Sue name tag and I'm 100 percent sure it's fake.

"I've gained weight," Portia says. "My shorts are getting tight, so we have to stop eating this crappy food."

"It's been less than a week. You aren't gaining weight, you're retaining water," I say.

She ignores me. "Tomorrow I'll find a place for us to eat salads with vegetables instead of fried meat."

"That sounds great," I say.

"I'm serious," Portia says.

"Oh, I know."

Krista is the only one who doesn't laugh. Her mood, which had started out pretty good today, has deteriorated ever since the museum. This is not the road trip of her dreams.

"Just tell me," she says. "Are we going to stop at every creepy, violent attraction along the way?"

"Not *every* one," Eddie says.

"But there are more," she says, burying her head in her hands. "This is the weirdest road trip ever."

She's right, it is, and that's not even including Grandpa's ashes.

"You don't have to be here," Eddie says to Krista. "You can fly home. Enjoy yourself while we finish this trip."

She lifts her head, staring at Eddie like she forgot that part. Krista isn't really a part of the trip. "That's true," she says.

"You should just go," I say. "Why force yourself to be miserable?"

Her eyes brighten a bit. "I mean, we're probably halfway done anyway, right?"

"Something like that," I say.

She wants to go. Eddie lives in a nice house on the beach. It's the same one he lived in with Tracy and now with Krista. It's modern, with clean lines and lots of windows facing the gulf. With a new wife and an expensive house like that, it's no wonder Eddie needs this inheritance.

"It probably wouldn't be a big deal to

drop me off at an airport, would it?" Krista says.

"Not at all," Eddie says. The idea is gaining traction for her, and for him. He's starting to look relieved she might be gone soon. "It's barely a detour."

Lie.

I say nothing. It's better if Krista gets home as quickly as possible. Whining never helped anything, and she's been doing it a lot.

Eddie turns to Felix. "You could go, too. No reason for you to traipse around the country like this, either."

"Yeah," Felix says. "But I wouldn't feel right about it, not with that truck following us. I'd probably just worry."

Krista's face changes. She's remembered the pickup.

I could kick Eddie. And Felix.

"I forgot about that," Krista says. "If I left, I'd just sit around wondering if you guys were okay." She turns to Eddie. "I'd probably be calling you all the time, driving you crazy."

He sees his mistake. Swallows hard. "You wouldn't have to do that. We'll be fine."

"No, no. I'll stay," Krista says, looking like she'd rather do the opposite. "I should stay."

"Great," Eddie says. "Whatever you want."

"So what's next on the list?" Krista says, rubbing her hands together. "The town with the most gruesome serial killer? The museum of horrible ways to kill someone?" She looks at Eddie. He turns to me.

"Beth's the one who remembers everything," he says.

Portia motions to the waitress, pointing to her beer mug. "I swear, I don't know how you do it," she says to me. "I try to block it all out."

I smile. I do remember everything, that's true. Really, it isn't that hard.

It also helps to have the book I brought. Everyone thinks I'm reading a big family saga because that's the cover I put over the journal. Felix won't touch it because he only reads nonfiction. Family sagas aren't his thing.

TEXAS

STATE MOTTO: FRIENDSHIP

In the morning, I go walking with Felix. It's only the second time I've joined him since the trip began, and that's disappointing. I had such high hopes for myself on this trip.

The first thing we do is check the tires on the car. They're fine.

We walk for twenty minutes, chatting about a work problem back home. His problem, not mine. Felix likes to talk them out, perhaps to make sure he is handling things the right way. Perhaps because it makes him feel smart. Even after all these years, I don't care which reason is right. When he's satisfied with his chosen course of action, we return to our room.

I notice it right away.

My phone. Every night, I put it facedown

on the nightstand. This is out of habit, and on purpose, because if I see the blinking light indicating I have a message waiting, I have to read it. Usually it's work, and it can wait until morning. To avoid reading or sending e-mails in the middle of the night, my phone stays facedown.

Now it's faceup. Light blinking.

Felix heads straight for the shower, not noticing anything, and I don't stop him. I want to be sure.

I try to remember if I looked at my phone before we went out for the walk. What I do remember is rolling off the bed and into my clothes, pulling on my shoes right before we left the room. If I had looked at my phone and saw the light blinking, I would've read the messages. I would've looked at Instagram to see if he had posted anything.

I check the time the new ones came in. Maybe it was while we were walking, and I'm wrong about this. Maybe I did check my phone before we left.

Nope.

All of the new messages arrived in the middle of the night, after I went to sleep and before we left. Even the spam.

I immediately check my bag and wallet. Nothing is missing. All money and credit cards are accounted for, and so is the book.

Still, someone has been in this room.

I don't mention my phone or the room to anyone, not even Felix. Not yet. He'll think it's those guys in the truck, because right now they're being blamed for everything. I don't think they did it.

But I bet I know who did.

"I've got it," Portia says. We've just started on our way. "It's called RE-AL." She pronounces it with two syllables. "Healthy food, no grease."

Fantastic.

The restaurant is in a remote corner of Kansas, right near the border with the Oklahoma Panhandle. On the way there, no one mentions the pickup truck or lack thereof.

At RE-AL, we are greeted by the owners, who are young and hip and have New York accents. In the first few minutes, we learn that one is a former chef at a big NYC restaurant and the other worked in advertising. They fled New York for a cheaper way of life. I don't like the food or the faux New York style, but there's no grease and it's not barbeque. It's not even faux barbeque, so I don't complain about how tasteless the food is.

"I have to admit," Felix says. "This was a

really good idea. We've been eating the worst food."

"Although it does taste good," Eddie says.

Portia glares at him. "So does this."

"All the food on this trip has been delicious," Felix says.

We all nod.

Krista is a big fan of RE-AL. She even stays behind to chat with the owners after we're done. Felix goes to the restroom. Portia walks outside to check the tire again, which leaves Eddie and me alone. It's the first time since Krista sent me that text.

"Truth," I say. "Did you see that truck following us?"

"No. I told you I didn't."

I take one last sip of organic, natural caffeine-infused tea. "Krista seems to think you did see it."

Eddie rolls his eyes. "Well, of course I told her that. I'm not about to tell her she's wrong."

"Oh, I'm sorry. I didn't realize you're afraid of your own wife."

"I'm not afraid, I'm just avoiding a fight. You saw what she's like when she's mad."

I did, a couple days ago when she was spewing venom in every direction. "What was that about?"

"She's just jealous. Thinks I flirt too much."

"You do."

He shrugs. "Can't help it."

"You're such an asshole."

"So I've been told."

When I first heard the name *Cadillac Ranch,* I naturally assumed it was an actual ranch, the kind with cows and horses and pigs. Chickens running around. Dogs barking. Cowboys lassoing. That type of thing.

Instead it's ten Cadillacs half stuck in the ground and covered in graffiti. There is no ranch, no animals, no pasture. Just a sculpture, as Grandpa called it, and it had something to do with the open road and American cars and some millionaire who paid to create it.

How stupid, I said then. My opinion changed, though not because burying cars in the dirt was a good idea. It isn't, but there is something special about the place.

Last time, Grandpa brought the paint. This time, Eddie has it.

"Everyone pick a car and paint," he says.

We aren't the only ones here. Tourists are everywhere, mostly taking selfies with their own graffiti. I go straight to the third Cadillac from the left and look up at the

124

underside between the two wheels. I don't care whose picture I'm in, or if I'm in someone's way. Green paint, that's what I'm looking for. Even just a piece of it.

"It's been too long."

Portia. She is standing behind me and staring at the same spot.

"Probably," I say.

"Definitely."

She walks away.

I don't stop looking. I look for so long that I think I see a speck of the same green paint, buried under twenty years of graffiti.

This place was less crowded back then. Some took pictures, though not with phones. It was hotter than it is today, and there were more children because school hadn't started yet. Kids climbed all over the cars, inside and out. Portia loved it, I didn't. At twelve, I thought of myself as basically a teenager. Too old for such things.

I still remember the message on this car, though. Bright green paint, like a grasshopper.

I'm interrupted again, this time by Eddie.

"Stop," he says.

"I know, it's been too long," I say.

"And it's not why we're here."

But it's why I'm here.

Eddie motions to Portia, calling her over

to join us. She walks up to us, holding a spray can. Her index finger is now covered in black paint.

"What?" she says.

"I just want to make sure we're all on the same page," he says.

Portia looks at me, then up at the car. "About graffiti?"

"About this trip," he says. Add a few more years and a few more pounds, and he would look just like Dad. "We're here to put Grandpa where he wants to be. That's it."

"And collect our inheritance," Portia says.

"Exactly." He nods. "But that's it. We aren't here for anything else."

I am.

"Okay?" Eddie says.

Portia looks at me and shrugs.

I shrug back. "Okay."

Lie.

"Good." He claps his hands together, perhaps a signal of success. He and Portia return to their previous tasks while I find a can of green paint. Bright green paint. I have to stretch up on my tiptoes to write what used to be there.

Here I am

8/

126

I wasn't the one who wrote it the first time, but I know who did. The original message was just like that, with the date left unfinished. I paint it just like it was. My handwriting isn't the same, but it's close. It makes me feel better that her graffiti is back where it belongs.

Back where *she* belongs.

You knew about her. Even if you didn't consciously know, you knew because it's how these stories go. It's a law. Maybe even written in stone by now.

There's always a missing girl.

Our motel near the Cadillac Ranch is the worst yet. Given where we've been, that's saying something. The Whirly-bird has always been a dump, from the paper-thin walls to the walk-up window that serves as a check-in desk and a place to buy cigarettes. Maybe other things as well. They have to be doing something to stay in business.

"Tomorrow I want to stay in a decent place," I say. "It doesn't have to be fancy, just clean with real towels, maybe a coffee-maker."

"Sounds good to me," Felix says.

"And for once, Portia should have her own room. We can afford that for one night."

"Aren't you a princess," Felix says.

I smile. "Bow next time you say that."

"Will do," he says. "That was cool today. The Cadillacs."

"Yeah, it was."

Lie.

"What did you paint?" he says.

"Just the usual. Initials, the date. The 'I was here' thing."

"Me too."

It's late. Felix is already in bed and shutting down his laptop. The day has been a long one and I should be tired. Instead, I stand up so fast it startles him.

"You okay?" he says. Just like I knew he would.

"Fine. I just want to get a soda from the vending machine. Maybe walk around a minute. It's stuffy in here."

"Oh." He looks at me, then at the door. "You want me to come with?"

"No, no. You get some rest. I'll be fine."

"Take your phone."

I do. I bring my phone and my wallet, and as soon as I walk out of that musty room, I take a big gulp of cool air.

There's nothing around, nothing to see except a clear sky. Five cars are in the parking lot; one is ours and the others are scattered in front of a few rooms. All have out-of-state license plates. More road-trippers as unlucky as us to stay here.

Right by the street entrance, there's an old wooden chair. Functional, yet ugly. It looks like someone put it out for the trash but no one picked it up. I don't have my disinfectant spray; however, the wood does look cleaner than the ground. I sit.

Here I am
8/

I've always wondered if she was going to add more. Her name, maybe. I don't know why. Even if she did, it was probably nothing. Some silly, rambling thing. Something a seventeen-year-old girl thought was important enough to memorialize in green paint on a Cadillac. That's why I painted it again: because it deserves to be there. Her words should be where she wants them.

Felix doesn't know about her, the same way he doesn't know about our parents or about what happened on the first road trip. I'm not going to tell him unless I have to.

My phone buzzes. I don't look at first, assuming it's Felix, but it's Portia. She says:

Eddie thinks you're losing it

I answer:

He's assuming I ever had it?

Nice. You're up?

Outside. Look for the wooden chair.

Minutes later, I hear her footsteps.

"Scoot," she says.

I do. We share, each with one butt cheek on and one off.

"What did he say?" I ask.

"It was after dinner. He pulled me aside and asked if I thought you were okay. I said you had never been okay."

"Thanks."

"Welcome. Then he went on and on about how you were staring at the car, looking for her graffiti. Maybe looking for her. He thinks you're going to drive yourself crazy if that's what you're doing."

"Mmm."

"Mmm?"

I shrug. "It's weirder that he doesn't give a shit about her. That he isn't looking at all."

I glance over at her and it hits me, again, how young she is. I swear she could pass for twenty. "He needs the money," she says.

"We all need the money."

"I mean, he really needs it." She pauses, scraping the ground with her thick leather boot. "I've heard him arguing with Krista about it. And a couple of nights ago, he was yelling about a judgment and lien."

131

It's that big house of his. Eddie's money problems are much worse than mine, and much worse than I originally thought. "No wonder he's so protective of Grandpa's ashes," I say.

Portia laughs. "He sleeps with that box next to the bed."

"No."

"Yes. I mean, I need the money, too. But not like that."

Just enough for her to pay off the student loans and stop stripping. Get out of that crappy apartment. Stop living with a roommate who sells something. Drugs. Maybe herself. The inheritance is more than enough.

"I don't think this is all about money," I say. "Grandpa could've just given it to us. He wanted us to go on this trip for a reason."

"Eddie doesn't care."

"Do you?"

She looks out at the dark street like a car might appear. It doesn't. "Yes and no? Like the thing with today, the paint. The Cadillacs. I remember that day, and I remember the fight and the green paint and she was yelling about not finishing. But I don't really know what happened, I was too young to understand." She shrugs. "It's been twenty years. I can't imagine knowing would change anything."

I disagree with everything she said. "Maybe you're right," I say.

She pats my arm, like she's the older one. "Of course I am. Now let's go back into this shitty motel and get some rest."

I almost stop her, almost tell her about someone coming into the room at the last motel. "You go," I say. "I'm not tired yet."

I watch her walk back to the motel. Portia was only six during the first road trip. She missed a lot and doesn't remember half of what happened.

I do. Not only what happened, but also what we were like. We are right back to being who we used to be.

Portia, too young to know what she was seeing. Me, wanting to see everything, know about everyone. Especially her. Eddie, blinders on, looking straight ahead, not admitting she existed.

And her. Nikki.

The firstborn. Our older sister.

Nikki with her wild, flaxen hair, her blazing eyes, her body constantly in motion. Here, there, everywhere, all at once.

And I have her journal.

I'm Pretty Sure It's Tuesday.
What Are You Thinking about Right Now?
That asshole at the Cadillac Ranch. He was old — as old as Dad — and he stood behind me staring the whole time I was trying to paint. Finally I had to say something, because what girl wouldn't, so I told him to fuck right off. Just like that.

All of a sudden, I'm the bad guy. I'm the bitch who cursed at a stranger and no one cared that he was the one staring at my ass. I told him to stop and he said if I was going to dress like a slut then men were going to stare at me. I called him an asshole and all of a sudden his wife — HIS WIFE — showed up and told me to stop yelling. By the time Grandpa even noticed something was happening, it was all out of control. The asshole and his wife were there with, like, a whole posse of friends and they all were yelling about me being the troublemaker.

Grandpa bought it. No surprise there, the adults always do. Oh, something bad happened? Must have been Nikki. Something got stolen? Nikki. Someone ran away? You bet your ass it's Nikki, because who wants to stick around to hear that all the time. That's why I run away so much.

Sometimes I wonder why I haven't run away from this trip yet. First, it's because of Beth. If I'm not around to protect her, it's not like Eddie will. He'd protect Portia because she's so young, but not Beth.

Second, it's because of what Grandpa did to Grandma. I've known about it since she died, and I might be the only who knows what he did to her. Someone's got to pay him back for it.

9 Days Left

About that pickup.

I stayed outside last night for another fifteen minutes or so, more than enough time for Portia to get back to her room.

I hadn't seen a car drive by all night, not a single one, and then I saw the truck. Black with the double-cab and oversized wheels. The front windows were tinted and rolled up so I couldn't see the driver or passenger.

Still, I knew. The back window was rolled down a few inches. As they passed by, a wisp of cigarette smoke escaped. I caught a flash of that auburn-haired woman in the back.

I sat right in that wooden chair and watched it, too shocked to move, until I could no longer see the taillights. Everyone was right about the truck: It was really following us. When it was gone, I ran inside to tell Felix.

He was asleep, but not for long.

136

"It's here," I kept saying. I said it until he responded.

"What's here?"

"That pickup. It just drove by outside."

He jumped out of bed and ran to the window. "I don't see it."

"It was on the road, driving by."

"You called the police?" he said.

"Because a truck drove by?"

Felix looked at me, his white-blond hair sticking out in all directions. It always looked like that after he slept. "Yeah, I guess that doesn't make any sense."

No, it did not.

I didn't call the police, I called Eddie.

"I saw it," I said. "That truck is definitely following us."

"Jesus Christ."

Back and forth, like a seesaw, this is what my mind feels like the next morning. The first thing I do is go outside and check the tires on the car. They're fine. I stand and stare at them, not thinking about the tires but thinking about that woman in the back. Thinking about how easy it is to dye your hair.

Felix comes up behind me. He slips one hand around my waist and offers me a cup of coffee with the other.

"Is that from the vending machine?" I say.

"No. It's from the check-in window. Only fifty cents."

I sniff it. Not bad.

"Just drink it," Felix says.

I do, and it's not the worst.

Krista joins us in the parking lot, though she didn't stop for a fifty-cent coffee.

"What's happening? Is it flat?" she says.

"No," I say. "Tires are fine."

"Imagine that." Eddie. He's right behind Krista, carrying their roller bags. He doesn't like to ruin the wheels by pulling them across cement.

Krista gives him a dirty look. He ignores it.

Portia shows up last in her usual outfit: T-shirt, shorts, sunglasses, no makeup. "What's everyone standing around for?" she asks.

"Waiting for you to tell us where we're eating," I say.

She waves her hand, dismissing all those healthy notions. "This is Texas."

No one answers that. We load up our things, I down the rest of that coffee, and we get in the car.

It doesn't start.

Again Eddie tries, and again the car doesn't start.

138

Felix checks under the hood and figures out the problem in minutes. Not a dead battery, not out of gas — nothing normal has happened. The starter relay was removed. I can't pretend to know what that is or how it works, but without it the car won't start. And car parts don't remove themselves, not even in Texas.

"Sabotage! We're being sabotaged!" Krista yells. Repeatedly.

Yes, it seems we are.

"I saw the truck last night," I say.

"I knew it!" Krista yells.

Eddie glares at me in the rearview mirror. No, he didn't tell her because he obviously knew she would act just like she is. So did I, but the fact that the truck really has been following us makes me feel unsettled.

And very curious about the woman in the back.

Eddie talks a Lyft driver into picking up the starter relay and bringing it to us, then passes the phone to Felix to describe what we need. The Lyft fee will be more expensive than the part, but less than having the car pick us up to go get it ourselves.

"We have to call the police," Krista says, taking out her phone. She has the oversized kind, like a small tablet. The cover is mint green.

"The police?" Portia says. "Jesus."

"The car's been vandalized. *More than once,*" Krista says.

"We can't prove anything," Felix says.

"Yeah, they'll probably throw us in jail," Portia says.

Krista's head whips around to face her. "For what?"

"It's Texas. I think they can arrest you for anything here. Probably just for annoying the police."

"But we *have* to —"

"Wait, just wait." Eddie walks up, hands in the air like he's stopping a boxing match. "I'm not getting stuck here waiting for the police. It's not like they'll do anything."

"We're just going to let those Alabama assholes keep doing this? Are you serious?" Krista says.

"Let's just get the car fixed. We'll all go to breakfast and figure out what to do."

Eddie turns to me, nodding his head once. He remembers. So does Portia. We all remember what happened with the police in Texas.

What Is Your Greatest Strength? Weakness?

Wow, okay. These are some useless questions because no one would get them right about themselves. That's pretty much impossible. But here goes . . .

Other people would say my greatest weakness is not being able to keep my mouth shut. I say it's my greatest strength, because who wants to be one of those people that keeps everything inside and then has a heart attack at 40? Not me.

But it does get me in trouble, even if it's not my fault. Example one, yesterday at the Cadillacs, when everyone blamed me for that asshole staring at me.

Example two, today at the museum.

Grandpa parked the van and we went in. It was another weirdo place just like all the other crappy, weirdo places Grandpa has brought us so far. This one was called the Devil's

Rope Museum. I mean, honestly.

I saw them first. It was that couple from yesterday, the same asshole and his angry wife, so I went and stood right next to them and waited for one of them to see me. The wife did. She looked over and her eyes got huge and she nudged her husband.

I admit I was a bitch, because who wouldn't be? I said something like, "Oh looky here, it's the asshole" and yeah, I had that tone. That's what Mom calls it. That tone.

But damn if I was going to keep my mouth shut about that pervert. I just didn't realize all hell would break loose the second I opened my mouth. The asshole said I needed to stop following him (as IF) and the wife said I was stalking them. I yelled back, their friends joined in with them, and the next thing I know the police show up.

Apparently they're always close by in Texas. Someone at the desk dialed 911 and the police just appeared.

They blamed me for starting all the trouble. I MEAN ARE YOU SERIOUS, but yes, they were, and they kept saying "This is Texas" like it meant something. They questioned me, they questioned Grandpa, they even questioned Eddie and Beth, but at least they left Portia alone. Paranoid much, Texas?

After a billion questions and a bunch of calls

to whoever was looking things up, yes I had to admit I'd run away several times. Yes, maybe I shoplifted some things and got caught, like 1% of the time, but no I wasn't a stalker. I wasn't dangerous. I pretended to be a dumb teenager because that's what they already decided I was.

They also searched the minivan, I guess to make sure we weren't secretly drug mules or something, and that's when they found the gun. I didn't even know Grandpa had one. I mean, sure it was legal and registered and all that, so of course the police let him keep it. But still, it would've been nice to know it was there. What if Portia found it? This van is so not childproof.

8 Days Left

Our breakfast feels like a meeting of the Five Families, except we're just one family with a lot of opinions.

Krista: Call the police.

Eddie: Keep going. Ignore them.

Portia: Find the pickup, confront the people inside.

Felix: Establish a schedule for watching the car throughout the night. We don't know what these people want or why they're following us, so we should be vigilant.

They all turn to me and I keep eating my toast. It has the perfect amount of butter and raspberry jam — the first time that's happened during this trip.

Eddie taps his index finger on the table. "We just need to get this trip over with," he says. "Then we can all go on with our lives."

Yes. I agree with that. My life will be a million times better after this trip.

"I'd rather not wake up dead one morning because of those psychos," Krista says.

Neither would I, but yes, I get her point.

"Screw it," Portia says. "We should put nails in *their* tire."

Yes. That, too.

Felix shrugs. "I told you my idea. Make the schedule."

He really likes schedules. We have dozens of them on our refrigerator at home.

"Well," I finally say, "since we really are being followed and apparently sabotaged, then I guess we have to go with Felix's idea. Let's watch for them, and when we see them, we'll decide what to do."

Felix nods.

"Good," Krista says.

"Fine with me," Portia says.

Eddie rolls his eyes. "Whatever."

"As long as we do call the police," Krista says. "Like they say, we shouldn't try to approach them on our own."

The more Krista speaks, the more I dislike her.

"Fine. Perfect. Let's just figure it out and get going," I say.

Krista looks around at everyone, as if gauging the mood of the room. "Are we all good? Everyone okay?"

I stare at her, realizing maybe I've been

wrong. Maybe Eddie isn't with her just because she's so young and pretty. Maybe he's also with her because she reminds him of our mother, because right then Krista sounded just like her.

Mom always had to make sure everyone was okay, including at all our family meals. That's how I remember her: walking around the table, checking on each one of us, making sure we had what we needed. She always wore the same kind of perfume, and I always smelled it when she leaned down beside me. Before she would settle down and eat, she would say "Are we all good?" just like Krista did.

Even when Mom had big news to share, she had to make sure we were okay. And for Nikki, Eddie, and me, Portia was the biggest news of our lives so far. Mom and Dad sat us down in the dining room — the formal one — and right away Mom let us know we weren't in trouble. Nikki visibly relaxed.

"We have great news," Mom said. "I'm pregnant."

That's how she told us about Portia. I was six, Eddie was eight, and Nikki was almost twelve.

Eddie and I stared at Mom, unsure of what this news meant for us.

"Are you okay?" Mom said.

"Pregnant?" Nikki said. "You won't even let me get a dog."

"A baby is not a dog," Mom said.

"But why? What's wrong with just us?" Nikki said.

"Nothing's wrong with anyone," Dad said.

"It will be great," Mom said. Her voice was tight, like she was angry. Maybe at us, maybe because we didn't give her the right reaction. "Everything will be great. I promise."

I didn't know if it would be or not. I was the youngest, and sometimes it was horrible because there were so many things I couldn't do. But being the youngest wasn't the worst thing, either, because I got a lot of attention. I knew that would change.

Nikki narrowed her eyes, stuck out her chin. "I'm not changing diapers."

"No one asked you to do a thing," Mom snapped.

Nikki smiled like she had won.

"So are we good?" Mom said. "Everyone good?"

We all said we were, just like we all said it to Krista.

Felix scribbles out a car-watch schedule on a napkin. Five-hour shifts, long enough to give the others time to rest but not long enough for the person on watch to fall asleep. So he says. I swear to God, Felix and his schedules. It can be maddening.

I bet if he sees the truck, he'll take a picture of it and nothing else. The flat tire and missed starter relay didn't faze him at all. He's not even close to his breaking point. If he has one.

"Felix," Krista says. "We can just put the schedule in our phones. You don't have to write on a . . . napkin." Her nose turns up as she tries to stop him.

"Let me just finish," he says.

More scribbling. Sometimes the best thing to do is ignore Felix, which is exactly what I do until we leave.

Next stop: Devil's Rope.

Yes, we're still in Texas. Grandpa was right about it swallowing you up, because we are staying in this state for not one but two stops.

Devil's Rope is what the Native Americans called barbed wire, and yes, there's an entire museum devoted to it. That didn't seem very exciting when I was twelve, but it turned out to be amazing. Barbed wire changed everything.

We learned about how it was used in the nineteenth century, when people could just settle on a piece of land and call it their own. The barbed wire was how people marked their territory, and it also kept the cattle in, otherwise they would just roam around. That's why cowboys hated it, along with the Native Americans. So many animals died when they walked into it, hence the name *Devil's Rope.*

I remember walking out of that museum

149

in awe of how important barbed wire was to our history. Even more important than Bonnie and Clyde.

But before I could voice this discovery, Grandpa ruined it.

"There's another reason why they call it Devil's Rope." He turned to us, one eyebrow raised. "The harder you try to get out of it, the worse it gets."

Nikki snorted. "Kind of like this road trip."

Grandpa raised his hand. I thought he was going to hit her, but she ran off before anything could happen. That's when she saw the couple from the Cadillac Ranch.

Today we tell Krista about the museum before we get there. She's already upset, and no one wants her to completely lose it. Whatever that would look like.

"Devil's Rope?" Krista says. "Jesus, what a name."

"It's not what you think," Eddie says.

She rolls her eyes.

I get a text from Felix. He is sitting right next to me.

Seriously, what was the deal with your grandfather?

150

My grandma died not long before the trip. He wasn't thinking real clear.

Felix nods as he reads it.

That explains a lot.

It does and it doesn't. Since he doesn't know anything about Nikki, I can't tell him that she was Grandma's favorite. I can't tell him how she was the one who took care of Grandma while she was sick and dying and Grandpa couldn't handle it. I can't tell him how much Nikki hated him for what he did to her.

So I don't text him back.

The museum is the same as I remember, only it's bigger and has more displays. Just as we had been fascinated by it, so are Krista and Felix. Especially Felix. He insists on reading about every display, which keeps us here for quite a while.

"I take it back," Felix says as we leave. "That's a pretty awesome place."

"Not bad," Krista says. "Not what I thought."

Eddie puts his arm around her as we walk out the door. Portia waited outside, again, and she shakes her head at us. No truck.

Eddie heads back to the interstate, the

same one we've stayed near. And yes, he's still the one driving. The only one ever, no matter what anyone else says. Because that's who Eddie is.

"North?" Krista says. "Again?"

"Yep," Eddie says.

We all sit in the same place every day. Sometimes it feels like the same road, the same scenery, like we're going around in circles. Our clothes change, though. No one wears makeup anymore except Krista, and she's down to only lip gloss. Portia's black nail polish is chipping and she hasn't fixed it.

I take out my laptop, decide maybe I should get some work done. Every night I download my e-mails to skim through them, because looking at my inbox puts me to sleep. Now, after multiple cups of coffee, it still makes me sleepy.

Before this trip started, I looked at my e-mails first thing in the morning and read them before I was even at work. After one week on the road, I'm wondering how I do this every day.

Maybe that's what I'll do with the inheritance. Forget the bills and the house and anything sensible. I'll quit my job and do something that doesn't involve staring at a computer.

This idea gives me a lot to ponder during the drive, as I once again avoid reading all those unopened e-mails. Instead, I think about what else I could do. I could train dogs, trim trees, deliver packages, wrap presents, ride horses, or join one of those now-defunct circuses. Read about barbed wire.

Nikki and I can do all of this together. Or we could just hang out on the beach. After I find her, we can do whatever we want.

Last time we left the Devil's Rope Museum, I wasn't daydreaming and the car wasn't quiet. Everyone was mad, either yelling or huffing or pouting. Grandpa was furious at Nikki for getting detained by the police for making a scene. He thought it was her fault, just like the police did.

We were back in the car and Nikki was in the passenger seat, practically tied down with the seatbelt. Arms crossed, mouth tight, face red. Nikki was angry about being blamed for everything again. Grandpa was angry the police almost called our parents.

"Do you know what your mother would do to me?" he yelled at her.

He had a point. Mom was always mad about Nikki these days, and getting a call from the police wouldn't help anything.

"I *told* you," Grandpa said. "I *explained* that your parents are trying to work things out. Don't you want them to stay together?"

"I don't care," Nikki said.

"That's not nice."

I couldn't see Nikki roll her eyes, but I knew she did.

In the back, Portia was crying. She had no idea what was going on, but all those policemen scared the hell out of her.

Eddie had his head down and earphones on, the sound turned up to a thousand. NIN blasted loud enough for all of us to hear.

"Turn that shit down!" Nikki yelled.

Eddie didn't hear her, didn't look up.

"Language!" Grandpa screamed, even though he swore all the time.

"Who cares?" Nikki said. "Nobody cares if they get divorced. Nobody!"

Portia cried harder.

"I care," Grandpa said.

"No you don't," I said. "You didn't want the police to call them because we aren't supposed to be here."

Nikki's head whipped around to face me. "What?"

"Beth," Grandpa said.

"No, what did you say?" Nikki asked — no, demanded.

So I told her. I told everyone that Grandpa had taken us, and our parents never gave him permission.

I said it for a lot of reasons. Because they were yelling and Portia was crying. Because Eddie wanted nothing to do with any of it. Because Nikki had been so upset ever since the Cadillac Ranch. Because I wanted attention. Because I wanted *Nikki's* attention. Ever since she became a teenager, it was impossible to get.

And because I really did think Grandpa would've hit Nikki if she hadn't moved away from his fist.

That was the moment everything changed — for our trip, and for us. A shift in perception about what we were doing and why we were there. You know that switch — when you realize the hunter is being hunted, the predator is the prey.

"He *stole* us?" Nikki said.

"Beth," Grandpa said. "You're being ridiculous. You just spoke to your parents last night."

I ignored him and spoke only to Nikki. "Haven't you noticed the way he's always standing right there when we're on the phone? And how Mom always sounds like she's about to explode? And," I said, leaning closer to Nikki. "Why do they keep ask-

155

ing where we are? Why doesn't Grandpa tell them?"

Grandpa banged his fist on the dash more than once. "Stop this right now!"

Nikki's eyes lit up, like she had just found the last piece of a puzzle. "Holyyyy shit. You're right."

Eddie took off his headphones. "What's happening?"

"We've been abducted," Nikki said.

The car lurched to the side, taking all of us with it. Grandpa pulled off the road and he turned around in his seat. He had never been a good-looking man, or maybe he was when he was younger but not when I knew him. He had ruddy skin, a bulbous nose, short legs, and a long torso. "Nobody has abducted you."

"Then why do you hide your cell phone?" I said.

"Cell phone?"

The stunned look on his face convinced Nikki. She smiled as big as I'd ever seen. Even Portia stopped crying.

"Oh my God," Nikki said. "This is awesome."

"Awesome?" Eddie said. "What's so awesome about it?"

Nikki didn't answer. She just kept smiling.

156

What Is Your Worst Habit?

Obviously it's that I'm too trusting. I trusted Grandpa when he said Mom and Dad wanted us to go on this trip, even if he was an asshole to Grandma. I trusted Beth would always tell me everything. I trusted that I hadn't been abducted.

Wrong. Wrong. Wrong.

Oh, and I trusted Grandpa was an okay man until Grandma told me he wasn't. Not even close.

The only good thing here is that other people are trusting, too. No one has a clue what I'm planning right now. Even if they suspect I'm up to something, they probably think I'm just going to run. I'm not.

Also, if you asked my mom this question, she'd say my worst habit is causing so much trouble. Most of the time, I don't even start it. I just get all the blame.

OKLAHOMA

When I said Nikki was close to Grandma, it was an understatement. Nikki practically lived at their house the last couple of weeks, when we all knew Grandma was about to die. Her cancer was so bad that the doctors stopped treatment and sent her home.

I went over there, too, just not as much. Grandma couldn't get out of bed and was only awake for short periods of time. The bedroom already smelled of death.

No idea how I knew that at my age, but I did.

If Nikki noticed it, she didn't say anything and never would have admitted if it bothered her.

Nikki and Grandma had one big thing in common: They were both the oldest child of four. That's why she always gave Nikki better presents, more gift money, and bigger slices of pie at dessert. Grandma used to say the firstborn had it the worst, because parents had no idea what they were doing yet. They had to experiment.

"I'm your guinea pig," Nikki used to say to our parents. "Firstborns are always the guinea pigs."

Grandma told her that and no one could talk her out of it. Our parents also couldn't stop her from skipping school to stay with Grandma during those last days.

What I didn't know about, didn't even think of, was the medication.

I didn't realize Nikki was the one who kept it organized, who made sure our grandmother took the right pills at the right time not just for the cancer, but for blood pressure, thyroid, cholesterol, and pain. She kept the bottles all lined up and color coded on the nightstand because she was afraid Grandpa would screw them up.

A few hours after Nikki learned we had been abducted, we were in another motel room, still blocked by Grandpa's cot from leaving. And by his gun, because by then we all knew he had one. I never really believed Grandpa would shoot one of us, but a gun was so foreign to me that it was like a living thing. I was scared to get too close to it.

As I was about to fall asleep, I felt Nikki's breath in my ear.

"Follow me," she said.

I didn't hesitate.

The only place to go was the bathroom, and that's where she went. Once inside, she shut the door and turned on the light. Nikki had Grandpa's toiletries bag in her hand.

"I forgive you for not telling me earlier," she whispered.

"Okay. Thanks." That wasn't really what I wanted to say. I wanted to say I'd kept my mouth shut until I was sure because I was afraid she would laugh at me for being wrong, but it didn't seem like the time to say all that.

She sat on the floor cross-legged, wearing sweats and an old rainbow shirt she'd had forever. I always hoped to get it as a hand-me-down but she wouldn't let it go. Not yet.

Sitting in that bathroom with her reminded me of when we were younger and used to play together. We'd sit on the floor of her room forever. That's how it felt. We'd play with dolls or games or whatever we could find until Mom yelled at us to go to bed. Sometimes we didn't. Nikki would turn on a flashlight and we'd stay up after everyone else went to sleep.

That all changed when Nikki decided she was too old to play with me anymore.

The road trip brought it all back, and it started that night. She shared a secret with me and she hadn't done that in forever.

I watched as she took Grandpa's medicine bottles out of his bag, reading each label before setting it down on the murky white tile. I wanted to ask what she was doing but figured I was supposed to know.

"Okay," she said, her voice still a whisper. "Check this out."

She opened the bottles and showed me a handful of pills. Three of them looked similar, the other two didn't.

"So?" I said.

"So look." She dumped a few of one kind out in her hand and put them in another bottle. You couldn't tell which pill was which. Nikki did this again and again until they were all mixed up. "Now he's going to take too much Vicodin."

"Okay."

She looked up at me, her eyes shiny in the dark. "You know what that means?"

I shrugged.

She sighed.

"It means we're taking control of this road trip," she said. "And Grandpa won't be able to stop us."

I nodded, keeping my confusion to myself. What did she mean, take control? Were we going to call Mom and Dad and tell them to come get us? I hoped so, because who wanted to be abducted?

That isn't what Nikki did, of course. Didn't even consider it.

As I watched her switch all those pills around, I had no idea what she was really up to.

I think about this now, as Eddie drives us through the Oklahoma Panhandle. It's thirty-four miles wide, and links routes from the Texas Panhandle to Colorado on the west, Kansas on the east. We're heading west.

"There it is," Portia says.

I look up, having no idea what she's talking about. "The border?"

"The pickup truck."

Pretty sure all of our heads turn at once.

"Are you shitting me?" Eddie says.

Portia doesn't answer. She's leaning over the seat, staring out the back window. I climb over our seat to join her.

"Where?" I say.

She points. To our right, behind a silver SUV, is a black pickup. Huge, double cab, black-on-black wheels. No license plate in front, typical for the South.

"Is it them?" Krista says.

"Could be," I say.

"It is," Portia says.

We're on a two-lane road, in the right lane, and the silver SUV is coming up on our left side. "Slow down. See if they'll pass us," I say.

Eddie does. He's looking in the side mirror, watching the truck.

The car behind us honks because we're slowing down. Portia flips off the driver, who looks like a teenager. He can't move into the fast lane because the pickup blocks his way.

"It's going to pass," Portia says.

"Then they can't be following us," Eddie says.

No one answers him.

"Wait," I say. "They're slowing down."

"Waaaay down," Portia says.

The teenager gets into the fast lane and passes us. The truck stays back.

"Get off at the next exit," I say. "Then get right back on. See if they follow."

"You watch police shows, don't you?" Portia asks.

Felix answers for me. "Movies. She likes the movies."

"Just do it," I say to Eddie.

He does. He increases his speed until we're moving normally again. The pickup does the same. When the next exit comes up, Eddie turns off without using his blinker. Everyone watches out the back window.

I'm looking for the auburn-haired woman.

"Moved to the slow lane," Portia says.

Eddie stops at the first light. We're below the interstate now, waiting for the truck to come down the off-ramp, and I can feel all of us hold our collective breath. We do not exhale until the pickup appears.

They *are* following us.

Eddie swears under his breath. "Shit."

"Light's green," Felix says.

Eddie doesn't step on the gas. The next thing I know Portia's out of the car, storming toward the truck coming up behind us.

They stop when they see her.

Felix follows her out of the car.

Krista takes out her phone. "I'm calling 911."

"What do you want?" Portia screams loud enough to cause an avalanche.

The guy in the truck guns it, tires squealing, and takes off down the road. Away from Portia, away from us, and they go right. Away from the interstate.

Gone. Just like that, they're gone.

"The police are on their way," Krista says.

We wait, because that's what you do when you call the police and they have your name, phone number, and location. They have it before you even say a word, and this is true everywhere, even Oklahoma. Personally, I'm beginning to wonder about this state. Last time I was here was when I told Nikki about Grandpa and everything exploded.

At least this time it's only about the truck.

"I'll do the talking," Eddie says.

Krista starts to argue and decides against it. I exhale. And I send Eddie a text.

The cops are going to think we're crazy.

He reads it, turns to me, and nods.

Don't get me wrong, I'm scared of whatever that truck is doing, but I also know we have no information that will interest the cops.

Whoever is in that truck knows what

166

they're doing.

Before I have a chance to text all of this to Eddie, the cavalry arrives. Otherwise known as the Oklahoma Highway Patrol. Two of them, on motorcycles, roar up to us. Our car is now on the side of the road and we're all standing outside of it except for Portia, who has climbed back inside the car and refuses to move.

Both patrolmen are male and both wear — yes — aviator sunglasses.

Eddie introduces himself, establishing that he is our leader. Krista is at his side, arms crossed over her chest.

Portia sends me a text.

Don't let Krista talk.

I shrug, assuming Portia's watching from the truck. What does she want me to do — tackle Krista to shut her up? Yes, probably.

Eddie starts talking, explaining everything from Alabama to Oklahoma. He's using his charming voice, smiling and laughing, turning red like he's embarrassed his wife called the police for this kind of thing. A good effort, but it still sounds bananas.

And there is no way to stop Krista.

"They put nails in our tire," she says.

"You saw this?" says one of the patrolman.

167

The name on his badge is Feldman.

Eddie shrugs. "Not saw them, exactly. But —"

"Who else would've done it?" Krista says. "I saw one of them in the parking lot the same night."

"Which parking lot?" Feldman says.

"At a motel, not here, but I mean they've been following us for a while," Krista says.

"And the starter relay?" says the other patrolman. His name is Pineda. "Anyone see who took that?"

No one answers.

Krista huffs. "I mean, come on!" she says. "I don't have to see every little thing to know what's going on."

Portia was right for staying in the car, and I wonder if it was college or the strip club that made my little sister smarter than me. Or maybe it's because she's single. I'll have to spend some time pondering that when I'm not with law enforcement.

"What exactly would you like us to do?" Pineda says.

Eddie jumps in before Krista does. "Look, we probably overreacted. It's been a weird trip for us, and to be honest, we're all a little raw right now. Our grandfather passed away and we're bringing him to his final resting place. That's why we're on this trip."

The patrolmen exchange looks. Feldman turns and walks back to his motorcycle, pushing up his sunglasses as he goes.

Pineda sighs. "You should have taken a plane."

He isn't wrong.

Oklahoma is where strange things happen, both now and then.

Grandpa started feeling woozy from the pain pills along this same thirty-four-mile stretch, and he pulled over as soon as he could. Nikki and I laid him out in the back of the van. He was slurring his words like he had been drinking.

"We have to call 911," Eddie said. "Then Mom and Dad." He reached into Grandpa's pocket for the cell phone.

"I have it," Nikki said, holding it up for him to see.

"You call then."

Nikki shook her head. "We're not calling anyone. He isn't sick."

"Look at him. How can you —"

"He's had too many pills," she said.

"How do you know?"

"I switched them around."

She stared at Eddie, daring him to say something. He looked at me. I looked to Grandpa, who was out of it but not unconscious. He understood what Nikki had said.

"Why?" Grandpa said.

We were in the van, pulled over in the parking lot of a fast-food restaurant right off the interstate, and we all stared at Nikki. Even I had no idea. I never asked her why because I didn't want to look stupid.

"Because of what you did to Grandma," she said.

"What are you —"

Nikki held up her hand to shut him up. "Don't. She told me everything."

Grandpa tried to sit up. "I don't know what you're talking about."

"Oh, you don't?" Nikki bent down, sticking her face close to his. "You don't remember hitting her?"

Everyone was too stunned to respond. I know I was.

"It's true," Nikki said. "You slapped her, you shoved her, you even punched her a few times." She stared at him, her eyes hard. "She told me everything. She wanted someone to know before she died."

"No," Grandpa said.

"Yes."

Portia dove into my lap, wanting protection from whatever was going on. "What's happening?" she said. She tried to whisper and failed.

"What's happening is our grandfather is a horrible man," Nikki said. "He was an asshole to Grandma and he's been an asshole to us."

Grandpa slumped back down on the seat, looking like he was in shock. He didn't say a word. Eddie crossed his arms over his chest. Portia buried her head in my lap.

I didn't hate Grandpa before then. Never had a reason to. Then all of a sudden I did.

Only later did I learn that Grandma didn't think she was talking to Nikki. She was too delirious at the end. Grandma said all of those things because she thought she was talking to her sister, not her granddaughter.

But the stories were true. All of them.

Nikki, still with the phone in her hand, nodded at me. Once. A sharp, sure movement.

"This is our road trip now," she said.

Who Is the Person from History That You Would Most like to Meet and Talk To?

Dr. Lang already asked me this question. I guess it must be especially revealing or something. I knew he wanted me to say Jesus, Washington, or Lincoln, because those are the obvious choices. So I did. I said Washington because he was the first US president so he had a unique insight into our history. Unique insight — I said it just like that and Dr. Lang laughed, but screw him. He gets paid by my parents, or our insurance or whatever, so he's just an employee.

He hates it when I say that.

But if I had to answer honestly, I'd say I want to talk to the guy who invented Risk. I always thought Dad was being dramatic when he said Risk isn't just a game, it's a metaphor for life.

Each turn has three parts: Draft, Attack, Fortify.

So, first you have to draft your troops. Your

172

allies. My closest ally has always been Beth.

Attack. That's exactly what we did to Grandpa — it was just with pills instead of guns.

Then we fortified our position. We got Eddie to come around to our side, and Portia had basically nowhere else to go.

I don't say this often about my parents, but Dad may have been right about this Risk thing.

COLORADO

STATE MOTTO: NOTHING WITHOUT PROVIDENCE

We're now in Round Two of the road trip, which began where Nikki took control. Felix and Krista don't know this. They also don't know that where we go and what we do is about to change.

This time, Round Two begins with a decent place to stay.

Not long after entering Colorado, we check into our first Holiday Inn. It's the only place we've stayed that has interior hallways, a continental breakfast, and coffeemakers in the rooms. They also have a bar, which is where we end up.

It's dark, everything is made of particleboard, and the bartender is a bored-looking young woman who would rather be texting. The other customers appear to be locals.

They all know one another and seem to have a somewhat incestuous relationship with one another. If they weren't so intoxicated and so loud, we wouldn't know that.

"We sort of ganged up on him," Eddie is saying. He's half watching a football game on the TV and half talking to us.

Felix turns to me. "You ganged up on your grandfather?"

I shrug. We shouldn't be talking about this, which is why I'm not drinking much.

"Not in a bad way," Eddie says. "But we all told him we didn't want to go to any more places where people were shot or ambushed or memorialized in wax."

Krista sips her wine spritzer but says nothing — she's still surly about what happened with the police earlier. Portia is on her third vodka tonic and starting to get on a roll.

"I mean, how many of those 'so-and-so was shot here' places are there in this country? Why do we memorialize this? How come we don't have markers that say 'so-and-so was conceived here'? The way we stigmatize sex in this country is an abomination." She slams her glass down on the table for emphasis.

"Exactly," Eddie says, still staring at the football game. "No more death places, no more weird museums, and no more Bonnie and Clyde. We're really, really done this time." He pauses and motions to the bartender for another round. I go to the bar and bring them all back in one trip, a skill I learned in college.

"What's next, then?" Felix says.

Eddie smiles, showing off his dimples. "It's a surprise."

"I hope it's a good one this time," Krista says.

I hand her another spritzer, heavy on the wine.

"Oh, come on," Felix says. "Tell us."

Eddie won't budge, and he doesn't mention that we'll be doing some backtracking. There are a lot of reasons why this trip took so long.

"If you aren't going to tell us, then stop talking about it," Krista says.

"Done," Eddie says.

"Good. Then can we get back to the truck?"

I say nothing. The truck is on my mind, too, along with the woman in the back. I got bored watching Eddie tease Krista a while ago. Instead, I constantly glance around the bar, keeping an eye out for the Alabama Godfather.

"To the truck," Portia says, holding up her drink. Only Felix toasts her. Eddie and

Krista are too busy glaring at each other.

"We're doing the stakeout thing, aren't we?" Krista says.

Eddie nods.

Krista pulls out that napkin with the schedule, the one Felix wrote out and Krista now maintains. "Your shift actually started two hours ago," she says to Felix.

Felix shrugs. "I guess we all got a little excited about this luxurious hotel." He stands up and stretches. "I can see the car from a window in our room. I'll go sit in front of it." He kisses me on the forehead and walks out of the bar.

Krista watches us and then turns to Eddie, still glaring at him.

"You're beautiful," he says.

She melts a little. It's a physical transformation that begins in her watery, drunken eyes. "That's not going to work."

Lie.

Eddie holds out his hand and she takes it. "Time for us to go," he says.

She huffs a little, pouts a little, and finally takes his hand. They weave out of the bar and toward the elevator.

"Jesus Christ," Portia says, shaking her head.

"Yeah," I say.

"You want another drink?"

"Probably shouldn't. I've got second shift."

"Ah, of course."

Tonight she's wearing her signature boots with jeans and a faded Tulane shirt. She looks like she should be a student, not a dancer on her night off. No judgment.

"Coming?" I say, standing up.

She points to her drink. Not empty. "When I'm done."

I pause, probably due to some provincial idea that women shouldn't hang out alone in random hotel bars. I'm sure it came from a list of rules written by a man, so he could weed out the good girls from the bad ones.

"Jesus. Go already," she says.

I go. If she can handle drunk tourists in New Orleans, she can handle Nowhere, Colorado.

Just as I head out, I stop and look back. Portia has already moved from our table to the bar, and she starts talking to the bartender.

She'll be fine, I tell myself. If the people in that truck wanted to hurt us, they would've done it by now. Even as I tell myself this, I walk back to her.

"You sure you'll be okay?"

Portia laughs. "I'll be fine. I promise. Get out of here."

I leave.

Our room is on the third floor, overlooking the back parking lot. I take the stairs hoping the walk will wake me up a bit. I'm not exhausted, but the thought of staring at our car for several hours is getting me there quick.

The second-floor landing has a window overlooking the side of the building. Nothing there except a road to drive from the front of the building to the back parking lot. Beyond that, a small green space and a path that leads to the street. This is where I see my husband.

Felix is hard to miss, even in the dark. His light hair and skin still stand out. He's standing on the footpath, not quite hidden by the trees on either side of him.

What strikes me is the glow. Not the glow of a phone screen, the burning glow of a cigarette.

Felix does not smoke. Never has.

7 Days Left

Instead of marching outside to confront Felix about the smoking, I decide to test him. I wait until he's done with his cigarette and comes back into the hotel, then give him time to get back to our room. By the time I walk in, he's already sitting by the window to watch the car. He stands up and stretches like he's been there for a while.

I lean in to give him a kiss. His breath smells minty fresh with a hint of beer, but I get a whiff of cigarette smoke from his shirt. "You smell like cigarettes."

"I know," he says, turning up his nose. "I went out to check the car and walked by a whole group of smokers."

"That must be it."

He takes a shower. I take my seat at the window. Up until I saw him smoking, I had no intention of watching the car half the night. Now I'm too keyed up to sleep.

The thing is, we can't smoke. We work at International United — *International Goddamn United* — and they don't hire smokers. They have far more health problems, which means the company has to pay more for insurance, and we were tested for tobacco before being hired. No-smoking policies are legal and companies like IU enforce it. Felix isn't just putting his health at risk; he's putting his livelihood at risk. Then who would have to support him?

His wife, perhaps? The one with the inheritance?

In the time I've known Felix, I've only caught him in one other lie. Yes, only one, and that was five years ago. One lie is nothing. My family lied on a daily basis. You couldn't win at Risk without a little lying.

Felix didn't even lie about anything important, either. Just a bachelor party that got out of hand. I knew about the party, though not everything that happened at it. A more forthright man told his girlfriend about it and she told me.

The smoking is different. It's not a lie by omission, like what I do. When I told him why I wanted to move to Central Florida, I said it was for work and that was the truth. It just wasn't the *whole* truth.

This, on the other hand, is an outright lie.

181

Felix was smooth about it, too — no stumbling, no stuttering, none of the signs I've learned to look for. Thinking about this keeps me awake throughout my shift, during which I see nothing. No one goes near our car. I think about my phone in that motel room, wondering if it was Felix who had turned it over and not some unknown intruder. Maybe he's been lying about a lot of things.

Still up?

Eddie, texting to see if I'm on the job.

I'm awake. All quiet.

He responds with a thumbs-up emoji and says:

I don't give a shit about those guys from Alabama. I'm just sick of finding our car damaged. Time + Money.

Eddie can be a real asshole, but sometimes he's the only one who makes sense.

Three hours of sleep is all I get. In part because of my shift, in part because of Felix's alarm. He set it to get up and walk this morning. I don't go with him. Instead,

I wonder if he smokes when he walks alone.

I wish I never saw that because I don't want to think about this now, in the middle of our trip. Today I have to think about the aliens.

Nikki had never shown an interest in them before, had never mentioned little green men or UFOs. She didn't even like *Men in Black,* but all of a sudden she wanted to look for aliens in the middle of Colorado. A place known as the UFO Watchtower had just opened and Nikki drove us there. She was seventeen and knew how to drive, although her license had been revoked because she got too many tickets.

Nikki not only took control of our road trip; she also took control of the music. She liked it loud. As she roared down the highway — as much as a minivan can roar — she blasted her favorite songs by Oasis, Radiohead, and Garbage. Especially Garbage. Her favorite song was "I Think I'm Paranoid."

Grandpa started refusing all pills, even the real medication, no doubt in an effort to sober up and take back control of the trip. Underestimating Nikki was one of his many mistakes. She dissolved the pills in water and he couldn't refuse to drink that. Not unless he wanted to die.

I sat in the passenger's seat next to Nikki, my head halfway out the open window. Eddie and Portia were in the back seat, and Grandpa was all the way in the back, not saying a word. The rest of us talked about what aliens looked like.

"I hope they aren't green," Nikki said. "I hate green."

"Me too," I said.

"I hope they're black and blue," Eddie said. "That'd be cool."

"Purple!" Portia yelled. "With trunks, like elephants."

"And polka dots," I said.

Nikki said no. "I hate polka dots."

"Me too," I said. "What about stripes?"

She shrugged.

We ate a mountain of candy, enough to make us sick, and we still ate more. The night before, we had pizza delivered to our motel. Nikki also made us call Mom and Dad because, at that point, we didn't know if the police were looking for us or not. Nikki didn't think they were, because we were still in the same car with the same license plate and no one pulled us over during the trip. We had a whole conversation about it while eating the pizza.

"Bet Mom won't call them," Nikki said. "She's not going to put her father in jail."

"Dad might," Eddie said.

"No way. He's not going to make Mom mad," Nikki said.

Eddie started to feel sick from all the junk food. He was laid out across one of the seats, holding his stomach. "Why don't we just go home? Why are we even staying on this trip?"

"We can't," Nikki said. "I'm not done yet."

"Done with what?" I said.

Nikki nodded toward the back seat, where Grandpa was knocked out. "I'm not even close to being done with him."

We all looked at her, waiting for more.

"This is for Grandma," she said.

I sided with Nikki because I always did. If she had a plan, I would follow. "Nikki's right, let's keep going. Mom and Dad have no idea we've figured out what Grandpa did. They think we're having fun," I said.

Nikki nodded. "That's the key. We act like everything is fine and normal and we're just having fun with Grandpa. And . . ." She held up a finger like she was pointing at us. Giving us an order. "No hinting about where we are. Pretend Grandpa is right there."

She dialed the number and spoke first, saying Grandpa was standing next to her.

Not a lie. He was next to her, and he was asleep.

She passed the phone to Eddie, who said the usual everything-is-fine-we're-having-a-great-time and then passed the phone to me.

I was too enthusiastic — although at the time, I didn't know that. I was just trying to impress Nikki.

The last one was Portia. She didn't say much, but at least she wasn't crying anymore. No one knew how much she understood or what she thought about any of this, but she did trust Nikki.

Nikki gave her very specific instructions about what to say. "Everything's great. So fun. I ate M&M's today."

Random phrases, the kind of thing six-year-olds spit out for no reason. Sometimes Portia was really good, other times she wasn't. I held my breath as Nikki put the phone up to Portia's ear.

"Hi," she said. "Great, so fun. I love M&M's."

Good enough.

We made it through the first night on our own. That's how we thought of it — as being on our own. Grandpa was asleep most of the time, and when he wasn't he looked a little afraid. Couldn't blame him. I also thought he deserved it.

Our only problem was money. We were almost out of it.

On the first trip, I didn't see any aliens or UFOs. Now the UFO Watchtower is much larger, more crowded, and it has a campground, a rock garden, and a gift shop, but I still don't see any aliens or UFOs.

"It's daytime," Portia says. "Hard to see UFOs when the sun's out."

"Is that right?" I say.

She nods, raising the binoculars up to her eyes and gazing upward. I'm shocked she even brought binoculars. For aliens.

"I had no idea you believe in UFOs," I said.

Portia gives me a bored look. "I just don't believe we're the only ones around. There has to be other life out there." She takes out her phone and glances at it. Someone is calling but I can't read the name. "It's my roommate, I better take this. Be right back." She walks so far away I can't hear anything she says.

I turn to Felix. "What about you? Do you believe?"

He shrugs. "Sure, why not?"

I've been asking him questions all morning, trying to catch him in another lie, trying to figure out if I know him. It's typical for him to go along with whatever is easiest when he doesn't care. Aliens don't rank very high.

"Do you?" Felix asks me.

No, but who cares about the truth at this point? "Sure," I say.

"You do not," Eddie says. "You made fun of it last time."

"I was twelve."

"Still."

It's true, I made fun of this place and the whole idea of it, but it was mostly because Nikki put me in charge of Grandpa. I wanted to be with her but was stuck with him. We couldn't leave Grandpa by himself in the car, so we had to help him to the platform, and I was in charge of standing by his chair, keeping him propped up. He wasn't asleep but he wasn't really awake, either.

So no, I never saw any aliens and I didn't believe in them. Bet Nikki didn't, either.

Just below us on the platform, Krista is walking around the rock garden. Discarded

189

items are strewn about, notes, tchotchkes, articles of clothes have been left as energy gifts to the vortexes. There are two here, near the watchtower, along with a circular view of the sky.

Next to me, a group of older women take this all very seriously. The watchtower is a pilgrimage for them twice a year and they have pictures from all the trips. One of them shows me a picture of glowing dots in a dark sky. UFOs, they say. The women have seen many of them.

Maybe that's what Felix is. An alien. You think you're married to a human only to find out he's from another planet. That would change things up.

"You okay?"

Not Felix. It's Krista. She's back from the rock garden, looking tired and hung over but she's in a good mood. It's a nice surprise, and when I nod to her, she smiles wide. Happy up to her eyes.

"I love this place," she says.

"You believe in aliens?"

"Why not?"

Why not.

Eddie is standing behind her. He's wearing sunglasses, making it impossible to gauge his reaction. I can guess, though.

I introduce Krista to the women on the

pilgrimage to get her out of the way. When Felix leaves to find the bathroom, I finally have a minute with Eddie.

"Tell me the truth," I say.

He raises an eyebrow. "It's a good thing Krista doesn't say things like that, otherwise I'd start running."

"Have you ever seen Felix smoke?" I ask.

"Smoke? You mean weed?"

"Cigarettes."

He shakes his head. "Never. Why?"

"It's probably nothing."

A lie, mostly. If it were nothing, I wouldn't have searched through his bag when he went out for a walk.

I'm not the kind who snoops. I've never felt a need to search through Felix's phone, computer, or e-mail. My thing has always been if he's going to do something bad, he'll do it no matter what. No way to stop it, but plenty of ways to drive yourself crazy. Like I did this morning.

I didn't find anything. No cigarettes, no lighter, nothing. He probably took them with him on the walk, or maybe they're hidden outside. For half a second I considered rushing out to follow him.

I decided against it because I don't want to be that woman. That wife. You know who

I'm talking about because we've all seen her before.

One day, a woman appears to be in a healthy, happy relationship; the next day she's in a movie of the week. It's that dramatic. It's that quick.

I think it happened to Eddie's old girl-friend. He met Krista when he was still with Tracy. I hadn't seen them for a while, but out of the blue Tracy started e-mailing and calling, asking how I was, how Felix was, and had I heard from Eddie lately? It was so odd that I called Eddie to ask what was going on.

"Going on? What do you mean, going on?" he said.

"I mean, is Tracy okay?"

"What do you mean, is she okay?"

"You screwed up again, didn't you?" I said. He started to answer with another question so I cut him off. "Just tell me."

"I didn't screw up on purpose," Eddie said.

I hung up, not bothering to hear the details, already knowing Tracy had become That Woman. The one who searches through her partner's things because she thinks he's up to something. Because she *knows* he's up to something. And Tracy was right.

■ ■ ■ ■

At the moment, Eddie is listening to two alien watchers talk about all the ships they've seen. Felix, back from bathroom, is with them. I glance at the pockets of his khakis, looking for the outline of a cigarette box. Don't see one.

I barge in, too tired to be polite. "Can I get the car keys?" I say. "I have to get something."

He hands them over and says, "Be careful."

It sounds patronizing. Has he always been patronizing and I just never realized it?

Maybe.

Yes, I search through Felix's things. Again. This time I find what I'm looking for. Half a pack of cigarettes and a plastic lighter, old enough to have scratches. Not a one-time thing — he has a habit. Don't know how I've missed it.

When I get over the shock, I feel horrible. Not because of him, because of me. I'm out here searching through his things because I couldn't control myself. Because I couldn't get this cigarette out of my mind, so I searched until I found proof and it doesn't matter that I had to invade his privacy. I did it anyway.

Why didn't I go outside and confront him while he was smoking? Why wait until I had to sneak around, rooting through his bags?

I know why. It's because I've become the kind of wife I hate.

Day, Date, Blah Blah.
What Would Happen If It Suddenly Started Raining Puppies and Kittens?
What the hell kind of question is this? They would all die and that's horrible.

Really, I've got no time for this. I'm a little busy running this road trip, and these questions are pretty stupid. But when I get home I'm going to let the publisher of this journal know it's a piece of crap.

We get a hotel room about five miles away from the watchtower. The name is different and it's been remodeled, but at first I think it's the same place we stayed the first time. I realize it's not when I look out the window. It's on the wrong side of the road.

Portia is with us tonight, though she drops off her stuff and leaves right away. She's been acting odd since we got here, but I guess we all are at this point.

It's late afternoon, giving us time to rest and eat before going back to see the UFOs at night like we did last time. Nikki made us go late, after midnight, because she figured the aliens waited until most people were asleep. This time we'll go after dinner.

Felix wants to nap. I go for a walk.

On the other side of the road, there's a general store. That's what it's called: Paula's General Store. It has a little bit of everything, from food to paper towels, air filters to scissors. And cigarettes. They have generic, name brand, and e-cigarettes, along with the nicotine gum, lozenges, and patches. Paula's is a one-stop shop for all things nicotine.

I buy three packs of Felix's brand and three lighters, all blue plastic. The purchase makes me angry. Cigarettes are more expensive than I realized. Felix has no business spending this kind of money on them, especially if it might cost him his job.

Out behind the store, I open a pack, take out a couple of cigarettes, and throw them away. Next I put all three lighters on the ground and rub them against the cement, scratching them up. Some guy sees me and watches. Maybe thinking I'm crazy, maybe trying to figure out what I'm doing. I smile at him and he walks away.

When I'm done, I put everything in my bag and go back to the motel. Portia is outside talking to Krista.

"Where'd you go?" Krista says.

"Across the road. There's a general store over there."

Portia snorts. "Good shopping?"

"They have Flaky Flix cookies," I say.

"Shut up."

I shrug.

"No one has Flaky Flix. They don't make

them anymore," Portia says.

"What are Flaky Flix?" Krista says. Just as she speaks, Eddie comes out of their motel room. His hair is wet and he's wearing a clean T-shirt. I bet it took him five minutes to look that fresh and clean.

"Flaky Flix?" he says. "You're talking about Flaky Flix?"

"Beth claims the store across the road has them," Portia says.

Now I'm caught, because Eddie knows it can't be true. He looks at me and shakes his head, then proceeds to spout off the history of Mother's brand Flaky Flix cookies, right down to the date they were discontinued.

Portia glares at me. "Liar."

"So sue me," I say.

In our world, Flaky Flix were no joke — least of all to our mother. Those cookies were one of the few things she loved.

Nikki discovered them first. She found half a pack of Flaky Flix cookies at the top of a kitchen cabinet. It was summer and we were bored, so we set up a little sting operation to catch whoever was eating the hidden cookies.

"Count how many are left," Nikki said, handing me the package.

I was about eight years old. Nikki was thirteen and always gave the orders and I always obeyed. I counted seventeen cookies. She counted them herself and confirmed.

"We have to set up a schedule," she said. "After dinner, we'll keep track of who comes and goes and try to count the cookies in between."

This was a little trick we learned from Mom. A few years earlier, she set up a similar trap to figure out who was messing with the garden figures she had placed around the backyard. We all said it wasn't us, it must be the deer or possums or some other wild animal. She didn't believe it, and she was right not to. Her little trap with a video camera caught Eddie knocking the figures over and crushing the flowers underneath.

We used a similar plan, although we didn't have a camera so we had to take turns watching in real time.

One evening, I was sitting in the family room when Nikki waved at me from the hallway. She was practically jumping up and down, and we both ran upstairs.

Now that she was thirteen, her room was in transition. Part child, part teenager. The lavender she used to love had made way for her new colors, black and red, and her toys were being replaced by clothes, rock band posters, and fashion magazines. She had stopped inviting me in so often. Tonight was special.

"Mom," she said. "It's Mom."

"No way."

"Way." Her eyes were so bright they could've lit up the whole house. "We have to mess with her."

I shook my head. No one made Mom angry on purpose, that was an unspoken rule in our house. "We'll get in trouble," I said.

"Oh come on."

"We can't."

"Stop being a baby," Nikki said.

I didn't want to be a baby. More importantly, I didn't want Nikki to think of me as one. It was also because the cookies were our secret. Eddie didn't know, and Portia was only two years old. This was ours.

Nikki wanted to do to Mom what she had done to Eddie. Mom messed with him the same way, only hers was even worse. She stomped on one of the garden figures and on her flowers, leaving behind giant fake footprints to make him believe there was a wild animal in the backyard. His reaction was caught on camera, and it became one of our favorite holiday videos.

Nikki's plan wasn't nearly as bad. All we did was move the cookies to the same shelf but in a different cabinet. At first, anyway. Another time we put it on top of the refrigerator, then inside the freezer. Watching Mom's reaction was the best part — if we were lucky enough to catch it.

I saw her find the cookies in the freezer, and it felt like I could see what she was thinking just from the expression on her face. Surprised at first, then confused. She picked up the package and opened the cabinet to where they were supposed to be. More surprise at the empty top shelf. Finally, her brow furrowed hard, causing so many wrinkles. Her mouth turned down, her lips pursed.

Worried. So worried. I could almost see her wonder if she had put the cookies in the freezer but didn't remember doing it.

I ran upstairs to tell Nikki and we both laughed. It was so rare to fool Mom. Unheard of, actually.

Our game didn't last long, though. Summer ended and we went back to school, and Nikki no longer wanted anything to do with me or Mom or anyone else at home. No, I didn't know the word *gaslighting.* I didn't know there was a name for what we were doing or for what Mom did to Eddie.

I do, however, know I'm about to do the same thing to my husband. And yes, it's to punish him for lying.

Anyone who claims they never gaslight their spouse is lying.

I'm still looking for the pickup truck every chance I get, but there's been no sign of it, not since we tried to confront them on the road. Eddie and Felix have no problem taking credit for getting rid of them, either.

Eddie first brings it up at dinner and the conversation continues at the watchtower. He and Felix continue to tell whoever will listen, including a group of younger guys who stopped by while on their own road trip. They're half drunk and ready for a good story. Eddie and Felix are full-on drunk and ready to tell it.

"Ever been to Alabama?" Felix says. "Because that's where these guys are from. Swear to God they followed us all the way from there."

"What'd you do?" one asks.

"*They* ran *us* off the road. When we called them on it, they got pissed."

Eddie nods his head, confirming this is

correct. Portia rolls her eyes but doesn't mention that their story *isn't* correct. She confronted them.

"That right?" one of the guys says. He's a big, athletic guy with a beard and he's wearing a lacrosse shirt from Clemson.

"That's right," Eddie says.

"Seems a little weird they would follow you for something like that."

"Right?" Felix says. "That's what I thought until I saw them."

"They put nails in our tire," Eddie says. He sounds like he's bragging about it. "And they stole our starter."

"Starter relay," Felix says.

"Exactly, the starter relay," Eddie says.

Clemson doesn't look convinced. "Huh."

His friends, who had been rather enthusiastic about this story, go quiet.

"Cool story, bro," Clemson says. He turns away from us, his eyes scanning the rest of the platform.

For a second, I think Eddie is going to let this go. Then I remember who he is. Years ago, he was that Clemson kid, only his shirt said Duke.

"Come on," I say. "Let's find some aliens."

"You think I'm bullshitting you," Eddie says to Clemson.

"No, actually. I think if you were bullshitting you would've come up with a better story."

Ouch.

"Cool, cool," Felix says. "Have a good night, guys." He leads Eddie to the other side of the platform.

The Clemson kid turns to me. "That guy your husband?"

"Brother. The blond one is my husband."

"Your brother's a bad liar."

He is, no doubt about it. "And you're an asshole," I say.

Clemson's eyebrows shoot up. "Wow, okay. Who hurt you?"

"Does it matter?"

Clemson turns to Portia. She is drinking a soda can of vodka and Sprite and doesn't look at him. He checks her out in a blatant way, and he takes a step toward her.

He starts to introduce himself. "My name —"

"No," Portia says.

"Can I at least —"

"No."

"Would it help —"

"No."

"Wow." Clemson shakes his head. Laughs. His friends do as well. "A whole family of assholes."

"Right?" another guy says.

"I'm starting to believe the story about those guys following you. Must have done something to deserve it." He walks off, his friends follow.

Eddie. He really is an asshole, especially when he's drunk. All of a sudden he's back, so is Felix, and neither one looks happy. "Now you're hassling my sisters?" Eddie says.

Clemson turns. Smiles. "I'm not hassling anyone, old man."

This is when I realize the vortexes and the watchtower really do work. We've become time travelers, sent right back to high school. On cue, our head cheerleader appears.

"What's going on?" Krista says. Not sober. Drinking the same thing as Portia, only hers has Diet Sprite.

"Nothing," I say.

"Actually, these guys are hassling Beth and Portia," Felix says.

Oh no, Felix. No, no, no.

Eddie snorts. "That's because they're Neanderthals. I mean, they go to *Clemson*."

"Excuse me?" Clemson says. "Where did you —"

"Duke. I went to Duke."

Clemson laughs. "Well, it all makes sense

206

now. I've heard you Duke boys are all in-bred."

The first punch is thrown by Eddie, which is no surprise. His ego — and his anger — always get the best of him, drunk or not. Insulting his alma mater is the easiest way to make Eddie mad enough to hit someone.

But against Clemson, he doesn't throw the last punch.

The fight ends when a large man steps in and says "Chill out" in a voice that makes everyone stop. Clemson's friends stop cheering him on, Krista stops screaming, and I stop glaring at Felix long enough to realize those police sirens in the background aren't coming from a TV.

I can't blame whoever called them. The watchtower is a place to look for UFOs, not get in a bar fight. And I can't blame the police officers for being so pissed off, considering it's Sunday and the Broncos game is on.

Eddie is arrested, along with the Clemson kid. He's more surprised than any of us. The rest of us go to the tiny local police station and sit in the lobby, waiting to pay whatever the bond is. I turn to Clemson's friends because I just can't help myself.

"Hard to believe this is the first time your

friend's mouth has gotten him arrested," I say.

Felix's jaw drops. So do Clemson's friends. One of them, another guy with a beard, calls me a bitch.

I snort. "Now I see why the other guy is your leader."

"We don't have a leader."

"Oh, okay. Whatever you say."

Portia laughs. Sometimes we are a family of assholes.

You can blame that on Grandpa, he started it.

The night ends exactly as it should: with Eddie in jail.

We go to bail him out, and we're met by one of the pissed-off patrolmen who arrested Eddie and Clemson. He's smiling.

"Come back in the morning," he says. "No one's getting out before a judge sets bail."

One of the Clemson guys shakes his head and says, "We are so screwed."

"Call a lawyer," another says.

"You call one."

When we all walk out of the station, they're still arguing about whether or not to call.

Krista is quiet. Too quiet. So it's not

surprising when she bursts into tears on the way back to the motel. I'm in the front seat, the designated driver, and Felix is next to me. Krista is in the back with Portia, who makes a halfhearted attempt to comfort her sister-in-law.

"He'll be out tomorrow," Portia says. "It's no big thing, really. He'll just have to pay a fine."

Krista cries harder. Portia looks at me and shrugs. Felix chooses this moment to keep his mouth shut.

"Eddie will be fine," I say.

"I know," she says, gasping for air. "I know he'll be fine. He's always fine."

I say nothing, sensing it isn't the time to mention this isn't the worst thing Eddie has ever done.

When I drive up to the motel, Krista takes a deep breath and pulls herself together. "I just can't believe I married such an asshole."

Ah.

Well, shit.

"Yeah," Portia says. "Eddie is that."

Krista laughs a little. "Yeah."

Before we get out of the car, I look at Portia in the rearview mirror. She nods.

"Hey, I'll stay in your room tonight," she says to Krista.

"Oh, you don't have to."

Felix steps in. "I think that's a good idea. With that truck and all and what's happened to the car, it's better that none of us are alone. Just in case."

Can't disagree with that.

Portia comes to our room to get her bag. We're both pissed off at Eddie. I can see it in her eyes and feel it in my heart, but ever since Krista started crying we've kept our mouths shut. I wish her luck. She rolls her eyes.

Felix is already in the bathroom, and I remember the lighter hidden in there. Bet he's about to find it.

What's the One Thing You Would Do Differently If You Could?

I probably wouldn't have come to this UFO place, because there's nothing here to see. It's all a big letdown and that sucks. Not that I believe in UFOs, I just thought we'd see something that could be a UFO and that would've been exciting enough. Didn't happen.

But I don't regret taking over this trip, and I sure as hell don't regret drugging up Grandpa. He deserves it. All of it, and more.

211

Felix stays in that bathroom for a while. I figured he would, so I settle in by the window and check Instagram. He hasn't posted anything today, which makes me a little nervous. I wish I could check on him, but I'm not in Florida.

That's when I remember Eddie is supposed to be watching the car tonight. Can't do that from jail.

I imagine Felix in the bathroom, wondering how his lighter ended up on the floor by the toilet.

Did it fall out of my pocket? Did I put it IN my pocket? I thought it was in my bag.

It is not in his bag. I have his lighter now, along with his cigarettes.

I do this sometimes — imagine what he's thinking. Usually it happens after we have an argument, and I try to picture what goes on his head.

She's wrong, she's being stupid, she's a bitch.

Should I apologize?

No, she should apologize. I'm not saying a word. Not this time.

It's been a while, though. She must be really mad.

Okay, maybe I should apologize. Just this once, though. I'm not doing it again.

More often than not, Felix apologized first.

When he comes out of the motel bathroom, Felix gives me a half smile and walks over to his backpack. As he checks the front pocket, he says, "You're not going to bed?"

I point to the parking lot. "Someone has to watch. It's Eddie's shift."

"Oh. Right." He doesn't find what he's looking for in that pocket. Glances around the room.

"Lose something?" I say.

"Phone charger." No hesitation.

Liar.

He goes to his suitcase and rummages through it. "Who's got the next shift?" he says.

"Krista."

"You really think she's going to watch?"

"No. You can use my charger."

He stops looking. "Cool, thanks."

"It's right there on the dresser."

Felix plugs in his phone and sits down on one of the beds. "I should take Krista's shift," he says.

Convenient. More time to look. More time to smoke. "If you want."

"Yeah. We should keep watching, at least for another day or two. Until we're sure they're gone."

"Okay." I look out the window, and I wonder if Eddie is in the same cell as Clemson. I wonder if the police are keeping an eye on them. When I turn back to Felix, he is eyeing the nightstand with the broken, crooked drawer.

Good guess, but no.

He doesn't look inside. Instead, he goes back to the bathroom. Those missing cigarettes will drive him crazy because he won't find them. Not until tomorrow.

6 Days Left

We have to go through a series of legal this, that, and the other to get Eddie back. They can't release him from the jail until he appears before a judge, so we're sent to the courtroom two blocks down. It's another tiny building, nothing much to it. Hard to believe this is where justice prevails.

Clemson's friends also show up. They sit on the opposite side of the courtroom, which means they're about five feet away.

It all happens very fast. In a small town like this, there aren't many cases. The only other one is a guy who got so drunk he slept on the hood of his car. Public drunkenness for him, and a fine.

Clemson and Eddie aren't so lucky. They get a lecture from the judge. A long-winded one, because it may be the only thing this judge has to do today. It all comes down to misdemeanors: criminal mischief, public drunkenness, disturbing the peace. The fine is $500 each.

The whole escapade has been expensive, annoying, and time-consuming. The definition of Eddie most of the time.

The only surprise comes after it's all over.

Eddie walks outside with Clemson. Together. They are smiling and laughing, and at one point, Eddie smacks him on the arm like they're teammates. Clemson's friends look as surprised as we are.

"What the hell?" Krista says.

When they reach us, Eddie turns to Clemson and offers his hand. "It's been an honor going into battle with you."

"Wouldn't have had it any other way," Clemson says.

They shake hands, bump fists, then slap each other on the back and part ways. Eddie turns to us, arms out and smiling. "Hey, guys!"

Krista glares at him. Arms crossed, back arched. "Are you kidding?"

"Oh, don't be mad. This will be a great story one day."

"Asshole." She turns around and walks back to the car.

Eddie follows, saying, "Come on . . . I mean, you have to admit it's a great story."

She admits nothing. Krista is starting to

grow on me.

The money came from us — Felix and me. We paid Eddie's $500 fine because we had room on our credit card. Krista did not.

Back into the car, Eddie is in the driver's seat. "No car problems, I assume?"

"No," I say. "No problems other than you."

"And no truck sightings?" he asks.

"None," Felix says.

"Didn't think so."

Krista's head swivels around to face him. "What's that supposed to mean?"

"You know, Derrick and I got to talking —"

"Derrick?" she says.

"Derrick. From Clemson. Well, I mean that's where all those guys graduated from. They aren't as young as I thought."

"Who cares about their age?" Krista says.

"Anyway, we had a lot of time to talk — obviously — and Derrick explained to me what he meant about the truck thing. Why he thought the story sounded so weird. And yeah, he said it totally wrong and he didn't have to call us assholes, but the fact is he made sense."

We're on the road now, but not on the interstate. Eddie has pulled into a drive-thru fast-food place. He orders a mountain of food and asks us if we want anything.

Today, this is breakfast.

Soon the car smells like it's been dipped in grease. Eddie parks so he can eat, stuffing food in his mouth while explaining Derrick's theory to us.

"I told him how it all started, about how you guys saw the truck, how the tire was flat again and the relay starter had been taken. It's funny, you know, how a person who isn't involved can see it all so clearly. How each thing that happened has a dozen explanations for why it had nothing to do with what happened in Alabama." He stops to take another bite of his breakfast sandwich. "Like the tire. Maybe we really did hit nails. Or the relay starter. There we are, in some rundown motel in the middle of nowhere, and maybe someone needed a relay starter for their own car. Or maybe someone sold it to make a couple dollars."

"We *saw* the truck," Krista says. "I *saw* the guy in the parking lot."

He shrugs. "You know how many black trucks there are in this country? And the guy you saw? It was late. Dark. Could've been any old guy who happened to be around, for God's sake." He shakes his head, bites on a hash brown. "We took a bunch of things that had nothing to do with one another and we mashed them together into some kind of story."

That last sentence doesn't sound like Eddie. He's just echoing Derrick.

Krista knows. "Bullshit."

"Wait a minute," Portia says. "Doesn't this mean you broke the rules?"

"What rules?" Krista says.

"Oh my God," I say, looking at Eddie in the mirror. "You went to jail. Grandpa said —"

"We couldn't go to jail. Yeah, I know," Eddie says. "But this isn't what he meant. You know that. One night in jail isn't *prison.*"

Maybe, maybe not. But it's something to consider.

For the first time, I notice the car smells. Maybe it's because our dirty clothes are piling up in our bags, maybe it's because we spend so much time sitting in the same spots. I roll down the window. Portia gets most of the air. It hits her in the face and she moves to the other side of her back seat.

"I hate Colorado," she says.

"Same," I say.

"Same!" Krista yells.

Felix shrugs, Eddie doesn't say a word. Probably too busy thinking about his new bromance with Clemson.

"Seriously," Portia says. "Nothing good has ever happened to us in this state. Nothing."

She is thinking of Grandpa, of Nikki, and I can't disagree with her. I also don't want anyone to ask.

"What happened here before?" Felix says.

Too late.

"Food poisoning," Portia says.

I glance back at her, she doesn't look at me.

She continues. "We were all cooped up in the motel room like we were quarantined or something."

"For how long?" Krista says. She also turns around in her seat, now facing the back. It's the first time she has said anything since we picked up Eddie.

"Days," Portia says. "It felt like weeks."

To a six-year-old, it probably did. She didn't even understand what was happening. As far as she knew, Grandpa was sick, Nikki was in charge, and we were stuck in Colorado.

And Grandpa was a bad, bad man.

Now that I'm an adult, I understand how betrayed I felt. Between the kidnapping and the abuse, my grandfather wasn't who I thought he was and never had been. Our grandfather was a man who hit his wife.

At twelve, I couldn't say all that, couldn't put what I was feeling into those kinds of words. If I had to describe my feelings right then, I would've said my grandfather was a monster.

I didn't have to say that out loud because Nikki did.

■ ■ ■ ■

We were out of money and needed more, and the only way we could get it was with Grandpa's debit card. All we needed was the pin number.

Nikki asked for it, and he gave her the number 4-2-5-9. She ran down to the corner store to get some cash. Or so we thought. A few minutes later, she ran back in, all out of breath and puffing anger everywhere.

"Wrong number," she said to Grandpa.

He was lying on the bed and he looked pretty bad. Smelled, too. "No, it isn't. The number is four, two, nine, five."

"That's not what you said."

"Yes, it is. Four, two, nine, five."

Nikki ran out again. I have to admit, I thought he just mixed up the numbers. With all the pills he was drinking in the water, it seemed reasonable he would do that.

A lot more time passed before Nikki showed up again. She wasn't out of breath and didn't yell. She sat down next to Grandpa on the bed and took his hand in hers.

"I know what you're doing," she said. "The third time I get that number wrong, the machine is going to take the card."

Grandpa said nothing.

"So give me the real number or I'll call our parents and tell them what you did," Nikki said. She stopped for a minute, gauging his reaction. There wasn't much of one, and it always made me wonder how much Mom knew about her father. I hope she didn't know about Grandma. Though if you knew our mother, you'd know she would never tolerate such a thing. Not for one second.

But Grandpa hitting Grandma wasn't what Nikki was talking about.

Nikki turned to Portia, who was sitting on the other bed playing with her dolls. "I'll tell Mom about how you touched her."

Grandpa looked horrified. Too horrified to speak.

Eddie had been sitting at the desk but was now on his feet. "No way," he said to Nikki.

"I swear," she said.

"You're lying," Eddie said.

"No."

That was me.

"He did touch her," I said. "I saw it."

Yes, Nikki was lying, and yes, I knew it. I lied with her. Maybe I was as angry as she was with Grandpa, or maybe I didn't want her angry with me.

We were in it together, allies in a secret mission. We were always playing Risk.

Portia didn't understand what we were saying; she wasn't even paying attention. We didn't tell her, either.

She knows now, though.

It feels like it takes forever, but we finally cross the border and get out of Colorado.

"Wyoming barely has enough people to be called a state," Portia says. "But at least it isn't Colorado."

She has talked more today than she has the entire trip because her soda cup has more than soda in it.

"Remember last time we were here?" she says. "We thought we were driving in circles."

She's not wrong. Wyoming is a state of empty roads, beautiful mountain views, and — now — a ton of fracking equipment. It wasn't here before.

We make one stop for lunch at a deli, another in the afternoon for gas. The station and a variety of stores are all nestled within the hills, the only signs of modern life other than the road.

We get out to use the restroom and stretch our legs. Portia and I go across the street to the package store, which is the only place to buy hard alcohol in Wyoming. She stocks up on vodka.

"You all right?" I say.

Her eyes are remarkably alert, given her daylong buzz. "Yeah. Why?"

I shrug, and add in snack cakes, chips, packaged cinnamon rolls, and cigarettes.

"Nice," Portia says.

The man at the counter doesn't glance my way, but Portia gets his attention. Could be the cutoff shorts, the long legs, or the fact that she's carrying enough alcohol to kill a few people. Could be that she's twenty-six.

She sees him look and she smiles at him. "Don't suppose you give bulk discounts?"

"Depends. Am I invited to the party?" His voice is deep, his smile a leer. I don't know how Portia can do what she does.

"I'd love to invite you," she says. "But we aren't staying. Just passing through."

"Your loss," he says.

"I bet it is."

He discounts our whole purchase by 20 percent. Now that, my friend, is power.

Outside, it's warm but not hot. Eddie stands around waiting, the gas already pumped, while Krista sits in the car and ignores him. Felix is "in the bathroom" and I already know what that means. While

225

Portia climbs into the car, I have a second alone with Eddie. He motions for me to come closer.

"You don't really think I broke the rule, do you?" he says.

So he is worried. "I don't know. I didn't make the rules."

"It was one night."

"You're right. One night."

"Yeah," he says, nodding his head like he's trying to convince himself he didn't break the rule. "One night."

We move on, and the roads look the same, the landscape looks the same, the only difference is the vodka in my soda. Portia rambles on about a club in New Orleans that none of us have been to, but at least her voice fills the air. Otherwise we'd be sitting in Krista's anger and the faint smell of cigarettes.

The alcohol relaxes me a bit. I start to think — to hope — all the bad things are behind us. The guys in the truck are gone, Eddie is out of jail, and the car is working just fine. We're still here, still driving, and everything is looking pretty good. Not that I want to jinx it, but I almost can't help myself.

We're north of Casper when we stop for the night. Eddie pulls into the Western Sun

226

Lodge and for the millionth time Felix remarks about how everything is the same all over.

"Agreed," Krista says. "I'm not convinced Wyoming is any better than Colorado." Her first words since we left that state.

Eddie doesn't respond, doesn't react. He goes to the back and starts unloading the suitcases. As I get out of the car, I hear Eddie say, "Guys?"

His tone is off. I may be intoxicated, but I know off when I hear it. "What?" I say, moving a little faster. As soon as I step around to the back, I see. All the suitcases are out of the car, on the ground, and the spare tire cover is up.

The side compartment is empty. No wooden box, no anything at all. Grandpa's ashes are gone.

WYOMING

STATE MOTTO: EQUAL RIGHTS

If you've ever wondered what would get you kicked out of a place like the Western Sun Lodge, start by losing your grandfather's ashes. Follow it with a brother who loses his mind over said ashes.

"Are you fucking kidding me? You *left Grandpa in the car last night*?" he screams.

Portia. Slurring. "We were a little busy, given that you were *in jail.*"

Eddie turns to Krista. "You saw me bring that box in every single night and you forgot?"

"Stop yelling at me," she says. Krista walks away, throwing one last bomb over her shoulder. "You're the one who got arrested!"

"Nice, you dick," Portia says.

"I mean, she has a point," I say.

228

Eddie continues to yell. "What happened to watching the car?"

"You missed your shift," I say. "You were in jail."

"So you just bailed?"

I hold up my hands, trying to halt the conversation before it gets more ridiculous. "Felix and I tried, but you know, people get tired. I may have nodded off."

"You nodded off?" Felix says. He sounds annoyed at this.

"Yes, I am human. I do sleep," I say.

"ASSHOLE!" Krista yells from across the parking lot.

Eddie punches the side of the car.

"Stop," I say to him. "Listen to yourself. You think someone broke into the car and stole a box of ashes."

"That looks like exactly what happened."

"Have you looked in the suitcases?"

Eddie sighs. "Why would —"

"Have you looked?"

He lays down the roller bags, opening each one in the quickest, roughest way possible, shoving aside the clothes in search of Grandpa's ashes. I think about stopping him and doing it myself, but I'm too intoxicated and can't be bothered. I was the one who suggested it, after all.

"Nope . . . Nope . . . Nope . . ." He says

this over and over, like it's a mantra.

Felix leans in and whispers, "You have to admit it's pretty weird."

"I know."

"Don't touch mine!" Portia says. She opens her own suitcase and shows Eddie that there are no ashes hiding inside.

Eddie looks through the whole car, throwing out whatever gets in his way. Snacks, garbage, water bottles, sweaters. When he finds the vodka bottles, one empty and one half full, he looks at Portia. "Really?"

"I didn't drink it all by myself."

"What the hell?"

The voice doesn't come from any of us. It comes from a very large, very shirtless man storming across the parking lot. He is unkempt in that just-woken-up way and not happy about it.

"What the hell?" he says again.

Portia is the only one stupid enough, drunk enough, to answer. "What the hell what?" she says.

"What the hell is all this noise about? For Christ's sake, I've got customers here."

"You work here?" I say.

He looks at me with so much scorn that I physically feel it. "I don't *work* here, I own this lodge. And you idiots could wake the dead."

"Do you have zombies here?" Portia says. "Or are they vampires? Because I'm pretty sure those are the only two dead things that can be woken —"

"Out," he says. "Get out now."

Eddie hears this, and sticks his head out of the truck to say, "I'm not going anywhere until I find our grandfather."

The man hesitates. "You've got five minutes to find him."

"I'm going to need our money back," I say.

He's already walking away, waving in the direction of the office. I motion to Felix to get our money, and I tell him to keep his eye out for Krista. No idea where she is.

Portia puts her suitcase back together, a slow process given her condition. I look into the back of our SUV. It's empty, and the tire cover is pulled up.

Something on the ground shines in the sun, catching my eye. It's right by the back tire, not far from the suitcases, including Portia's. And Eddie's.

I pick it up and put it in my pocket.

"You find anything?" I call to Eddie. He's rummaging around in the front.

"No."

I turn to Portia. She shrugs.

"It's not like anyone knew what we had,"

I say. "And Grandpa's ashes aren't worth anything to anyone but us."

Eddie gets out of the car and leans against the bumper. "They're worth a hell of a lot, though."

"Who's going to know?" Portia says. "Ashes are ashes. They all look the same."

"That's a messed-up thing to say," Eddie says.

"This is a messed-up thing we have to do."

"Grandpa was still pissed off," I say. "Until the day he died, he was pissed off at all of us."

"*He* was pissed?" Portia says.

She's right. We all have good reasons to be pissed off about that trip.

"What if we really are being sabotaged on purpose?" Portia says.

"Why?" Eddie says.

"Because he was crazy? Because this is exactly the kind of sick game he would play?"

I think about this, though my brain isn't moving as fast as it should. Someone else comes to mind, but it isn't Grandpa.

"You think he's made this trip impossible for us," Eddie says.

"Why not?" Portia says. "Maybe he's got people following us. Probably those guys in the truck."

"Maybe they're being paid," I say.

Eddie looks up at us, like a light bulb just went off in his head. "You know, you might be right. Maybe Grandpa is having us followed to make sure we stay on track."

"And to screw with us," Portia says, rolling her eyes like it's obvious.

Eddie thinks about it, nodding his head. "It's possible."

"Duh," Portia says.

Eddie doesn't respond to that. He walks off toward the office, leaving Portia and me alone.

It's dark now, and there's only one light in the Western Sun Lodge parking lot. The black dye on her hair has faded, lost its shine, and it looks like burnt charcoal. She looks down at the ground as she says, "You think Grandpa's messing with us, don't you?"

"Not necessarily," I say.

She looks up. "No?"

"There's someone else it could be."

Portia looks stunned, like she sees a ghost. Or is thinking about one.

"No," she says. "It can't be Nikki. I mean . . . no. That's insane."

Except it's not.

Stealing the ashes is exactly the kind of

thing Nikki would do. I know this because I know her better than anyone. Always have.

If You Could Be Any Animal, What Would It Be?

Right this second, I'd say a cheetah. That's the fastest thing ever, and it has to be faster than this van. I swear sometimes it feels like a horse and buggy. Not that I'd really know what that's like, but still. Slow.

But that's not the ultimate animal I'd want to be. For that, it has to be a lion. Because who doesn't want to be king of the jungle? It'd worry me if someone said anything other than a lion. And it has to be the male lion, too, because of the mane. I want the mane and I wished the female lions had it, too.

Everyone gets lions wrong, too. They always said the female lions hunt while the males just kick back and wait for their meal. When people went out to study lions, that's what they saw — the females hunting while the males stayed back — so it had to be true. It's not.

Once they got better cameras and better lenses and people started filming them from above, like from helicopters, they saw the male lions hunting, but only in the tall thick grass where they can stay hidden. Mom was the one who told me that, and then she said that nothing is ever what it seems.

After getting kicked out of the first motel, we end up at the Peak Valley Inn. Once again, Eddie pulls apart the car to look for the ashes, and he talks to himself the whole time.

". . . Checked into the motel . . . Left them in the car when we went back to the watchtower . . . No one brought them inside for the night . . ."

Crazy? Yes. But at least he isn't yelling, and neither is Krista. She's the first to disappear into a room. Portia starts to say something to Eddie, but I drag her away. She's staying in our room tonight, and as soon as we get inside, she passes out on the bed. I don't even get a chance to spray it with disinfectant.

"Guess she's not coming to dinner," Felix says.

"I don't think anyone is."

It's just us. We walk across the street, to a

fast-food-type place called Buffalo Burger, leaving Eddie in the parking lot mumbling to himself.

As Felix and I sit down with our buffalo burgers, twice-fried onion rings, and sodas, I realize this is our first meal alone since the trip began.

Felix chuckles. "Not much of a meal."

"Are you kidding? Look at this thing." I hold up my burger, which has a thick slab of meat and oily, melted cheddar cheese. "Now this is a buffalo burger."

"Only the best for my wife."

The best, but not always the truth. It's important to know the difference. If my family hadn't played Risk so often, it would have taken me a lot longer to learn that.

Nikki was obsessed with Risk. Even after she discovered boys, she still wanted to play. One of the last times was just a few days before the road trip.

Mom, Dad, Nikki, Eddie, and I all played. Portia watched.

During the first half hour, Nikki took control of an entire continent. Eddie helped her. They had an alliance until they didn't, because the next continent she went after was the one he needed.

"You said Australia wasn't your thing," he said.

"Sue me."

Nikki said that a lot. *Sue me.* Especially when we played Risk.

That night, Australia was her thing and she took it over quick — with my help, of course — because her goal was to wipe out Eddie.

Next, she came after me. It didn't matter that I had helped her.

"Alliances never last," she said.

Dad taught us that. He was also the one who stopped her that night, because he had his own secret mission. His was to take over Asia, but to get there he took over Australia for strategic purposes. Europe, too. Nikki was almost out when Mom saved her. She swooped right in, with me as an ally, and we took out Dad.

"But why?" Dad asked Mom.

She shrugged. "Because I could."

Despite all of these takeovers, no one completed their secret mission.

That was the last time we ever played Risk. After Nikki was gone, no one ever brought it up again.

Felix doesn't mention Grandpa's missing ashes until I take my second bite of the buffalo burger.

"You haven't said anything about the ashes," Felix says.

He's right, and it's because nothing about the ashes makes sense. "Eddie has pretty much covered that topic. Why have everyone panicking?"

"You're panicked about it?"

I finish eating an onion ring before answering. "I'm disturbed. The tire and the starter thing, maybe I can rationalize. But Grandpa's ashes?" I shake my head. "I don't know."

"You think it was those guys in the truck?"

"Could be. The only other option I see is that Eddie did bring them into the room in Colorado. Maybe Krista didn't bring them back out, so they're still sitting in that room."

Felix thinks about this, nods. "Especially if he hid them in the room. She might've forgotten all about them."

I laugh a little, though it's hardly funny. "We all forgot. And those ashes are the reason we're on this trip."

Felix doesn't say anything, and neither do I, but I know we're both thinking the same thing. If the ashes are really gone, will the lawyer know? Will he refuse to give us the money?

"There's something else we need to talk about," Felix says. "But don't get mad."

I freeze, holding the buffalo burger halfway to my mouth. "That's the worst way to start a conversation."

"Sorry."

"What's wrong?" I say. "Is this about us?"

"No, but I find it strange you think it is."

"What else would I think? You said we needed to talk. That's what people think when you say that."

He sighs and throws his napkin down. I think if he ever threw anything heavier, it would shock me. Even the napkin tells me this trip is getting to him. It's getting to all of us, but Felix shows it on his pale face. Those dark circles under his eyes stick out like bruises. "I'm still talking about the ashes."

Of course he is. Who would talk about their marriage at Buffalo Burger?

Actually, Felix might.

He did propose right outside of an Applebee's, although at the time we were both still in college and buried in bills, so going out to eat anywhere was considered a treat. I've always thought it was a funny story and have told it many times at dinner parties, especially when anyone asks about my ring.

When he kneeled down and asked me to

marry him, he held out a silver ring with a green stone in it. Not an emerald, just green quartz that resembled one. I still wear it. Now the ring looks like an antique because the silver is so tarnished — yes, you guessed it, just like our marriage. That was too easy to miss.

But having my marriage end at Buffalo Burger would not be a good story. That's the story of a tragically bad romantic comedy. On the upside, the food is already paid for.

"Oh, sorry," I say. "I thought you were talking about us."

"No." He slurps up the last of his soda and clears his throat. "I just wanted to throw something out there. I'm not suggesting anything."

"Go ahead. I won't be mad."

"Did you ever think that whoever is sabotaging us is also traveling with us?"

Why yes, Felix. I did think of this. With over $3 million at stake and two siblings I almost never see and hardly trust, I'd be an idiot if I didn't consider it. As you already know, anyone can be the villain. There could even be more than one.

"I don't know why Eddie or Portia would sabotage the whole trip," I say. "Then no one would get any money."

Felix nods, says nothing.

"What?" I say.

"Oh, I'm probably just being paranoid. I just keep thinking about the tire and the starter relay, and now the ashes. I can't imagine those guys in the truck would do that."

He's not being paranoid. A few hours ago, I might've said he was, but I haven't told him what I found near the car, right after Eddie searched through the bags. I haven't even taken it out of my pocket. It's still there, damn near burning a hole through my jeans.

The button. A large, round, golden button.

I wish we had never kept it.

The Peak Valley Inn has a platinum-level vending machine. No empty spaces, no fading wrappers, no cracked plexiglass. A good mix of salty and sweet, plus individual packs of laundry detergent, toothpaste, and tampons. I'm so inspired that I do my laundry in their coin-operated machines, and it's so impressive that they work, I almost feel bad for underestimating this motel.

While listening to the washer fill with water, I take the button out of my pocket. I can still see the engraving on the front. The finish has worn off in a few spots, but most of it still shines. It looks the same size, feels the same weight. I keep telling myself it can't be the same button but I know it is.

I take out my phone and send a text to Eddie and Portia.

Whatever happened to the button?

I hop up on the washer to sit and wait for their responses.

When Felix and I got back from Buffalo Burger, Portia had woken up from her stupor and went out in search of food. Eddie was either fighting with Krista or making up with her. Maybe neither, since he answers my text first.

Why?

Then Portia:

Yeah, why?

Neither answer reveals a thing, but I know at least one of them is lying by omission. Has to be.

No reason. Being on this trip just made me think about it.

Eddie doesn't answer. Portia sends a text only to me.

You okay?

I say:

Sure. Probably still buzzed or something.

Weirdo.

True.

I don't answer again. I just hold it in my hand while my laundry cycles through wash. When it hits rinse, I get another text.

You okay?

This one is from Felix, who's probably worried because I've been gone so long. Maybe he needs a cigarette and can't find them because I took them all.

To be honest, I'm getting a little tired of gaslighting him. He should've figured it out by now. I'm disappointed that he hasn't.

5 Days Left

It looks warm outside but it isn't. In Wyoming, the sun is a liar. Our first road trip was in August and I swear it was cold then. Now it's September and it's even worse. I brought a jacket for this and am not happy about putting it on. We don't have these problems in Florida.

First thing in the morning, Eddie is at the car and rummaging through it again. This must be the tenth time.

"Find anything?" I say.

"No."

"This feels like the Arctic," Portia says. She walks up behind me, wrapped up in layers and a hoodie pulled tight around her head.

"Have you been to the Arctic?" I say.

"I have now." She calls out to Eddie. "Find anything?"

"No."

"I can't believe we lost Grandpa," she says.

"Nobody lost him. He was stolen," Eddie shoots back.

She whispers in my ear. "Nobody stole Grandpa."

"No?" I say.

"Why would anyone steal ashes?"

I shrug.

"Hey," Eddie says to me. "Why did you ask about that button?"

Eddie is in the middle row, where Felix and I usually sit, and he appears to be looking under it. "I don't know, I was just thinking about it," I say.

We're interrupted by Felix. He's rolling his bag across the cement and the wheels are so loud they probably wake up whoever is still asleep. "Chilly out here," he says.

I nod. The rest of us have already had that conversation.

Felix lifts his bag into the back. "Find anything?" he says.

"Not yet," I say.

"Screw this," Eddie says. "It's not here."

We could've told him that yesterday, after the first search, but he had to come to this conclusion on his own. Sometimes that's the only way.

Once our bags are in the back, we've checked our rooms one last time, and we turn in our keys, all of us pile into the car and get in our usual seats. Portia buries herself in the back. Felix and I sit side by side; he's already on his laptop and I'm avoiding mine. Eddie cranks the heat up high and starts to drive out of the parking lot.

That's when I realize the passenger's seat is empty. "Wait, you forgot Krista."

"No, I didn't." Eddie keeps driving.

Out of the corner of my eye, I see Portia lift her head.

"Where is she?" I say.

"She left," Eddie says.

"Left?" I say.

"Left. She called an Uber and went to Casper. She's flying home today."

Silence.

It goes on so long that Eddie speaks again. "We had a huge fight. She was pissed off and didn't want to be here anymore. End of story."

I turn around to look at Portia. She shrugs and lies back down.

"You mind if I get in the front?" Felix says.

"Nope."

Eddie stops the car and Felix looks at me. I wave him off, and he gets in the front. I have the middle row to myself.

I'm not upset she's gone, and I know

Portia isn't either. If it had been Tracy, who I knew a lot better, things would be different. Eddie is the one who should be upset, considering Krista's his wife. He should be the one chasing her down to the airport and begging her to stay. In theory, anyway.

In reality, he will do no such thing. Neither would I. Ashes or no ashes, we have to keep going if we're going to finish this trip the way we're supposed to.

We stop for food and gas before heading toward our next stop in northern Wyoming. When we have a second alone, I ask Eddie if he's okay. He shrugs me off, insisting he's fine.

"Krista can be . . . difficult," he says.

I choose my words with care. "She's a little emotional."

"More than a little."

We both smile.

"Is there more to the story?" I say.

Another shrug. "She might have looked at my phone. Maybe she saw Tracy called."

Tracy. The girlfriend he blew off to marry Krista. "Jesus Christ."

"She called *me,"* he says. "I can't control that."

I walk away, refraining from calling him an asshole. Again.

An hour or so later, our new arrangement

250

feels normal. Almost like Krista was never here.

251

Any Idea What You Would like to Be When You Grow Up?

Not a parent. Seriously, what a pain in the ass. Everybody's bored and hungry and someone always has to go to the bathroom.

Grandpa's still pretty out of it, because the only water he gets is the kind with pills in it. On our last stop, I also bought some NyQuil, so if he gets extra thirsty he can have some of that.

Once or maybe twice I've looked at him and wondered if I'm doing the right thing. Then I think of when Grandma told me about Christmas a couple of years ago. She got mad about how much he spent on presents, and he got mad because she was telling him what to do. And physically, he was the stronger one.

She didn't win that argument.

The way I remember that Christmas is different. Mom and Dad always had a big Christmas thing with a bunch of food and presents, and Grandma and Grandpa always came over for it. I didn't even run away during the holidays. But two years ago, Grandma and Grandpa didn't come because she was sick. The flu, they said. It wasn't that. She just had too many bruises to show up.

When she told me the real story, I asked her why she stayed, because that's what didn't make sense to me. Who stays for that? Who doesn't hit back? It was crazy.

She said she knew that. Grandma also said she had no idea why she stayed, she just did.

That made me hate him so much more. It's the whole reason why I agreed to come on this trip, because from the start I knew it was all about him.

Except now I've got a new problem. One I don't want to fucking deal with and I sure as hell don't want to write about.

■ ■ ■ ■

PART 2

■ ■ ■ ■

It seems we've reached the middle of this story, and given the recent fight between Eddie and Krista, this seems like a perfect time to tell you about my parents.

I'll start by saying my father is dead. We don't talk about him and we don't talk about our mother either, because she's the one who killed him.

When it happened, I was going to school in Florida, Eddie had already graduated from Duke, and Portia finished high school a year early. She left for New Orleans before her first semester at Tulane even started — that's how badly she wanted to get away from home. My parents were living alone together for the first time since Nikki was born.

The story, as Mom told it, goes like this:

They were in the kitchen, making dinner, when Dad brought up Nikki. My parents had been searching for her ever since she

257

disappeared. They had hired private investigators to hunt down every lead, and they even paid a computer specialist to create pictures of how she might look today. Every year. They had a new picture made every single year.

If you met them, you wouldn't know this. You wouldn't know that all their money was gone, their house was mortgaged, and they had nothing in retirement. You wouldn't notice anything unusual about them at all.

Nikki's room upstairs was left intact, right down to the nineties rock band posters she had plastered all over her walls.

The evening our mother killed our father, he'd had enough. He walked into the kitchen and said, *Honey, we have to stop. We've spent years looking for her, we've spent everything we have trying to find her, and we can't keep doing this.*

I don't know if that's how he really said it, but that's what Mom claimed in her confession. The thing is, I can imagine it. I can see Mom in the kitchen, preparing dinner, still in her work clothes but wearing slippers instead of her heels. I can see Dad, his shirt unbuttoned at the neck, his slacks wrinkled from sitting all day. Maybe even the beginning of stubble on his cheeks. Grey stubble.

His hair had turned completely grey by the time he died.

Mom didn't answer him, so he tried again.

We have to move on, he said. *We have to accept she isn't coming back.*

Still, Mom said nothing.

Paulette, he said. *We have to face the truth. Nikki is dead.*

She had been standing at the kitchen counter, slicing bell peppers. She turned around, the knife still in her hand, and she swung it at him. The blade grazed his stomach, slicing his shirt open, but the wound didn't kill him.

The next nineteen did.

Someone next door heard him yell and called 911. The police found her sitting at the table, drenched in blood, eating raw bell peppers.

Was it wrong? Who's to say? What's the right way to act when your child disappears?

This is why we never talk about Mom.

Grandpa disowned her. Not just verbally, but legally. He didn't help with her defense, didn't try to get her committed instead of sent to prison. Instead, he claimed she was never his.

He wouldn't listen to any of us: not me, not Eddie, not even Portia. Even when I

259

reminded him that Mom could have called the police on him, that she could have put him in jail for kidnapping us but she didn't, our grandfather wouldn't budge. Mom got nothing.

With no money and a public defender, Mom didn't try to fight the murder charge, didn't even try to claim insanity. She confessed to everything in exchange for life in prison instead of the death penalty. Felix doesn't even know. It all happened right before I met him, and I told him both my parents were dead.

Mom wouldn't see us, either. She refused all visitors when she was awaiting sentencing, so all we could do was sit in her court appearances, watching her from a distance.

"This is so messed up," Eddie said. He said that every time we saw each other and every time I talked to him. He said it during the small, private service we had to bury our father.

I cried. That's what I did. I cried for my father, for my mother, and for everything they had gone through because of what happened on the trip. I cried for every lie I told them and every secret I kept. Most of all, I cried for all the years we had lived without Nikki.

Portia was more succinct. The only thing

I remember her saying is, "That road trip ruined everything."

True.

I saw Mom just once. A week after she had been transferred to Arrendale State Prison in Georgia, her lawyer contacted me and said she wanted to see me. I flew up that day.

The woman I saw was not my mother. She was a shell of that person, a ghostly figure who looked like someone pretending to be my mother. I don't think I did a good job hiding the shock.

We were separated by a thick pane of plexiglass, and we spoke through a phone. I had so many things to say, to ask, to tell her, but she picked up the receiver and spoke first.

"Beth," she said.

"Mom."

She stared at me. Her eyes were bloodshot but the blue color of them was clear. As clear as I'd ever seen them. She leaned forward a bit and spoke under her breath.

"Find her. You find Nikki, and don't come back until you do."

My jaw dropped, and before I could say a word she hung up the phone and stood up. I tried to get her to sit back down, but she walked away. She didn't turn around even when I yelled.

I never got the chance to tell her that I had been looking for Nikki. I had always been looking for her. I had never stopped.

The day passes in a scenic haze, like we're driving through a postcard. Without Krista to complain, or lead a cheer, we are silent and bored. Last time we weren't because Nikki made sure of it. Halfway into the drive, she bought two disposable cameras. One was for us to have fun with.

I still have some of those pictures. There's one of Nikki and me sitting on the hood of the minivan, the sun shining down and making us squint. Both of us are sticking our tongues out at Eddie, who took the picture.

Another picture is of all four of us — the kids — and we're all lying down on a bed in a motel room, looking up at the camera. An early selfie, I suppose. That was near the end of the trip, and the first time I saw that picture I was shocked at how wild we looked. In just two weeks, we had gone from well-groomed suburban children to near feral. Our hair was unkempt, our faces a mixture of tanned skin and peeling, sunburnt noses. By then our clothes were dirty and we barely bothered to wash. Nikki wore oxblood-colored lipstick she bought at a drugstore and it made her look unreal.

The second disposable camera was for Grandpa. I don't have the photos from that one.

We haven't taken many pictures of us on this trip. There was one at the beginning, when we first started out, and another at that hotel bar. Felix has taken a bunch of pictures of the scenery but not of us.

I almost feel bad about it now that Krista's gone. Not too bad, though.

Lunch is at a roadside hot dog stand, and that's where Eddie corners me about Krista. He waits until Portia is on her phone and Felix is in the bathroom. Or he might be smoking, because I put cigarettes in his bag this morning. Yesterday he checked for them at least a dozen times.

"Hey," Eddie says, motioning for me to follow him. He leads me away from picnic tables. "Can you text Krista?"

"Why?"

"I just want to make sure she got home okay. She's not answering mine." He sighs.

"She's not really talking to me, so I didn't think she would."

"How bad was this fight?"

"Bad. She wanted me to leave, too. Said our marriage was more important than any inheritance."

"Did Tracy call again?"

He shrugs.

I don't say anything, so he says, "I can't control what Tracy does."

He's right — he can't — but knowing Eddie, this is partially his fault. "Okay, I'll text her."

"Thanks."

"You want me to ask her if she has the ashes?" I say.

Eddie gives me the finger as he walks away.

I type and retype a text several times before sending it.

Hey, Krista, I just wanted to check in and see if you got home ok? Sorry we didn't get a chance to say goodbye. This road trip has been so stressful for all of us.

I think a minute, then send her a second text.

P.S. Yes, my brother can be an asshole.

It's true. It's also true that the last thing I

want to do is encourage her to come back and join us.

The rest of the afternoon is just like the morning. In the front, Eddie and Felix talk about sports, bad sitcoms, and standup comics. Several times I hear Portia giggle and it's not because they're funny. It's because they're ridiculous.

She sends me a text:

Are we sure this is better than listening to Krista?

I reply:

I think so? Ask me again tomorrow.

Honestly, at least she was entertaining. This is like listening to random guys on a podcast or something.

She has a point. And she says:

You know, I think Eddie is lying about the ashes.

I ask:

What do you mean?

I think he's hiding them.

I disagree but keep my mouth shut. I've already told her who I think is behind it.

Up front, the guys move on to discussing their favorite cartoons as kids and I put on my headphones. White noise drowns out their voices and I doze off for the rest of the drive, and I don't wake up until the car jolts. A dirt road is the only way to get to the ghost town.

Nikki didn't really know what a ghost town was. That's my theory, anyway; otherwise, I'm not sure we would have gone. We all thought it was a haunted place filled with castles and old Victorian houses. And ghosts. Lots of ghosts.

When we hit the dirt road, Nikki started singing the *Ghostbusters* song. Eddie and I joined in, but Portia didn't know the words. She just pretended she did.

She was also scared. At one point, Portia whispered in my ear. "Will the ghosts hurt us?"

"No. They're nice," I said.

"Like Casper?"

"Sort of."

She nodded, her hair covering half her face. It hadn't been brushed that day.

"Don't worry," I said. "It'll be fun."

Lie, though I didn't know that when I said it. I believed ghost towns had ghosts, but they don't. They have empty buildings and stories about miners who worked there a hundred years ago. Like Mom said, nothing is what it seems. It was true in so many ways that day.

During the drive up, when Portia was scared, I reached into Nikki's bag to get her CD Discman. Nikki had stopped singing by that point. She was concentrating on getting up the hill, and I thought some fun music would keep Portia calm.

I searched around in Nikki's bag, never expecting to find a pregnancy test.

I watch Felix searching the Internet on his phone, looking for information about the ghost town. Refresh, scroll, refresh, scroll.

I pull out my phone and check Instagram. He's working today, and even posted a picture of his giant coffee cup. For a second, I forget about the mountain that we're about to drive up.

When the incline starts, I put on my seatbelt. Portia climbs back to her seat and does the same.

The road hasn't improved since last time, although we're in a better car for it. Last time we bounced around, in part because Nikki had no idea how to make this kind of drive. If anyone had seen us, they would've stopped us from even trying. I grab the plastic handle above my head.

I used it last time, too. One hand gripping the handle, the other rooting through Nikki's bag.

I close my eyes, thinking back to when I found that pregnancy test. I remember thinking it must belong to Mom — she must be pregnant again and Nikki had found this test. But that made no sense because why would Nikki take it, and why would she bring it with her? It also didn't make sense that the test belonged to Nikki, yet that seemed to be the only answer. She would've had plenty of chances to buy it; there were so many times we stopped and she ran into the store to get something, leaving me with Grandpa and the others.

So it was hers, then. Had to be. I swear I can still feel the shock of that moment.

Or maybe it's the road.

"Jesus," Eddie says.

I open my eyes and see the mountain.

Eddie slows down and tries to avoid the bumps. He also tries to avoid the steep drop-off on one side of the road. The old town of Kirwin is in the mountains, and this is the only way to get there.

"You remember this?" I ask Portia.

She nods, looking as scared now as she did then, which is a little surprising.

Portia never saw the test in Nikki's bag. Her eyes were squeezed shut.

Felix looks up from his phone, sees the mountain on one side and the cliff on the other. He puts the phone away. "Service is gone," he says.

"Ya think?" Portia says.

No one answers. No one says anything. It feels like we are balancing, hovering in the air in a place no one, certainly no car, should be. Yet somehow we keep going.

The town is at the very top. A jeep is what we should be driving, maybe an ATV. Or a helicopter.

Behind me, Portia whispers, "This is where the ghosts live. At the top."

I smile. That's what Nikki said when she saw how scared we all were during the drive up. She was scared, too; she was just better at hiding it.

"All the ghosts," I say.

"Even Grandma."

Yes, Nikki had said that. I believed it. We all did because we wanted it to be true. No one cared what Grandpa thought about seeing Grandma's ghost. He was just the asshole who hit her.

The drive also made him sick. He vomited when we got to the top, although that was probably due to the pills and the NyQuil. Bad mix.

Now Felix is the one who looks queasy. He has one hand on the dashboard, the other clenching the seatbelt.

271

I pat him on the arm. "Exciting, right?"

"Almost there," Eddie says.

"Jesus Christ, your grandfather brought you guys up here?" Felix says.

I don't answer that. No one says another word until our car makes that final lurch up to the top. I exhale because that's what you do when you escape death, or at least feel like you did.

Another dirt road brings us to Kirwin, where two hundred residents once lived and worked mining both gold and silver. We get out of the car and stare at the buildings. They're all boarded up, every last one. If there are ghosts, we can't see them.

It's spooky, though. Spookier than I remember as a kid. Now I can imagine the people who used to be here, can envision them walking, working, growing food, and praying at the little church. What I can't imagine is the same thing, day after day, without any relief in sight.

Not so different from life now.

Felix is the only one who hasn't seen Kirwin before. He glances around, still looking a little sick from the ride. "Seems like we could've done this with a drone," he says.

It takes a second, but everyone starts to laugh. A big laugh, the kind you feel deep in your belly, the kind that makes you

272

double over and try to catch your breath.

Sometimes Felix makes me laugh this hard. I might miss that.

What Are You Most Grateful For?

Having a brain. I can't imagine being stupid.

I'm also grateful for Beth, not that I'd ever say that to her. But really, this wouldn't work without her, because someone's got to keep an eye on everything when I'm driving. If Eddie wasn't so into his NIN world, maybe he'd help out, but of course, he's not. Trent Reznor's got his attention.

I'm also grateful for *Thelma & Louise*. Grandma and I used to watch that together. She loved it, but I never understood why until she got sick and told me what Grandpa did to her. Then I got it. She was Thelma, the one with the horrible husband, and all she wanted to do was run away and get back at him. At everyone. When I finally understood why she liked that movie, I told her I'd be Louise. So that's what I'm doing.

I just wish she was still around. I wish she was on this trip, so she could see that I'm get-

ting Grandpa back for her. I told her I would.
  I promised.

We all knew the trip up to Kirwin was long
and treacherous and the drive down wasn't
any better, but we also knew we had to do
it. We worked under the assumption that
our whole trip was being tracked.

The reality was we had no idea, we just
assumed, and no one wanted to chance
breaking the rules just in case we lost our
inheritance. For all we knew, there was a
camera in the car.

There were other reasons to go back,
though. The first was the air. Nothing like
it, at least not that I've experienced. This is
pure clean air, high up enough to avoid any
smog, exhaust, or any other sign of the
modern world. If you've never smelled that
kind of air, believe me when I say it's different.

However. I sure as hell didn't risk falling
off a cliff just to inhale air. We have a more
interesting reason to be here.

I point to a squat log cabin, the first one on the right. "Behind it. Fourth to the left, five back." It was all in the journal. Every place we visited was marked on a hand-drawn map inside the back cover.

Eddie and Portia started walking. Felix looked at me and said, "What's that?"

"The tree."

"The tree?" he says.

I nod but don't explain.

It was Nikki's idea. When we got tired of running around the abandoned town and started complaining about the lack of ghosts, she said we needed to leave our mark. "People will know we were here," she said. "Forever."

Eddie suggested carving our names on one of the buildings, but Nikki said whoever was in charge of Kirwin would get rid of that. This was a clean place — no garbage or graffiti — so we had to pick something that wouldn't get erased. The best we came up with was a tree, in part because they were everywhere. The whole town was sur-rounded by giant evergreens that had to be twenty feet tall and a hundred years old. We went with the odds. Kirwin was in a national forest and you couldn't just walk up and cut down a tree. We bet the tree, and our carving, would be here forever.

"What did you say?" Portia yelled. "Fourth to the left?"

"And five back," I said.

Before we carved anything, we all argued back and forth, like that old seesaw, about how big the carving should be, what the carving should say, where on the tree it should go. We wanted to be able to find it again, and to have others see it, but it couldn't be so ridiculous that the park rangers would get mad about it. Maybe they'd scratch it out or change it. Then we'd disappear forever.

"This is how we're going to live forever," Nikki said. "It's important to get it right."

No bad words, no weird pictures, nothing that looked offensive. The people in charge would get rid of anything like that.

She made the rules.

I had to give her credit, though. We were no longer thinking about ghosts; we were obsessed with living forever.

"Think about it," Nikki said. "In thirty years, if you bring your kids here, what do you want them to see?"

Not the symbol of some cartoon superhero. Not a slang phrase at the height of its popularity. Not a song lyric. One by one, we eliminated all the things we wouldn't want our kids to see, even though it felt like lifetimes would pass before any of us had kids.

Simplicity won the argument. We picked a tree, noted the location, and decided to put the carving at our eye level. Our initials, in order of our ages, in a straight line down the tree. Nikki started, then Eddie, me, and finally Portia. Nikki carved hers and ran off, back to Grandpa. He hadn't been out of the van since we got to the top because he was still so nauseous.

Below Nikki's initials, we each carved ours. Deep, too. That's what took so long — we had to carve everything deep enough to last forever.

When we were done, I went back to the van to get Nikki. All the doors of the car were open to air it out, and Grandpa was sitting up in the back eating a box of crackers. Those pills made him do everything slow, even chewing looked difficult.

Nikki sat beside him, and she was whispering in his ear.

She looked up at me and said, "What?" It sounded like a demand.

"We're done," I said.

"Oh. Cool."

Nikki grabbed the camera and followed me, leaving Grandpa where he was. I hesitated at first, wondering if Grandpa would try to leave. But then, where would he go on top of a mountain?

Nikki took a picture of the tree with the disposable camera, but I don't have that photo. We split all those pictures up after the film was developed, and no one gave them to the police when Nikki was reported missing. We were the only ones who knew the cameras existed.

It takes a while to find the original tree. Maybe because more have grown. Maybe because they aren't in straight lines so counting four over and five back isn't as easy as it sounds. Anyone who claims all trees are unique needs glasses.

"We carved our initials on a tree," I tell Felix.

He smiles. "That's cute."

When he says things like that, I'm convinced I wouldn't miss him.

Eddie finds it first. The leaves and branches crunch under our feet as we all make our way through to where he's standing. Or kneeling, because we were a lot shorter when we made that carving.

Portia kneels down beside him. I come up behind the tree, so I can't see the carving yet. I can only see Portia's face.

"What?" I say.

She looks up at me, points at the tree. I walk around and look at it.

The carving is just how we left it, though it's weathered. Discolored. Nikki's initials at the top, followed by the others, and the year at the bottom.

NM
EM
BM
PM
1999

That should've been it.

The last carving on the list is this year, 2019. It's fresh and deep. Like it was added yesterday.

"It was just some kids, I'm sure," Eddie says. "We're near Yellowstone. Millions of people come through here."

We are on our way back down the hill because we have to make the drive before it gets dark. It's September, still daylight savings, so we've got the time. In another month or two, it would be dark by now.

"Oh, I'm sure," Felix says. "That carving could've been done a week ago. Probably a month ago. The place is probably swarming with kids in the summer."

"Obviously," Portia says.

"Has to be," I say.

Lie. Not for one second do I believe this is a coincidence. This is pure Nikki, just like the missing ashes. She's playing with us.

But I can't say that in front of Felix.

We let him believe the NM initials belonged to our grandfather. It hasn't occurred to him that this was our maternal

282

grandfather and his last name was not Morgan. And he's not concerned at all about the extra carving.

"It doesn't matter," he says.

But that's Felix, always looking the wrong way. He continues to do this all the way down the mountain and even at the Barney's Steakhouse, where we stop for dinner. The steaks are too big to eat in one sitting, the baked potatoes are saturated with butter, and the vegetables are scarce. We have big mugs of beer and we don't talk at all.

Felix is too busy checking the news or his e-mails or looking for the black truck outside.

The rest of us are texting one another. Eddie sends the first one.

Who was it?

Portia answers.

Well, since I've been with you for the past week, safe to say it wasn't me.

Eddie says:

Wasn't me.

I cut off another piece of steak and put it

in my mouth before answering.

What about Krista?

He scoffs.

On a mountain? Not likely.

I say:

Nikki?

We all pause to take a sip of beer, a bite of food.
Eddie answers first.

For Christ's sake, it's not Nikki.

He has always believed she's dead. A tree carving isn't going to change his mind.
I say:

Then who? Who else would know?

Portia says:

Grandpa.

Before he died, or as a ghost?

Eddie says:

He has to be messing with us. That's why he set this whole thing up. The ashes, too. It's all to get back at us.

I say:

Sure. Except Grandpa never saw the tree. He stayed in the car the whole time.

That shuts everyone up.

It's my night to pay for the motel. Tonight we're at the Coyote Run Inn. Eddie picked it on purpose, given that Grandpa used to call us the little coyotes.

"Seems like a sign," Eddie says.

A sign of what, he doesn't say.

The motel looks like all the others except for the coyote motif sprinkled everywhere, from the sign to the numbers on the doors. When I go in to pay for two rooms, it hits me that Eddie and Portia will have their own. She won't have to stay with Felix and me anymore.

This feels weirder than I expect it to. If nothing else, Krista was a buffer — a pawn, so to speak, kind of like Felix is. Since neither one knew the truth about the first trip, or about Nikki, we couldn't talk about it in front of them. For Eddie and Portia, that barrier is gone.

Felix leaves our room twice, no doubt to smoke. He must have bought a new pack. Vaguely I think about putting one of the packs I have into his bag, like he had missed it, but I don't have any energy left for Felix's smoking. Sometimes there are too many battles to fight, and his smoking is the least important.

What I'm thinking about is Grandpa.

At one point, we were alone together. We had just come down the mountain from Kirwin, and as soon as we hit civilization, Nikki stopped at a gas station. Portia had to pee so bad she was almost crying, and she jumped out of the car as soon as it came to a stop. Nikki ran after her, and Eddie wasn't far behind.

That left me and Grandpa. He was slightly more lucid, given that he had eaten crackers and drunk some real water. At least he wasn't sick anymore.

I climbed to the back and looked over the seat at him. His eyes were sleepy but as clear as I'd seen them since Nikki took over.

"Hi," I said.

"Hi." He sounded hoarse, like you do when your throat is scratched from throwing up. He held up an empty bottle of water.

286

"You have any more?"

I hesitated, and then gave him mine. He drank what was left in one gulp.

"Why'd you hit her?" I said.

He froze. As foggy as his head must have been, he knew what I was asking. His answer would reveal the truth. I trusted Nikki — more than anyone, ever — but I wasn't stupid. She did know how to exaggerate.

All at once, Grandpa's face changed. A tiny smile. No, a hint of a smile. It was in his eyes. And it scared the hell out of me.

What he said made it even worse.

"Because I could."

"Because you *could*?"

He blinked. His face changed, the smile gone, the eyes sleepy once again. "Because I couldn't *help it,*" he said.

The first way was right. *Because I could.*

I wonder how many bad things have been explained by such a simple phase, a simple idea. Because I could. Because no one stopped me. Because it was easy. All the same answer, and it really means *because I wanted to.*

"I guess that's why Nikki has done this to you," I told him. *"Because she could."*

He glared at me and I glared back. I wanted to tell him that I hated him and didn't want to be anywhere near him. And I certainly didn't want him around Nikki. Or her baby.

But I kept that thought to myself, because I always kept Nikki's secrets.

Almost always.

If You Could Live in a Movie or TV Show, Which One Would You Choose?

A week ago I would've said *The X-Files* but after seeing nothing at the watchtower, I'm pretty sure that aliens are BS and there's no point. Then maybe I'd say *Poltergeist* except there aren't any ghosts.

Yesterday, I would've said the only answer is *Buffy.* Who cares if vampires are real? I just want to be a slayer.

Today is different. Today I'd say *Beverly Hills 90210,* because if I'm going to be a mom, I want to be a rich one.

In the middle of the night, in the middle of nowhere, someone blasts music so loud it makes the windows vibrate. I jump out of bed, convinced the end of the world is nigh.

Felix sleeps through it.

The music, I realize, is coming from a car. The headlights shine through the window as the car drives out of the motel parking lot, and then it's gone.

Silence returns, though not to my thumping heart. Sleep won't come back anytime soon.

I pick up my phone, which is facedown on the nightstand, right as it's supposed to be. I haven't found it faceup since that one time. I also haven't gone on another morning walk with Felix.

Coincidence? Perhaps.

Still no text from Krista. She hasn't responded to me at all.

No interesting e-mails. Nothing new from

him on Instagram. I check the news, which I haven't looked at in days. Being on a road trip is like being in limbo, sort of like flying before they added Wi-Fi. I read about a celebrity wedding, hoping it will put me to sleep, when I hear the bass.

The music. Same song, same volume, I recognize all of it. The sound is faint but getting closer.

That damn song.

I get up and stand near the window so I can see the car. Since whoever it is seems determined to wake everyone up, I feel obligated to see who it is.

Yes, I do want to see if it's the black pickup.

Yes, Felix is still asleep.

The headlights come first, along with the thumping music and rattling windows. Only when the car turns and drives through the motel, not into it, do I see the car.

It makes me gasp.

Not a truck or a sports car or a sedan. The car blasting that music is at least twenty years old, with dulled paint and no license plate. A minivan.

Exactly like the one Grandpa had on the last trip.

I rush out, not even bothering to put on shoes, and flinging the door open so hard it bounces back at me. I see the back of the van as it drives out of the parking lot.

I'm not the only one.

Portia has come out of her room, also barefoot, and she looks like she just woke up. "Did you see that car?" she says.

I nod.

Felix is finally awake. He comes up behind me, scaring me half to death when he says, "What happened?"

I glare at him. *Now* he wakes up.

The music fades into the background as the van drives farther away, and as it does, I hear the pounding of my own heart. "Twice," I say to Portia. "It came through twice."

"I know. I heard."

"Is Eddie awake? He's supposed to be watching tonight."

She sticks her head back in the room. The light floods out when she turns it on. Pause. Her head pops back out. "He's not here," she says.

"What's happening?" Felix says.

"You heard her," I say. "Eddie isn't in the room."

"He's right there."

Felix points.

Eddie is across the parking lot, coming from around the back of the building.

Dressed, with shoes on, at one o'clock in the morning. He stops when he sees us.

"What?" he says. "What happened?"

Felix throws up his hands. "That's what I've been trying to find out."

"Where were you?" I ask Eddie.

"Taking a walk around the motel, keeping watch."

"Didn't you hear that car?" Portia says.

Eddie shrugs. "What, that music? I heard it. The whole state probably heard it."

I step closer so I can look at his eyes. "You didn't *see* the car?"

Eddie is wearing his Duke baseball cap, but it doesn't hide his blue eyes. The color is so strong, so clear, it looks fake.

"No." He sounds offended, like he knows I'm accusing him of something but doesn't know what. His eyes don't move, his pupils neither contract nor dilate. "Why?"

I turn to look at Portia. She's looks at Eddie, who's staring at me. Everybody watching everybody, like a game of Risk.

We do not break eye contact until Felix speaks.

"What are you guys *doing*?"

"Nothing," I say. "We aren't doing anything."

But what just happened is everything.

The van. Same color, same make, same age. Not the same van, though. It can't be. Grandpa got rid of his the second the trip was over. It's probably sitting in a junkyard by now.

The last time I was in Grandpa's van was when we left the desert. It was late. We were all tired and dirty, and we all smelled like smoke.

When I close my eyes and imagine it, I can still feel the heat on my face. From the sun, yes. The desert sun is the strongest I've felt, like I was being baked in a pan under the broiler. Day in and day out, the desert will wear you down.

It wasn't just the sun, though. On that day, the heat came from the fire.

Imagine a giant fireplace, then multiply it times a hundred. You can't get too close unless you want to lose your eyebrows.

That was surprising enough, but even more surprising was the noise. Fires are *loud.* The cracking, the breaking, the sound of the flames being whipped up, the small and large explosions as everything that could burn did. I had to scream to be heard.

Do You Ever Wish You Could Read Minds?

Obviously.

But being invisible would be so much better. Imagine how easy things would be if you could just disappear and reappear whenever you wanted. You wouldn't have to spend so much time strategizing or building allies and doing everything step by step.

If I could be invisible, I'd know what everyone was saying about me behind my back. I'd know if they thought I was ugly or if my outfit sucked or something. And I'd know what Cooper is up to whenever we're on one of our breaks. He says he doesn't hook up with anyone else, but maybe he's lying.

I'd also know if Mom and Dad were really going to get divorced. I don't know if it would matter, but I still want to know.

4 Days Left

If I were the tortured soul of this story, I'd wake up screaming because of a nightmare. Inevitably it would have pickup trucks, cigarettes, evil tree carvings, and a dead grandfather wearing a Clemson shirt. Instead, I sleep through the rest of the night and wake up feeling pretty darn refreshed. Invigorated, even.

My morning gets even better when Felix takes a shower. I take the opportunity to steal his cigarettes and replace them with a different brand. Even though I'm tired of this, it's like I have to stick with it.

You'd think I'd have better things to do with my time right now, given all the weird things that have happened, but Felix deserves this. If he's going to lose his job because of smoking, he might as well lose his mind along with it.

That's how aggravated I am with him. Not

just because of the smoking, but because he can't figure out why he keeps misplacing his own things. Here I am, making it as obvious as possible, and he doesn't have a clue.

When I'm in the shower, I imagine Felix finding that pack and wondering if he's losing his mind.

This is exactly what happens. I can see it on his face when I come out of the bathroom. "You okay?" I say.

He looks at me, blinks his glassy eyes. "What happened last night? What was that car you were chasing?"

"I wasn't chasing anyone," I say. "That music woke me up and I was trying to tell them to turn it down."

"You ran out there barefoot." He says this like I ran out there naked.

"I was mad. They woke me up." I sound much calmer than I feel. In reality, I am freaking out about what happened. In a good way.

Felix looks like he's going to argue but decides against it. Interesting. Usually he doesn't even get that close to arguing.

This morning there is no music outside, no minivans in the parking lot. Just a cold morning in northern Wyoming and a few people who need more sleep. Felix is the only one who makes small talk. He does it as we pack up the car and he does it again when we stop for breakfast.

Since no one else is talking, Felix launches into a description of a true crime documentary series he watched just last month. It involved girls that had been kidnapped, dismembered, and sprinkled around the cornfields in Oklahoma.

No one interrupts.

Felix babbles on, maybe trying to convince himself he's not losing his mind. He describes the whole documentary, episode by episode. Eventually he gets to the point, which is that the police knew who did it but pretended they didn't have a clue.

"Totally shocking," he says. "I didn't know until they revealed it. Up until they made the arrest, the media had zeroed in on this one man, a teacher, but it wasn't him at all. It was a totally different guy."

"Wow, honey," I say. "That sounds like an amazing story."

Yes, I'm patronizing him. And I'm wondering if he was like this when I met him. It was a couple of weeks after I returned from Georgia to see my mother in prison. I just remember that he was kind and easygoing and different than everyone in my family. But maybe he had always been this annoying and I never noticed.

Eddie pays for breakfast because I paid for the motel. Portia doesn't even bother offering anymore unless it's just for coffee or snacks. And gas — she has paid for gas.

Felix talks about work as we walk back to the car. Sherry got promoted, Allan got demoted. Hortense the cow (their department mascot) was stolen by finance, who then traded it to marketing in return for an as-yet-to-be-named favor. Oh, and our numbers looked pretty good this month, but not great.

A month ago I would've been right there with him, trading stories and gossip and wondering how the company was doing. A month ago, I went on morning walks with Felix every day before work. A month ago, I was thinking about bills, my weight, my health, and the likelihood of having time to run errands on my lunch hour. A month ago, I had a husband who didn't lie to me.

Now I know that not having kids with Felix was the right decision. Is the right decision.

That's not what I'm thinking about, though. What I'm actually thinking about is more important than my marriage.

The pickup truck was one thing, along with the flat tires and stolen starter. Even someone coming into our room at a sketchy motel to look at my phone wasn't that unbelievable. All of that could be explained. It wasn't like the guys in the truck actually hurt us. They never even tried. It was just weird, like the year carved into the tree. Anyone could've done that. Even Krista's sudden disappearance was easy — and no one was complaining she was gone.

Last night was different. Or rather, everything *looked* different, like seeing a room through a peephole and then seeing the real thing.

Not because of the van. A lot of people knew what kind of van Grandpa had. Plus it was all over the local news when Nikki disappeared.

The location was a little weirder. Wyoming was a desolate, sparsely populated state. What are the chances?

The song was what did it. Eddie, Portia, and I knew that song. We could sing it word for word, even now.

"I Think I'm Paranoid" by Garbage was blasting out of that van.

The only people who know this are sitting right here. Plus Nikki.

She's here. I knew it. I always knew it.

MONTANA

STATE MOTTO: GOLD AND SILVER

Today is the longest single-day drive of our trip — both times. Nikki wanted to get out of Wyoming to have some real fun, and not the kind you have at tourist sites and odd museums.

Screw history, she said. *It's all boring.*

Roller coasters were a much better idea. The biggest theme park in the area was over nine hours away and we couldn't wait to get there. On the other hand, nine hours was a long time to be cooped up in a car. All kinds of things could happen in that amount of time.

Grandpa was still drugged, though neither unconscious nor sick, and he always looked like he was watching TV. Even in the car, he stared out of the window like he was watching an episode of *JAG*.

I gave him his breakfast, which came from a drive-thru. He used to like breakfast sandwiches, or at least he acted like it, but now he was a zombie who couldn't taste anything.

I couldn't look at him without thinking of what he'd done to Grandma. Everything I remembered about her was warm and sweet and filled with apple juice. She always gave us apple juice. Even if you could hit her, why would you?

However, as mad as I was, he looked pathetic. He was drinking a constant stream of pain pills and that made him woozy enough to slur his words. When he wasn't trying to talk, he stared off into space, and he looked terrible. Unkempt hair and clothes, days of stubble on his chin.

"Hey," I said. "You okay?"

He turned to me, his eyes dull, his skin so very white, and he laughed. It was so unexpected it made me jump. Grandpa laughed so hard he had tears in his eyes. No one else saw, or heard, because Nikki had the music up so loud.

"Why are you laughing?" I said.

That made him laugh all over again. I waited until he stopped.

"I can't believe you asked if I was okay," he said, wiping his eyes. "You're holding me captive."

I shook my head, gesturing to his body. "You aren't tied up."

"You're right, I'm not tied up." He sighed so hard it made the seat rumble. "But I'm still a captive."

Well, yes. He was, I'll give him that. Our threats about Portia were keeping him here instead of running whenever he had the chance.

"There's something wrong with your sister," he said.

My first thought was Portia, who was in the seat in front of us, playing with an Etch A Sketch. She looked fine.

"Not her," Grandpa said.

Nikki. Up in the driver's seat, singing along to the music, bouncing around in her seat trying to dance. Seemed normal to me. "She's not sick," I said.

"She's sick in the head."

This was all a little vague for my young mind. Nikki was my sister. She was wild and fun and a little crazy. And pregnant. But not sick. There's a difference, and I knew it even then.

He lowered his voice and said, "Do you know about the camera?"

I nodded. We had been taking a lot of pictures with that disposable camera.

"Not that one," Grandpa said. "The other one."

"The second camera? We haven't used it yet."

"She has."

I shook my head. He was wrong, because I just saw the first camera earlier in the morning. It still had pictures left. There was no reason to start another one.

"So you don't know about the other pictures," Grandpa said.

I did not. "Tell me."

"They're . . ." His face scrunched up into a ball of wrinkles. "They're vile."

Vile. The word made me think of vomit, but that wasn't what he was talking about. I knew, or thought I knew, but even I couldn't believe it.

"Are they . . . Are they pictures of Portia?" I asked.

He nodded once, closing his eyes as he did.

"She took them," I said, thinking out loud, working through what he was saying. Vile pictures of Portia were what kept him here, what kept him from trying to get away or get help.

That's what he said, anyway.

It took me a few seconds to process what he was saying, to assess it, and then to remember that this was the man who hit Grandma.

"Liar," I said.

"Beth, I swear I'm not lying. Your sister . . . She isn't right."

I shook my head at him, at every word he said. "You're the one who isn't right."

"Please —"

"Shut up."

I went up a seat, to where Portia was sitting. "Let me," I said to Portia, grabbing the Etch A Sketch. It wasn't really hers, anyway. Originally it had belonged to Nikki.

"Hey," she said.

"Just wait." I spent quite a while with that thing, creating a bad replica of our house back home, including the imaginary dog I had when I was little because Mom didn't allow pets. Portia sat right next to me, her arms crossed and her bottom lip pushed out. The girl could pout.

She eventually got tired of waiting, because she leaned forward and poked Nikki on the arm. Nikki turned down the music and said, "What?"

"Beth took the Etch A Sketch," Portia said.

"So?"

"So I was *playing* with it."

Nikki looked into the rearview mirror.

"Then why did you let her take it?"

Portia blinked, her eyes wide. "Because she's —"

"Because you let her," Nikki said.

Portia didn't answer, nor did she grab the Etch A Sketch. She didn't do anything except continue to sit by my side until I finished my picture and gave it back to her.

That was my fault, and I can admit that now. I underestimated Portia. Always have. Later that day, my things started going missing.

The first was a candy bar I had hidden in my bag. I had saved it from our convenience store stop the day before, but when I went to eat it, the bar was gone. Portia claimed to have no knowledge of said candy bar.

Next it was a T-shirt I loved, followed by some hair bands. Those I went looking for, and I found them in the pocket of her jeans.

"You took these," I said.

She shrugged. "No, I didn't."

"But they're in *your* pocket."

"I don't know how."

Like that, over and over, for the rest of the trip and the rest of her childhood.

Would she have become a little kleptomaniac if Nikki hadn't told her to take the Etch A Sketch?

I've thought about this a lot over the years,

wondering if you become something like that just because someone tells you to. You don't. You don't become a murderer because someone says "Kill that guy." That's not how behavior works.

Nikki may have given her permission, but there was a little thief inside of Portia all along. Just like there was an asshole inside of Eddie and a wild child inside of Nikki. And a liar inside of all of us.

Nikki was one of the best. There were no pictures of Portia, certainly not any that were vile. I asked Nikki about it that very night, after everyone was asleep.

She laughed. "Are you kidding? Of course there aren't any pictures."

"I didn't think so. He just seemed so sure."

"That's the point."

Liars that good are hard to find.

What is Something That Has Surprised You?

Oh, I can name more than one. Being pregnant is first. Whatever was supposed to happen in my life, it wasn't getting pregnant at 17, I can tell you that.

Grandpa being an asshole is a close second.

Our parents allowing this trip to continue is third. Although I guess it's somewhat understandable since they don't know what Grandpa did. Grandma said it didn't start until he retired — was forced out, actually — and all of a sudden he had no job and nowhere to go. I mean, part of me can't blame her for staying. What do you do when you're 64 years old and your husband suddenly starts hitting you?

Who the hell knows? Doesn't matter anyway, because he's the asshole.

One more thing. I think we're being followed.

No, I'm sure of it. That maroon Honda has been behind us for a while now.

When I look at Portia now, headphones on, listening to music, I wonder if she's really as broke as she pretends to be. Maybe it's all a lie. Maybe we've been paying her way because she's still stealing from us.

Eddie. Where had he been during that original nine-hour ride? In the passenger's seat, next to Nikki, doing a whole lot of sleeping. He woke up long enough to charm a truck stop waitress into giving all of us some free ice cream. As soon as we got back into the car, he went back to sleep after mumbling something about pulling a muscle while up at the ghost town.

That's when I turned my attention to him. Throughout the trip, he was our secret weapon. The one who could talk to anybody, young or old, into giving us a pass. If we were late checking out of a motel, we sent Eddie to talk to the manager.

I spent a lot of time watching him, trying

to figure out how he charmed people into giving him free stuff and, usually, becoming his friend at the same time. He did have a formula.

One, make fun of yourself. It makes you nonthreatening from the start.

Two, smile. Especially when you're asking for something.

Three, mix your lies with the truth.

Four, remind them how silly/stupid/forgetful you are, this is all your fault, and won't you be an awesome person and lend a hand?

This worked for him often enough that I tried to copy it. I practiced making fun of myself, I memorized jokes, and I practiced a half-dozen smiles so I'd have a lot to choose from.

Didn't work. People never responded the same way. It didn't matter how nice or sweet or cute I was, I never would've been able to convince that truck stop waitress to give us free ice cream.

Even at fourteen years old, Eddie was the guy everyone loved. I hated him because everyone loved him.

We were around five hours into our nine-hour journey when I kicked the back of his seat.

Nikki didn't notice, neither did Portia. I

didn't know it yet, but she was too busy looking for shit to steal.

I was about to kick his seat harder when I realized I could kick his arm. It was wedged between the seat and the passenger's door.

That woke him up.

He looked around like we had hit something. "What?" he said.

"What what?" Nikki said.

"Nothing, I guess." He curled back up to sleep. After about ten minutes, I kicked his arm again. And again.

The fourth time was the charm. That was when he figured out it was me.

"What the hell?" he said.

I shrugged.

"Stop it."

Obviously I did it again.

Eddie readjusted, making sure none of his limbs were reachable by my foot. I felt like I had won.

Now, as I sit behind the driver's seat, his left arm is visible. Maybe even reachable.

More than that, I still *want* to kick him.

Back then, it was because I hated him. I knew that. Now I know my hate was just jealousy, and I also know I feel it toward all my siblings. Every one of them ended up with some special skill. A superpower.

Eddie and his charming ways, Portia and

312

her ability to steal. Nikki, who got away with everything, even disappearing. What did I get, other than similar DNA? I can fade into the background. Let others have the spotlight.

Every family needs a dull bulb. Not everyone can be as bright as the sun. I've known for a long time that I'm not smart enough or charming enough to get all the attention. It's always worked for me, or I've made it work, but that doesn't mean I like it. Sometimes it makes me angry.

Right now, it makes me want to kick Eddie just like I did before.

I stare at his arm, at the seat, at the road in front of us. How stupid would it be to kick his arm while he's driving? What are the odds we'll get into an accident? And if we do, what are the odds we'll survive?

This is what I think about during our nine-hour drive.

"Beth."

Felix's voice snaps me back, making me want to kick him instead. "What?"

"Did you read your e-mail today? Your work e-mail?"

"No."

He hands me his phone, pointing to the screen. A company-wide memo was sent out this morning about a downsizing plan to reduce our staff by 15 percent. The first cuts were made today. I read down the list, not recognizing most of the names, but then I get to Linda McCormack. My supervisor. Next I see Danielle Bertram, one of my coworkers, followed by Adam Perry, our administrative assistant.

They're making cuts in my department.

Perfect. Felix is going to lose his job because he started smoking, and now my department is getting cut to shreds — and this is just the first round of layoffs.

It's a good thing I have an inheritance coming.

I can't help thinking about Eddie's night in jail, and once again, I wonder if that will disqualify him for his share.

Of course that means someone would have to let the lawyer know about it.

Are you okay?

Felix has texted me the same question several times, and each time I answer the same way:

Yes, we'll talk later.

Are you sure you're okay?

Yes, we'll talk later.

He squirms around in the front passenger's seat, turning to look at me so many
times I finally put on my headphones and
pretend to go to sleep. I don't even have
music on. Just in case Felix opens his big
mouth, I want to hear it.

Because the drive is so long, our lunch
stop is short. It takes place at an exit filled
with multiple gas stations and fast-food
restaurants, all within a one-block radius.

"Twenty minutes," Eddie says. "Get whatever you need and meet me back at this gas
station."

Portia takes the opportunity to load up on
alcohol while Eddie pays for the gas. They're
alone together in the convenience store, and
this is what I'm thinking about when Felix
asks me about the downsizing.

"Don't tell them," I say to Felix. "It's none
of their business what's happening at work."

"Understood."

"Did your department get cut?"

"One person so far."

I nod. He's right. We have no idea what's
coming next, and we aren't at the office to
hear the gossip.

"I'll check in with Sandra," I say. She's
my closest friend at work, and the only one

315

I'd talk to about this.

"We'll be okay," Felix says. He doesn't mention the inheritance, but I know he's thinking about it. That kind of pisses me off, given his new smoking habit. I now think of the inheritance as *mine,* not *ours.*

Strange what money can do.

He pretends to go find the restroom when he's really going to smoke. I walk across the street to Arby's and load up on roast beef sandwiches. We're going to need more than alcohol and tobacco to get through the rest of this drive.

While standing in line, I look out the window and see Eddie come out of the convenience store. Even from across the street, he is a good-looking man. I don't know how I got a brother who looks more like a model than a regular guy, but I did. Not that our parents were ugly, but neither was as good-looking as Eddie.

He's talking on his phone, gesturing with one hand like the other person can see him. He paces along the length of the car, alternating between talking and listening. Someone is making him agitated.

Portia comes out of the store next. She isn't classically good-looking like Eddie, but she does have long legs, short shorts, and boots. That's enough to turn the head of every man at the gas station.

She's carrying two bags from the store, one obviously with bottles in it, and she already has a cup in her hand. Maybe they serve mixed drinks at the convenience store. It wouldn't surprise me in Montana.

"Ma'am."

The girl behind the counter is pointing to my food, which is all bagged up and ready to go. I grab it.

Ma'am, my ass. Another reason to leave this state. They're too polite.

I stuff napkins and condiments into the bag, still looking out the window to see what else is going on. Felix returns from behind the store. Tall, lanky, and so very pale. Today he's wearing a Denver Broncos shirt and that orange color does him no favors. He puts a stick of gum in his mouth before returning to the car, and it pisses me off. Tonight maybe I'll take his cigarettes again. No, his lighter. It must be so much worse to have a cigarette but not be able to light it.

By the time I get across the street, Eddie has pulled the car away from the gas pump and into a parking space. He's back inside the convenience store.

"Coffee," Portia says. She's doing some semi-suggestive stretching behind the car.

I hand Felix a roast beef sandwich.

"No mayo?" he says.

Mayo.

That goddamn mayo.

You want to know why I cheated on Felix? Because of this right here.

I was at a bridal shower for a friend of mine from college. It was an after-work event because most of us had jobs and many had children. Saturdays and Sundays were out. The host was a woman named Clarabel. No kidding. She was bouncy and perky, the type who loved to organize things. A lot like Krista, actually.

We had drinks and finger sandwiches and fancy deviled eggs served on lace doilies while my friend opened her presents. Nothing about the shower was unusual until the stripper showed up, and then the shower turned into a bachelorette party.

He was dressed as a cop, sent to "investigate a noise complaint" and we all believed this. I know I did — never even noticed his bright eyes and big dimples. I thought he was a cop right up until he tore off his shirt to reveal his tanned, greased-up muscles. This guy had more than a six-pack. Had to be at least eight.

More drinks. Less food. The party lasted longer than I thought.

When the stripper finally stopped grinding on the bride, I called Felix and said I was on my way home.

"I'm going to stop on the way home. I need a burger or something," I said. "You want one?"

"Yeah, sure."

"I'll be home soon."

"Okay. Oh," he said. "And no mayo."

No mayo.

Felix has hated mayo since I met him. He says so every time we get sandwiches or burgers, veggie or real, doesn't matter. Even fish sticks and chicken nuggets, he says it. No mayo. And he said it again that night.

Like I didn't know.

That's why I stopped the stripper as he walked to his car. That's why I had sex with him in the back of mine. And I don't even have a thing about men in uniforms.

It was because of the mayo. Because he said it over and over again, like he didn't think I was smart enough to remember. Because Felix is just like that, always has been.

And here he is, still asking.

Every time Felix mentions mayo, I think of that stripper. This is why I can't be the heroine. A cheating wife is one of the deal breakers.

"No," I say, handing Felix the Arby's roast beef. "No mayo."

"Cool." He unwraps the sandwich and takes a big bite while climbing into the passenger's seat.

Eddie comes out of the convenience store with an oversized coffee cup in his hand. He takes a sip, makes a face, and takes another. I walk over and meet him halfway, so no one can hear what I say.

"Roast beef?"

"Absolutely."

"Only with cheese left," I say, handing him a sandwich. I lean in a little closer. "I forgot to tell you. I got a text from Krista."

His eyes widen, his head rears back. "You did?"

"Yeah. She said she's fine. Got home okay."

"That's it?"

"That's it."

Lie.

I haven't heard from Krista at all, but what I do know is that Eddie's reaction was genuine. He's not a good enough actor to fake that kind of surprise.

Have You Found This Journal Helpful?

. . . um, no? It's a way to pass the time and it helps put me to sleep. And honestly, now that I'm driving all day I fall asleep pretty fast, so it's not even that helpful anymore.

Dr. Lang would say this is just a tool and it's not the only one available, so I'll just go along with that for now unless I think of something else, but I probably won't.

I'm watching that Honda. One guy driving, no other passengers. I'm not about to tell anyone else about him, not even Beth, because the last thing I need is for everyone to freak out. I mean, it's just a guy in a maroon Honda. Maybe he thinks I'm cute. Wouldn't be the first time some old guy followed me because of that.

Bet he wouldn't think I was so cute if he knew I was pregnant.

Montana is called Big Sky Country, and that's a true statement. Big sky, open land, and long, long drives. It's also called the Treasure State, but I don't know anything about that. We've only driven through Montana, never stopped to look for treasure. Our destination is the strip of Idaho between Washington and Montana. Yes, that's right. Our *goal* is Idaho.

Last time, we had a moment in Idaho. A real, lasting moment that altered the course of our trip.

I'm hoping this visit is a lot less exciting. The drive there certainly is. I've already thought about all the things worth thinking about, so unless I start obsessing about one of them, there's no place for my mind to go. If I didn't have to look over my shoulder every five minutes to make sure someone wasn't stabbing me in the back, I would've fallen asleep.

Portia is the one who keeps it interesting. She combines her alcoholic beverages with Hostess cupcakes, so she gets buzzed pretty quick. Not a normal buzz, either. She's also wired from all the sugar.

She starts telling a story about her last boyfriend, a guy named Jagger. They met "at work."

"Where do you work again?" Felix says.

"A bar. It's called Young Guns."

Lie. It's called Young Buns.

Jagger worked at the same bar, but after they started getting serious, he switched shifts so they didn't have to deal with any weird shit. Her words.

They had lockers at work for their bags and wallets, and that's where the relationship began.

"I started finding little gifts at my locker," she says. "A flower, a little note telling me how beautiful I looked. I knew it was someone who worked there because of what he left. Like, one day I talked about how much I loved tangerines and the next day that's what I'd find. A tangerine."

"Wait," Felix says. "You didn't think that was creepy?"

Portia rolls her eyes while taking another swig of her drink. In the car, she uses a sippy cup. "*Of course* it was creepy. At the time, I mean. But I already told you this guy became my boyfriend, so obviously it didn't turn out creepy."

Felix nods, eyes wide. "Got it."

"Good," she says. "Moving on. This continued for a couple of weeks. I started looking forward to seeing what would come next, because the gifts started getting more elaborate. Like, one flower became half a dozen, or a one-line note became a whole poem."

She stops. I'm sitting sideways in the middle row, back against the door, so I can see both Felix in the front and her in the back. She's smiling.

"What?" I say.

"I was just thinking of the last gift. The one where he finally signed his name."

The whole time she is talking, I keep thinking the story sounds a little familiar. Like something out of a CW show or a Netflix series, the kind of thing I'd watch unintentionally. I assume she's lying, and that there never was any Jagger.

"Bluebells," she says. "He left me a whole bouquet of bluebells." Another smile, followed by a wistful glance out the window.

She is lying. I just had the source wrong. This story doesn't come from a TV show. "Your favorite flower," I say.

"Exactly."

This is Nikki's story. Close to it, anyway. This is how she met Cooper.

He left gifts at her locker, and the bluebell was her favorite flower. We heard it all, multiple times, because Nikki loved to talk about it. Portia stole parts of Nikki's story, made up the rest, and came up with her own version. Maybe she's too drunk to realize the story isn't hers.

Eddie laughs. "You're lying."

"Excuse me?" Portia says.

"There's no way that could happen. First, how many people work at this bar? How difficult would it be to figure out who was leaving all these presents?"

"It's a pretty big bar . . ."

"So if it's that big of a bar, how are there not cameras? In *New Orleans*? And why wasn't anyone worried that an employee was receiving all these gifts? Jesus, I think this guy broke a few stalker laws."

"I'm not lying," Portia says. I can't blame her for digging in and defending her lie. When you get caught, sometimes you have to.

Eddie snorts.

Snorts.

"Oh, okay. If you say so," he says.

Portia leans forward on the back of my

seat, getting as close to Eddie as she can without climbing over. "This is *my* story, not *your* story. I think I know what's true and what's not."

"Uh-huh."

"What do you even care? Like it matters who I date or how I got a boyfriend?"

"It doesn't matter," Eddie says. "I'm just not going to sit here and listen to such an obvious lie without saying something."

"Oh sorry, I didn't realize you had joined the truth police."

"I can't help if you're a terrible liar."

"You also can't help being an asshole."

Eddie shrugs in that nonchalant yet infuriating way. Portia lies back down on her seat. Felix stares at his phone. I can't tell if what I just heard was an act or a real argument, because they're both right. Eddie pointed out the obvious holes in Portia's story, yet at the same time, why the hell should he care?

"Check the GPS, will you? See how much longer."

Now Eddie is talking to Felix. Rather, he's ordering Felix around.

"Sure," Felix says, reaching over to the touchscreen in the middle of the dash. The same touchscreen Eddie has been using the whole trip.

"Is your hand broken?" I say to Eddie.

"Three hours," Felix says.

"Thanks."

Eddie does not answer me. Instead, he says, "We'll stop once more before we get there, so figure out now what you need to pick up."

Portia pokes her head up to give him a dirty look. She lies back down without saying a word.

In the rearview mirror, I see Eddie smile. He switches the music to an annoying song from the eighties. We've listened to this before and we've complained about it. Now he not only turns it back on, he turns it up.

All of a sudden, I realize what he's doing. He's done it before.

What Do You Most Fear?

Nothing. Most of the time, anyway. I really don't have time for deep introspection right now, I'm a little busy.

But I'm a little tired of that guy following us. I don't know if I'm scared, but I'm definitely annoyed. What I'd really like to do is pull over and ask him who the hell he is and what he wants, but I won't. Not with Portia and all the others around. If I was alone, I'd do it, though. I swear I would.

Nobody ever gives me credit for that — being brave, I mean. They always say I act without thinking and I'm impulsive and blah, blah, blah. How about brave? Why can't I ever be that?

On the first trip, I sat up front with Nikki on the second half of the drive through Montana. She needed a navigator she could trust, and Portia was too small. Eddie slept too much.

Nikki and I talked a lot during that long drive, and listening to her was my favorite thing. She was talking to me again, just like when we were younger. After a while, whatever thrill she got from taking over the trip started to fade. I was the one she told.

"I'm so tired of driving," she said.

I wondered if she was tired because she was pregnant. Mom wasn't overly tired when she was pregnant with Portia, but that was her fourth child. This was Nikki's first.

"You sure you're okay?" I asked.

"I just said I'm tired."

I waited a second, then said, "Have you talked to Coop?" Cooper, also known as Coop, was her on-off boyfriend. When they were on, she talked about him. When they were off, she would only say he was a big dick — "and not the good kind." I didn't understand that at first.

"Coop? He's a dick," Nikki said. She glanced over at me. "Why are you asking me that?"

I shrugged. "I don't know. I just thought you might have called him or something."

"I haven't."

"Okay."

We were both silent for a minute, and then she said, "It's just all this driving. I hate it."

"Lie. You love driving."

"Not anymore."

"You sure that's all it is?" I asked.

"*Yes.* Jesus."

No matter what I said, or how many ways I tried to ask, she never told me about the pregnancy test. And I didn't want to tell her that I snooped.

"Seriously," she said. "I think this is it."

I sat up and leaned in toward her. "What's it?"

"After we're done with the theme park, we have to call Mom and Dad."

I shook my head. "No way."

"We have to go home sometime," she said. "We can't stay out here forever."

No one said anything about forever. It was

just supposed to be until we got to the Pacific Ocean.

I didn't want to go home. For once, we were free, or as free as we ever had been. We could sleep, eat, and watch TV whenever we wanted. We could go anywhere, pretend to be anyone, and we weren't really doing anything bad — it's not like we had killed anyone. Nikki and I were in it together. We were partners. That was all I ever wanted.

"They'll come get us," Nikki said. "We won't have to drive home. I mean, you heard how angry Mom sounded last night. She'll fly here in a second."

That was true. I did miss Mom and Dad and my friends. I missed my bed, my room, my window. I even missed eating healthy food.

But I missed Nikki even more. At home, we weren't like this. She ignored me most of the time.

"Think about the stories you'll get to tell in school," Nikki said. "Everyone will be so jealous we did this." She looked over at me, a big smile on her face. "You can even say we did it together."

I think my jaw dropped. No, I know it did. Nikki had a rule that I was never supposed to talk about her at school or what she did. She said I'd only get her in trouble.

So I wasn't sure if I should trust her. "You're lying."

"I'm not. Promise." Nikki held out her pinkie. I couldn't remember the last time we pinkie-swore. Even then, we were a little old for it.

I fell for it anyway. That's how badly I wanted attention from Nikki. Maybe she was telling the truth. Maybe she just wanted me to help with her plan to get home. Doesn't matter now and it didn't matter then, because Eddie stepped in and ruined everything.

I should've known, should've listened, should've seen it coming. That's what Nikki said. It was all my fault that Grandpa and Eddie had staged a coup and forced Nikki out of power.

It happened so fast.

One day, Nikki was driving and we were going to ride roller coasters.

The next day, Grandpa was back in the driver's seat and Nikki didn't have anything to blackmail him into staying quiet. While I was up front talking to Nikki, Eddie found the second disposable camera — the one with the so-called vile pictures on it. That's all he needed to take control.

I can still see him holding it up, smiling.

Grandpa was right there, smiling right along with him, and he looked a lot more lucid. He turned to Nikki and said, "This was always *my* road trip."

Nikki screamed. It was one of those top-of-the-lungs, ear-piercing, horror-movie screams and I thought she was going to break all the windows in the van. When the screaming was over, the cursing began. It continued until Eddie threatened to gag her.

She shut up.

I hated Eddie more than I ever had, maybe more than Grandpa. Honestly, it never crossed my mind that Eddie would do such a thing. Not once.

But if it had crossed my mind, I wouldn't have told him about the camera. He didn't know anything about it until I opened my big mouth. It happened the night before, after Nikki was asleep. Eddie and I were the only ones up, and we were talking about the trip and the pictures we took, and I mentioned the second camera.

I thought he already knew about it. The look of surprise on his face told me he didn't.

So yes, the whole thing was my fault. The one time I shared Nikki's secret, I ruined everything.

I asked Eddie why he did it, why he

couldn't just let Nikki be in charge. Everything was going okay, we were on our way to the roller coasters, so why did he have to help Grandpa take control?

"Nikki's lying," he said. "Grandpa told me he never hit Grandma."

"He *did* hit her. Why else would Nikki do all of this?"

"Because she's a psycho."

Not true. Nikki had told me everything about Grandpa, all the details, and I knew it was true. If Nikki had been lying, she would have told me she was. Just like she did about the pictures of Portia that didn't exist.

"No," I said to Eddie. "That can't be why you did it."

He looked at me, almost surprised that I was arguing with him. "You don't believe me?"

"No."

He smiled and shrugged.

I should've known what he'd say.

"Because I could."

Now here we are again, the same place, the same long drive, and Eddie is ordering people around like he's in control of everything. That's how it sounds, especially when he pulls up to the Appaloosa Inn. The motel looks as bad as it sounds, right down to the burnt-out lights in the sign and the misspelling of "Cabel" TV.

"I have to make some calls tonight," Eddie says. "You guys can all stay in the same room."

Before anyone can say a word, he gets out and goes into the motel office.

"Such. An. Asshole." Portia emphasizes that with a scoff. "Is he going to take us somewhere to eat?"

I glance around the street, spotting a twenty-four-hour diner. Amazing how many of them are actually left in the country, and they're all located near motels like the Appaloosa. "There," I say.

"Oh perfect. This is just like last time. Another shitshow." She gets out of the car and slams the door behind her.

Felix looks to me.

"I'll explain everything," I say.

I know I have to. I have to explain to Felix why it was a shitshow last time we were here. Why we all rushed outside last night when that van drove by. There's probably more, but those are the biggest ones.

Our first moment alone is after eating club sandwiches at the diner. Eddie didn't come with us, Portia left to get some sleep, so it was just Felix and me, drinking weak coffee and sharing a piece of apple pie.

"Last time we were here, we all got sick from eating something at one of these diners," I say. "That's why Portia said it was a shitshow. Except it was more like a vomit show."

Lie.

Felix puts down his fork. "What happened last night?"

I've given this one a lot of thought. Had all day to come up with a creative story, but the truth is easier. Mostly the truth.

"It was the song that freaked us out. Did you hear it?" I say.

He thinks for a minute, shakes his head.

"Doesn't matter. Point is, we heard it a

thousand times on the first trip. If we had a theme song, that was it." I stop and take a deep breath. "So when that song woke me up, I ran outside. It wasn't like I gave it a lot of thought, I just did it. And I guess Portia did the same thing."

"Why didn't you just say that?"

"It was the middle of the night. I was confused . . . I don't know. It just seemed difficult to explain at one in the morning."

"I feel like you aren't telling me everything," he said.

"Well, you're wrong. There's nothing more to tell."

No, Felix, I'm not going to ever tell you about Nikki or her secrets. I've already learned that lesson.

I almost let Felix believe we're going to the theme park. It was the whole reason we originally drove so many hours in one day. Nikki said we had to get a good night's sleep so we could spend the whole next day at Silverwood. But Nikki was no longer in control, and the only time we saw roller coasters was through the car window as Grandpa drove by.

I still remember how that felt. It wasn't disappointment; it was something big and sharp and it hit me like a fist. It felt the same as finding out Grandpa had abducted us. At the time, I didn't recognize it as betrayal.

While I doubt the impact would be the same, I still tell Felix before we get on the road.

"There's no roller coasters," I say.

We're in the motel room alone. Portia is outside on her phone or drinking or whatever she does when she's alone. Felix is repacking his bag because it wasn't right the first time. He doesn't stop. "What do you mean?"

"I mean, we aren't really going to a theme park. We were supposed to, but then we never did."

"Was it closed?"

Easy enough to lie here, but I don't. "We just didn't go."

He looks frustrated now, maybe even angry, and it's no longer interesting. It's weird. "Then where are we going?" he says.

"Washington."

"Why wouldn't you just tell me that? Why are you keeping things from me?"

Because I can't explain why or how it happened, and I can't tell him what really happened on the trip. "I'm sorry," I say.

Anger flashes in his eyes. "You lied to me."

Yes, I did lie. And I have lied to him so

many times — about my parents, about the first trip, and about Nikki, by never telling him about her at all. I also lied about why I went to school in Florida.

Way back when we first starting dating, I told Felix I chose the University of Miami because of the weather, the beaches, and because I just wanted to be somewhere new.
Lie.
I moved to Florida because of Cooper, Nikki's boyfriend. He went to the University of Miami and stayed in the area after graduation. I went to the same school and did the same thing, right up until he moved to Central Florida. Felix didn't know it, but I applied for a transfer to an United International office in the same area. When it finally came through, I told him the offer came out of nowhere.
Lie.
And yes, International United came through for both of us, and we moved to the next town over from Cooper. It was all because of him. And, as always, because of her.
When I was in high school back in Atlanta, I thought a lot about where Nikki would turn up. If she hadn't been pregnant, I never would've moved to Florida.

Cooper went on with his life. He got married, had a couple of kids, and seems to have a perfectly normal life that does not include Nikki. Yet. He has no idea I've been right there with him, watching and waiting for the day his high school girlfriend shows up with the child he didn't know anything about.

Because I'm on this road trip, I can't see him in person. All I have is his Instagram.

3 Days Left

IDAHO

STATE MOTTO: LET IT BE PERPETUAL

Today's lie is about roller coasters, and I had no choice but to admit it. Felix is looking at me as if this is a much bigger deal than it is.

Before I can respond to him, Portia bursts in the door and she's visibly shivering. "Jesus Christ, it wasn't this cold last time." She stamps her feet like there's snow on them. There is not.

"You've been complaining about the cold for a while now," I say.

"I live in *Louisiana.* It's ninety degrees down there."

She looks up at me, then at Felix. We're both staring at her, not saying a word. "Oh God, you guys are fighting, aren't you? Yeah, you are, I can tell. Sorry, sorry." Before

341

either of us can stop her, she slams back out of the room.

This is how marriage feels. Being in it is one thing, looking at it from the outside is another.

"You're right," I say. "I lied."

He shakes his head at me. "That's not right."

"I'm sorry." I slip my hands around his waist and it feels like the most comfortable thing in the world. After years of being married, I know his body like I know my own, and I can feel him relax as his anger starts to disappear.

"You shouldn't have kept this from me," he says. "I'm your husband."

"I know. You're right."

"I don't like being lied to."

"I'm sorry." This doesn't seem like the right time to bring up *his* lies, but the hypocrisy of our conversation doesn't escape me. It pisses me off.

"I know you're sorry." He kisses the top of my head.

I lean back and look up at him. "You know what would be fun?" I say.

"What?"

"Let's pretend we *are* fighting."

"Why?" he says.

"Because . . ." I have to twist the idea

around in my mind the way Nikki would when she wanted something. "Because this trip hasn't been any fun and my brother can be an asshole and Portia is always drunk and I want to have some fun with them." I keep my eyes on his, never wavering at all. "Don't you want to have fun with me?"

He smiles, every speck of anger gone. "I'd love to have fun with you."

Score one for me. Thanks to Nikki.

Breakfast in Idaho isn't much different from breakfast in Wyoming except there are more potatoes. Actually, everything revolves around the potato, including the name of the place: Spuds.

Felix and I do not speak during the meal.

Portia notices. She talks the whole time about a dream she had, and it sounds like a convenient story. She also keeps looking over at Eddie, who alternates between nodding at what she's saying and staring at his phone. If he notices Felix and I aren't talking, he doesn't say anything.

Even when we're in the car, driving out of Idaho and into Washington, he doesn't pay any attention to us. That's no fun.

"Felix, where did you put the phone charger?" I ask.

He doesn't even look at me. "You had it last."

"No. You did."

"Well, I don't have it now."

Felix's tone is sharp enough to get Eddie's attention. He glances away from the road and at me. "Plenty of chargers around. You can use mine." Eddie nods toward the center console.

I reach over to get it, glaring at Felix in the process.

"Asshole." I say this under my breath. Felix doesn't respond.

I lean back in my seat, plug in the portable charger, and put on my headphones. The first text I get is from Portia.

You guys okay?

I say:

Yeah, just cabin fever.

We all have it. Not much longer now.

No, not much longer.

Thank God.

My mind has already started to drift to the end, to the desert.

344

Knowing where the trip ends is the biggest difference between the first trip and this one. Last time, we thought we were going all the way to the edge of California. This time we know we never made it that far, and I've still never been in that state. I've also never been back to Nevada.

Felix starts to eat a bag of chips, which normally wouldn't bother me. Today I decide it does. "Do you have to be so loud?" I say.

He rattles the bag, making even more noise.

"Really?" I say.

"Yep. Really." He puts a whole chip in his mouth and bites down hard, crunching unnecessarily with his mouth open. If we weren't pretending to be in a fight, that would piss me off.

"Nice," I say.

"All right," Eddie says, putting up a hand like a referee. "I don't know what's going on with you guys, but you sound like children."

I admit we're trying to provoke a response, I just didn't realize how patronizing Eddie would be. Now I do want to argue.

"No worse than you and Krista," I say.

"Ouch," Portia says, leaning forward like she wants a better view. "She got you there."

345

"She didn't 'get' me." Eddie throws her a dirty look in the rearview mirror. "She's wrong. Krista and I argue but we don't sound like five-year-olds."

"Yeah, your arguments were really mature," I say.

Eddie slams on the brakes and pulls off the road. He turns around, his blue eyes lit up like meteorites. "Look," he says. "I've tried my best with you. I've tried to be as accommodating as I know how, as laid-back as . . ." Portia opens her mouth to speak but Eddie silences her. "Other than one night in jail, I've done everything I can to make this trip easy, including paying more than my fair share." He looks at Portia.

She shrugs. Doesn't argue.

"Maybe you don't like me," he says. "Maybe all of you hate me. Fine. I don't care. We don't have to be friends. We don't even have to talk. What we have to do is get through this." He stops, takes a breath. "That's it. Let's just get through this."

What Do You See When You Look in the Mirror?

Someone who is screwed.

Someone who was too stupid to realize her own brother would align with the enemy. Of course he would. Of course. It's Beth's fault and it's my fault and neither one of us should have forgotten how easy it is for someone to sneak up on you when you aren't looking.

Like sperm. Those little things just sneak right up into you and bam, you're pregnant.

Or like that guy following us. I'm still the only one who knows about him.

347

WASHINGTON

STATE MOTTO: BYE AND BYE

For the rest of the drive, Felix and I speak only in essential terms.

I'm hungry.

I have to go to the bathroom.

Roll up/down the window.

Felix and I don't even text.

We do, however, keep an eye out for the truck. No one has seen it for a long time, and maybe it's gone forever, but looking for it gives us something to do.

I also keep an eye out for the van.

It's like this all the way to Colfax, Washington, home of the Codger Pole, and this is where Grandpa brought us instead of the amusement park. The pole is sixty-five feet high, made of wood, and it was carved with a chainsaw. I see the pole long before we get there, but I don't point it out to Felix. I wait until we park and walk up to it, so he can see it up close. He stares at it, up it, around it.

"Are those . . . faces?" he says.

"They are," Eddie says.

"Of *football players*?"

"Indeed," Portia says. "The Codger Pole is a giant phallic memorial to a football game."

True.

The Colfax Bulldogs and the St. John Eagles played against each other in 1938, and St. Johns won. Fifty years later, in 1988, they played again. With the same team.

Yes, they were about seventy years old, and yes, they played a game called the Codger Bowl. Colfax won, and all the players got their faces carved into a big pole. It's actually an amazing structure to see when you're standing in front of it, so there is that.

We aren't the only people here to see it, either. There are other tourists around, taking selfies and family photos in front of the pole.

"You came here instead of the theme park?" Felix says.

I avoid looking at Eddie. "Not my choice."

Eddie says nothing. Acts like he did nothing.

In truth, it's been a long time since I thought about how we ended up here instead of on the roller coasters, but his betrayal has always been in the back of my mind. It's why I would never fully trust him.

Back then, I don't know how Grandpa found this place in a world without smartphones, but he did. Maybe he had it all mapped out before he took us on this trip.

I can see Grandpa smiling now that he was back in charge, with Eddie right by his side. The three of us, the girls, lagged behind.

"Just wait," Grandpa said. "You're going to love this."

I already hated it, partly because it wasn't a roller coaster. Partly because of Nikki. She stood next to me, her whole body radiating anger, and I felt it the way you feel a chill. If I were her, I'd be angry at Eddie. He was the one who had betrayed her, who had betrayed all of us. We were supposed to stick together.

Grandpa stood next to the plaque by the pole. His smile looked wicked.

"Go ahead," he said. "Read it."

Nikki didn't just read it — she read it out loud for everyone to hear. I still remember parts of it, especially the last sentence.

350

The ghosts of our youth revealed glimpses of gridiron brilliance, unfortunately brief and few but even so, that glorious afternoon of fun gave us guys a chance to fulfill that dream every seventy-year-old kid secretly hangs onto: playing one more game.

And how many old rascals ever get to do that?

John Crawford
Codger Pole Dedication
September 15, 1991

Nikki finished reading and looked up at Grandpa. "*This* is what you brought us to see?"

"What?" Grandpa said. "You don't like the story?"

She rolled her eyes and walked away.

Nikki had a way of pissing people off. That day was no exception.

Now here we are again, standing in front of the same plaque, and Felix is the only one who hasn't read it. When he finishes, he turns to us and smiles.

"Cute," he says.

"Yeah, it's kinda cool," Eddie says.

Portia and I don't say a word.

351

We all walk around the pole, seeing it from every angle. At the bottom, the Eagle and Bulldog mascots are carved into it and painted, with the names of the teams written alongside. Above them, the faces of the players — wearing painted football helmets — are carved one on top of the other, also with their names. The pole is thick. It actually looks like several poles put together, and in total there are four rows of faces reaching up to the sky.

"I swear to God," Portia says. "The lengths men will go to memorialize themselves."

"Amen," I say.

"I bet they didn't have seventy-year-old cheerleaders at that game."

"You know they didn't."

Eddie sighs. "It's not to . . ." Whatever he was about to say fades out, and instead he just shakes his head.

"What was that?" Portia says.

"Never mind."

I glare at Eddie, not so much because of what he said now, but because of what happened before. We were enemies the last time we were here. And he kept making it worse.

Our whole excursion takes less than an hour. We go back to the car, drive south toward Oregon, and we don't stop until we hit the border.

A fairly peaceful, if quiet, end to the Codger Pole trip. The first time it wasn't.

Grandpa was pissed we didn't appreciate the Codger Pole. As soon as we got back into the van, he started yelling at us. "You can ride a roller coaster any damn time you want," he said. "I've been trying to show you *culture*. And *heritage*."

Nikki should have kept her mouth shut, but when did she ever.

"When did Bonnie and Clyde become culture and heritage?" she yelled. By then, she looked almost nothing like herself. Her blond hair had become blonder, but Nikki had stopped wearing as much makeup as she usually did, her clothes were a mess, and her nails were chipped. She looked like a kid instead of an almost eighteen-year-old. "When did a *fucking football game between old men become heritage?*"

Grandpa pointed at Nikki, the hate in his eyes visible. Tangible. "Shut up," he said.

"Yeah. Shut up," Eddie said.

Nikki crossed her arms over her chest, raised her chin, and said, "Make me."

They did.

OREGON

STATE MOTTO: SHE FLIES WITH HER OWN WINGS

Hells Canyon.

Of all the places in Oregon to go, of course Grandpa took us to Hells Canyon. Oh, and the name of the river that runs through this ten-mile-wide gorge? Snake River. Of course.

I have no doubt Grandpa chose it because of the name.

"You have to be prepared for this," Eddie says to Felix. "No motels tonight."

Felix nods.

"I'm not kidding. We're going to be in the wilderness."

"Actually, it's a recreation area," Portia says, reading from her phone. "It's the Hells Canyon National Recreation Area, to be exact." She smiles. She's particularly happy

354

because we're eating at an organic vegetarian restaurant. Oregon is full of them.

I take a bite of my black bean burger, which is delicious.

Eddie sighs hard enough to shake the table. "It's the wilderness," he says to Felix.

"Wait, are we camping?" Felix says. "Do we need a tent? Sleeping bags?"

"If you plan to sleep outside," Portia says. "I'll be in the car."

Eddie rolls his eyes. The disdain he has for all of us feels like last time. "We can't take the car out that far. We'll stop and get some supplies. Won't need a tent, though. The weather is nice."

Portia looks horrified.

"It's one night," Eddie says. "When did you become such a princess?"

"I was *six* the last time we were here. I didn't become a princess, I grew a brain."

Felix turns to me. "You know I have a bunch of camping stuff at home. I can't believe you didn't tell me." This is not part of our fake argument. The anger is back in his eyes.

"Sorry," I say. "I'm sure it won't cost much."

"I'm sure it will." He picks up his phone. I don't have to look to know he is looking up Hells Canyon to see what wild animals will be waiting for us.

A lot, actually.

"You know what?" Portia says, grabbing the check off the table. "Tonight I'm paying for dinner."

I am immediately suspicious — well, more suspicious than I already was — but I keep it to myself. Eddie doesn't.

"Did hell freeze over?" he says.

She smiles, not bothered at all. "Who knows — maybe we'll all get eaten by a bear tonight."

Felix glances up from his phone, still looking angry. "Then he's going to be disappointed by all the kale and beans in our stomachs."

His tone keeps us from laughing.

We stop and get clearance-rack sleeping bags, inflatable pillows, and a portable cooking kit. Felix is the one who remembers the bug spray. He walks up and down the aisles of the sporting goods store, searching for anything else we may need.

"We must need more than this," he says.

"One night," Eddie says. "It's just one night."

Felix snaps his fingers. "Toilet paper. We shouldn't go camping without toilet paper."

He's got a point, and I can't argue with

the extra blankets, either. Or the quick-pitch tent in case it does rain. And who would have a problem with bear spray? No one should ever have a problem with that. Even if it doesn't work, I like believing it will.

Eddie, ever the asshole, makes us pay because Felix picked out so much stuff. On the way to the car, Eddie continues to bark out orders.

"Remember, we have to walk to the campsite. I don't think you'll be able to roll your bags through that path."

Portia turns around and gives him a dirty look. "I'll be able to roll the bag, don't you worry."

"I'm not carrying it when the wheels break."

I ignore them. They can kill each other for all I care. Actually, that would make everything a lot easier.

No such luck. We all make it to the car alive and well, our arms filled with sleeping bags and blow-up pillows. Before Eddie lets us put everything in the car, he searches it. He's been doing that every day since the ashes disappeared. We still haven't talked about how to replace them, or what we were going to scatter in the desert.

"Nothing?" I say.

Eddie shakes his head, half annoyed and

half disappointed.

The drive isn't too long. Felix spends it reciting a list of wild animals that live in Hells Canyon. That would've been handy to know the first time around. Maybe we would've been more prepared for them. We heard more than we saw, including some seriously loud birds. Grandpa said they were owls.

And of course, the coyotes. We heard them all night, and Nikki said they sounded more like wolves, but Grandpa said she was wrong.

That night in the woods twenty years ago, everything appeared normal. From a distance.

We collected wood and Grandpa lit a campfire. Dinner was canned ravioli, warmed up and gross, although it tasted pretty good at the time. We toasted marshmallows on sticks after scraping off the outer bark. Well, Eddie scraped off the bark. Grandpa wouldn't let me or Nikki have a knife.

Eddie had started working on Portia, trying to lure her over to their side. That's what we had, opposite sides, and it had been that way for the whole trip. The groups changed, the power changed, but we had never been on the same side.

If you happened upon us at that moment, you never would've guessed all that. We gathered around Grandpa while he told gruesome ghost stories. Eddie tickled Portia, making her jump at the scary parts. All normal. But if you stayed too long, you might have noticed that Nikki's hands were tied up.

That's what Grandpa and Eddie did to her. She tried to run — tried to actually get out of the van as it was moving — but they stopped her. Tied her up so she couldn't get out. She stayed that way until Grandpa untied her hands so she could eat.

So you might have seen the rope around her wrists, and you might've thought that was a little weird.

Today, no one is tied up or being held captive. In fact, it's the opposite. We're all fighting to stay here. But like last time, we've never been on the same side. Not since the trip started.

Halfway there, Felix yells, "Wait!"

Eddie slams on the brakes. We all look at Felix, waiting for him to say something. Instead he does something worse.

Felix slams his fist on the dashboard.

Just like that, I'm a kid again.

I'm at home, hearing Mom scream and

yell and slam a door.

Then I'm back in the van watching Grandpa do the same thing. Hearing him say *Shut The Hell Up* all over again. I even feel the same level of fear, and I can't move, can't speak.

Violence always starts with the slam of door or a fist. It never ends there.

"What?" Eddie says to Felix.

"I forgot the soap," Felix says. He sounds disgusted, probably at himself. "We don't have any fucking soap."

"Oh God," Portia says. "We all stink already."

"No worries," Eddie says, patting Felix on the arm. "It's all good. Without you, we wouldn't have any of this stuff."

He continues driving and Felix continues to be angry at himself. I find myself watching his hands, wondering if he's going to punch the dashboard again.

The drive isn't long, thank God, so there isn't much time for anything else dramatic to happen. After Eddie parks the car and we gather our things, he barks out one more order. "Check your phones. I'm sure we won't have service once we leave the road."

We all pull out our phones. Three of us see the same e-mail from Grandpa's lawyer.

Dear all,

I hope your trip has been going well. I expect you'll be done soon?

Just wanted to drop a line and let you know we've had your grandfather's real estate valued. Assuming the real estate sells within 5 percent (plus or minus) of the appraised value, and that we sell the car for the average value of the make and model, the grand total of his estate is approximately $8 million. Rounded down, to be cautious.

I look forward to seeing you upon your return.

Regards,
Morton J. Barrie, Esquire

We all look up in unison. There might as well be a giant stack of money sitting at our feet, keeping us separated. It's so much money, more than enough to survive getting downsized. More than enough to disappear and start a new life.

The game is no longer Secret Risk. This is the real deal, the original version where the winner takes all. I can see it in their eyes. Greed is a real, palpable thing you see, smell, even hear, and it's all around me now.

But it's most noticeable in Felix. His pale

blue eyes have transformed into the color of money.

"All right, then," Eddie says. "Let's go camping."

There's a lot I remember about being in the woods, but there's also a lot I don't.

I remember walking through the woods, like we're doing now. I remember the open space next to a lake. Or the reservoir, as Grandpa said it was called. The food, the campfire, the marshmallows, and the ghost stories. Last, the hot cocoa, made with a double helping of chocolate and a bunch of marshmallows so it was thick and creamy.

The next thing I remember was being woken up by the sun. It was fully up, so bright I closed my eyes as soon as the glare hit. I threw the sleeping bag over my head and stayed there, although I didn't go back to sleep. I lay there for a minute until it hit me that everything was quiet. Grandpa usually got up early, but I didn't hear him at all.

I poked my head back out, shading my eyes with my hand. Everyone was still in their sleeping bags.

I stayed in my bag until I had to get up and pee. All at once I unzipped the bag and threw it off. That's how Mom always woke us up: She grabbed the covers and yanked. I put on my shoes and went into the woods. That's when I first realized I didn't feel well.

My head was heavy, almost like when I had a cold, but my nose wasn't stuffy and I didn't have a sore throat. Even as I moved around, I didn't feel quite awake. Like my head was filled with sand.

Back at camp, everyone continued to sleep. Portia had kicked the top of her sleeping bag off. She slept with all her limbs splayed out like she had all the room in the world. Grandpa made the biggest lump under his sleeping bag, his grey hair sticking out on top. Eddie was snoring now, and he was loud. The only one I couldn't see was Nikki. She was just a lump.

I pulled back her sleeping bag the way Mom would've done.

Nikki wasn't there. She had replaced herself with a pillow, a bunched-up blanket, and some of her dirty clothes. They were tied together with the rope that had been around her hands.

I screamed.

My fault, my fault, my fault.

After everyone woke up and saw the same thing I did, Eddie ran toward the road to try and find her. I started to run after him but immediately got dizzy and had to sit down.

"She couldn't have gone far," Grandpa said.

I stared at him, wondering how he could still underestimate her. If Nikki wanted to sail across the world, she would already be on a boat. She'd find a way.

"I don't remember," I said.

"Remember what?"

I put my hands on my head, which still didn't feel right. "I don't remember what happened last night. I just remember the cocoa."

He furrowed his brow, then looked up at the sky. Shook his head. "I don't, either."

"Don't what?"

"Remember. It's all just . . . a blur." He grabbed his bag and dumped everything out on the ground. He picked up his toiletries bag and went through the bottles. "Gone," he said.

"Your medicine?"

"My pain pills. Or what was left of them." He shook his head. "Jesus Christ. She drugged us."

"Nikki?" I said. Of course he was talking

365

about Nikki. "But she was tied up."

"Not while we were eating."

"But we ate out of cans. It couldn't have been —"

"The cocoa," he said. "I bet it was in the cocoa."

Possible. Maybe. "Wouldn't she have been drugged, too?" I said. She had her own cup. Grandpa had retied her hands in the front so she could hold it by herself.

"Seems like it." Grandpa walked back over to the where the campfire was. We'd sat on rocks around it the night before, and he knelt down near where Nikki had been sitting. "There's melted marshmallows here," he said.

My brain was slow and heavy, so it took me a minute to understand. "She poured it out?"

"Yeah. She did."

"It was me."

The tiny voice came from behind us.

Portia.

She was sitting on her sleeping bag, holding her stomach like it hurt.

"What was you?" I said.

"It was sugar. That's what Nikki said it was. She had a pouch of it in her bag, she told me to get it out and sprinkle it on the cocoa."

Now I remembered. Portia had put the marshmallows on top of our cocoa. And the pills. Nikki had them all crushed and ready to go, like she had been waiting for the right moment.

"She said it was powdered sugar," Portia said, her bottom lip trembling. "She told me it would make the cocoa even better."

"It's okay," I said. "You didn't do anything wrong."

She cried anyway.

So Nikki had really done it. She had managed to drug everyone — even *me* — and just like that, our story became stereotypical. Again.

There's always one of these nights, sometimes more than one. Happens every time. Someone is drunk or drugged or so sleep deprived they can't remember what happened. You know how that story goes because it's become a standard, a law, written in stone. Just like the missing girl.

That's how it went with us. We were all swept away by a good cup of hot cocoa, and no one could remember a thing. Nikki drugged us and ran.

No. She escaped.

I can say that now. She was a teenager who had been tied up by her grandfather and brother, so of course she escaped. At the time, it felt like she had abandoned me. I couldn't believe she didn't wake me up to go with her.

After I stayed by her side, even going along with her lies about Grandpa touching Portia, she left me behind.

Eddie burst through the trees, all out of breath. "I ran all the way to the car. Nothing." He bent over at the waist and put his hands on his knees. His face was pale. Sickly.

"She drugged us," I said.

He shook his head, looking like he was about to puke. "She's a bitch. She's always been a bitch." Eddie stood up and ran back into the woods.

Portia lay down and closed her eyes. "Sick," she said.

"I know," Grandpa said. "I'll get you some bread."

Nikki had done a lot to Portia on the trip. She had used her as a pawn, a weapon, an ally — whatever suited her needs at the time. But Grandpa had tied her up, for Christ's sake. Nikki had to do what she did.

Grandpa was the asshole. Everything Nikki did was a reaction to that.

I grabbed my bag to see if she had taken her stuff. She had given me some of her makeup because I had helped her put it on while her hands were tied, and it was still in the bag.

I also had the camera — the first one, the one we used to take pictures of ourselves. Eddie still had the second; it never left his pocket.

One thing had been added to my bag: Nikki's rainbow shirt. The one I always wanted was now mine, yet I wasn't happy about it. I didn't want it like that.

Nikki had also taken something. What I didn't have were my ashtrays, the two I had stolen from the motels, the two I had kept when Grandpa took the others. Both were gone, along with the shirt I had wrapped around them.

The button is gone.

The old one with the tarnished gold color, it's gone. At first, I think that I'm just missing it, that it must be here, but it isn't. I realized this as we repacked our bags before heading out into the woods, to the campsite, and now it's all I can think about. That damn button appeared and then disappeared without any explanation.

Felix doesn't know anything about it, so if he did go through my bag, I doubt he'd take an old button. He'd take the cigarettes instead — or at least wonder why I have them.

It would be easy to blame Portia since we shared a room so many times, but Eddie had access as well. There were plenty of times I left my bag in the car to use the restroom or go into the store. Anyone could have taken it.

I think about this as we walk single file

into the woods, even as I continue to argue with Felix. "You bought way too much stuff for one night."

"You buy too much stuff all the time," he says, half turning around to wink at me.

Now that we have our camping equipment, he's back to the pretend fighting, and he's really bad at it. I still wink back.

"Time out," Portia yells from behind us. "Hold the bickering until we get there."

I don't say anything else. All I hear now is the clink of the bottles in Portia's bag.

The walk isn't a long one. One minute we're in the middle of the woods, and the next we're in a small clearing in front of the water. This isn't one of the formal campgrounds, so there are no cabins, outhouses, or anything that looks like civilization.

The memories come back. I can see exactly how it looked then: where each of our sleeping bags were located, and off to the right, the woods where I last saw Nikki.

It makes me feel like crying all over again.

"Well, this is nice," Felix says, walking around like he's checking out another motel room. "I don't see any bear droppings or anything."

Lovely.

Portia looks at him like he's crazy.

"You didn't look for bear droppings last time?" Felix says.

"No," Eddie says.

Felix whistles. He's good at it. "You guys are so lucky to be alive."

"All right," Eddie says, cutting off anyone who thinks about continuing this conversation. "Here's how we're going to set this up."

He barks out orders about where everything should go, then Felix contradicts him, and I feel like hitting both of them with my can of bug spray.

Portia motions for me to follow her into the woods. She grabs one of her orange juice bottles and brings it along. We go just far enough that we hear them talk but they can't hear us whisper.

"Bears?" she says, unscrewing the top. She has premixed vodka with the orange juice. The smell hits me from a foot away.

"He's just being . . . Felix. That's how he is."

"Huh." She takes a swig of the drink and nods. "How long have you been with him?"

"So many years."

"Huh."

"You don't like him?" I say.

"Oh, he's fine, I guess. A little quirky, maybe."

Quirky. Yes, I would say he's quirky. And he can be uptight, finicky, and completely overorganized. And when you least expect it, he'll slam his fist on the dashboard. Maybe into other things, too. Maybe I've just never seen it.

"It's weird being back here," I say, changing the subject. Everywhere I look, I imagine us here as kids.

"I guess," Portia says.

"You don't remember."

She looks around, like she's trying to conjure it up in her mind. "I remember Nikki being tied up. I remember the ghost stories and the marshmallows and the cocoa." She stops and stares at the campsite in front of us. "That's about it."

"Yeah."

She starts to say something. Stops. Starts again. "Sometimes I think I remember but I don't know if it's real or I'm just making it up."

Felix looks at us through the trees and I wave him off, letting him know that we're fine. He doesn't have to come save us from any bears. "Like what?" I say, taking a gulp of the strongest drink I've had in a while. "What do you remember?"

"I think she said goodbye to me," Portia says. "I swear I can hear her whisper it."

I nod. "I bet she did. I bet she said goodbye to you."

Portia tilts the bottle and downs a lot more than a sip. She wipes her mouth with the back of her hand and chuckles. "I was joking," she says. "Nikki never said goodbye to me or anyone else. She was nothing but a selfish bitch."

I feel like I've been slapped.

"But you loved her," I say. "You *worshipped* her."

"Beth, she tricked me into drugging everyone. Into drugging *myself.*" Portia scoffs and shakes her head. "Nikki was a horrible person."

She walks away, leaving me in the woods by myself.

We don't use sticks for the marshmallows. Not this time, not with Felix around. He bought a set of metal spears made just for roasting marshmallows, because "I'm not eating anything off a stick because a bear could've peed on it."

Once the campfire is lit, we heat up our store-bought soup and eat it with our store-bought bread. For dessert, we roast marshmallows while drinking Portia's screwdrivers. I drink very little because the orange juice doesn't mix well with the marshmallows. I also can't afford to have another memory blackout. Once in my life was enough. Bad things always happen during blackouts.

"Your turn, Beth," Eddie says. He was finished telling a story about a ghostly fisherman who rises from the lake. "Don't make it stupid, either."

He didn't set the bar very high. Eddie's story was about as generic is it gets.

"Once upon a time, on a dark and moonless night . . ." I ignore Portia rolling her eyes. "There was a group of teenage boys who wanted to have some fun. Well, really they wanted to get laid, but since they were all virgins and didn't have any prospects, they had to come up with something else.

"They decided to break into their high school, because where else would teenage boys go? One of them says there's a broken window latch in his math class, so that's where they go first. It doesn't take much to get in, because the school is old and budgets have been slashed and who pays attention to window latches? Not this school."

Eddie clears his throat. I take it as a sign the story is stupid, but I don't care. I have a point to make.

"They went straight to the teacher's lounge, just to see what it was like. None of the students were allowed inside, and as far as the boys knew, no one had ever tried to get in. The lounge was like the black hole of secrets, and the boys wanted to be the first to know what they were.

"They were surprised to find the door unlocked. All these years, and the damn thing was unlocked. They walked right in, assuming it was empty. It was not.

"A whole group of teachers stood in the center of the lounge, huddled together like they were gathered around a campfire. Except they weren't. Instead, they were all smoking. The air was so thick it was hard to breathe. The teachers didn't see the boys until one of them coughed.

" 'Oh crap,' the boy said.

"All of the teachers turned around. Their eyes were hollowed out. They all had grey skin and sunken cheeks. Like they were dead." I glance at Felix, whose expression doesn't change. "One of the boys pointed at the teachers.

" 'They're . . . floating,' he said.

"He was right. The teachers hovered about a foot off the ground, and their feet looked like wisps of smoke.

"One of the boys said, 'They're ghosts.'

"The comment made all the teachers start puffing harder on their cigarettes. They also started moving closer to the boys."

"Do ghosts smoke?" Eddie said.

I ignored him. "The boys took off running back down the hall, but the smoke followed. They turned and found another hall filled with smoke, but they plowed forward, into the abyss.

"One boy screamed, 'Screw the alarm,' and they ran toward the front doors of the school. The first boy burst through the doors, setting off the alarm. All the others followed behind, but the boy who came out last was never the same. He started smoking that very night. Didn't stop, refused to even try. Within a month, he got kicked out of school for smoking on campus. The boy wouldn't do anything except smoke; he wouldn't go to any other school, wouldn't see his friends.

"His parents had to put him in an addiction center, but he was kicked out for smoking. Next they put him in a psych hospital. He's still there, still locked away in a room. He doesn't say a word. Never has."

I pause to glance at Felix again. Still no expression, no reaction to my story about his new habit.

"Oh shit," Portia says.

"All the boy does," I say, "is smoke."

Everyone stares at me.

"Was that supposed to be scary?" Eddie says.

"It was supposed to be creepy," I say.

No one responds.

Portia wiggles like she's shivering. "Jesus Christ. Who the hell thinks of smoking ghosts?" She stands up from her rock, brushes off her butt. "Now I have to use the facilities. If I scream, it's because I saw a smoking ghost."

"What did you think?" I say to Felix.

"Not bad, I guess."

Dick.

I roll my eyes and stand up, walking into the woods after Portia. Maybe Felix is still pretending to fight, or maybe he really is as quirky as Portia says.

She doesn't hear me coming because the guys launch into a loud, drunken conversation. I see her kneeling down and assume she's taking care of business. Instead, I see her slip something out of her pocket and hide it beneath a tree, under some leaves.

I wait until she's done before walking closer.

"Hey," I say.

"Oh hey." She whips around, the guilt in her eyes as clear as the nighttime sky.

"You forgot the toilet paper," I say.

She smiles. "Yeah, I just realized that."

We go back to get some and I make a mental note about that tree, so I can come back to it.

After we go to bed, I wait an appropriate amount of time for everyone to fall asleep. Half an hour, at least, and then I get up as quietly as I can. Using only my phone as a light, I make my way into the woods, toward the tree. It isn't hard to find. Earlier I noted a particular branch it had, the way it bent out like an arm with a broken elbow. Just as I'm about to kneel down, I hear him.

"What are you doing?"

Felix.

Goddamn Felix.

"Jesus Christ," I say. "You scared the hell out of me." Truth.

"I heard you get up and thought you needed to pee, but you didn't take any toilet paper," he says.

"So you followed me out here instead of saying something back there?"

He nods, like he doesn't understand the problem, and it's so irritating. All I want to do is see what Portia hid out here, but I can't get away from my husband.

Who is probably awake because he wants to smoke.

I do not get to check what Portia left in the woods. Instead, I have to pretend to pee and then go back to my sleeping bag, where I'm afraid to move. Almost like I'm being held captive by my overprotective husband.

And I don't like it one bit.

The music. I hear it again, that same song by Garbage. In the middle of the wilderness, that music wakes me up.

It's not loud and booming like it was last time. Now it's faint, like an alarm clock ringing in another part of a house. I glance around. The moon gives off enough light so it's not pitch dark. Everyone else is asleep. I slip out of my bag and stand up, checking to make sure I can see everyone's head and not just a lump in the sleeping bag. No one is missing this time.

The music stops.

It starts again.

When I move, I step on a rock. I bite the inside of my cheek to stop myself from screaming.

I put on my shoes and grab the flashlight Felix bought.

At the edge of the woods I turn it on, scanning through the trees. Nothing. No one is there, no movement, nothing but the music. I take a step forward because, yes, I can be an idiot. An idiot who wants to find her sister.

The music grows louder with each step. The same song, over and over, on a never-ending loop — sort of like this road trip. Appropriate. Ironic. You know what I mean. It still doesn't stop me from going into the dark woods alone.

Because at some point, we have to know. We have to find out.

So I move forward, clearing the leaves with my toe before I step down. Making as little noise as possible to not wake the others. I can't hide from whoever is out here, because I'm carrying a damn flashlight.

About thirty feet in, the music is loud enough to know I'm close.

"Nikki?" I say. Not a whisper, but not too loud.

No answer.

No movement, no breathing other than my own. I'm alone. I know this, I can feel it. All I have to do is find whatever is playing the music. A little digging through the bushes is all it takes.

A phone, the generic prepaid kind. The

same song, the only song, plays on a loop. It's the alarm going off again and again, not stopping until someone turns it off.

I should've known Nikki wouldn't just step out and reveal herself. She's not done playing yet. But at least I know she's still right here with us.

I turn off the phone, making the music stop.

Now I have a chance to see what Portia hid, but first I look back to make sure Felix is still in his sleeping bag.

I go to the tree and kneel down, rummaging under the bush at the base of it. This takes longer than I expect. It seems Portia was shoving something into the dirt, burying something, not just placing it on the ground. Eventually, I find something that doesn't feel natural. Well, not anymore. It feels like leather.

A wallet.

A billfold, actually — the kind men often carry in their back pockets. This one isn't empty, either. It's stuffed so full of credit cards it barely folds in half. I pull the first one out and look at the name.

IAN P. WELTON

No idea who that is. I pull out the next one.

JOHNATHAN RICKER

One by one, I take the cards out. All the cards have male names, and I wonder if she stole them back home, from customers at the strip club, or if she's been doing it on this trip. Not that it matters. She needed to get rid of them, and the woods are a convenient place to make something disappear.

Portia really is a thief, and she steals more than candy bars now.

And if she gets caught, she won't inherit a thing.

Two Days Left

Felix is up in time to see the sunrise. I'm up at the same time, which is a surprise to me, considering how little sleep I got after my walk through the woods.

At home, this is normal for us. Most mornings we get up at the same time to go walking, then we get ready for work and drive together to International United. This is our routine, our way of life.

Now everything feels different.

For example, the day before we left on this trip started like any other. Felix was up first. He was already changing into his walking clothes when I woke up.

"I'll come, too," I said, sitting up in bed.

"You don't have to. Get some extra sleep if you want."

I sat there, knowing I should walk because I would be sitting in a car for the next two weeks, but also wanting to sleep. And here was my sweet kind husband telling me to stay in bed, like he knew that's what I wanted to do.

Wrong. I was completely wrong. My husband wanted to go out alone because he wanted to smoke. He didn't give a shit about what I wanted or if I needed more sleep.

And what about all those times he offered to go out when we needed something? A run to the store, to the cash machine, to get gas . . . was he being nice? Or was he trying to find a moment alone to feed his nicotine habit?

Then there's the big question, the one I still haven't been able to answer. What else is he hiding? Besides, apparently, a temper. It's so clear to me now, ever since that slam of his fist. Maybe I've missed all the signs that spouses miss, but everyone else can see.

Jesus Christ, I've become the worst kind of wife. The stupid one.

This is what's going through my mind as I heat up the kettle and make us some instant coffee. Portia and Eddie sleep right through it.

I motion toward the woods with my hand and whisper, "Want to take a walk?"

He shrugs, as if he doesn't care, but I bet

he does. He wants that morning cigarette.

"We can take a quick swim, too," I say. "At least get clean."

He nods.

We sip our awful coffee as we walk in the dark, though somehow the fresh air makes me think it's better than it is.

"Best sleep I've had on this trip." He says this like I asked him about it. "I love sleeping outdoors."

I don't answer that. Even I have limits about lying.

"I never realized how much of the country I haven't seen," he says. "We can see a lot more when this is over. On our own, I mean."

"On our own?"

He puts his arm around my shoulder. "I mean, once all the bills are paid off — the student loans and the mortgage. We'll have a lot more money for vacations."

Student loans. *His* student loans. I worked three jobs every summer to not have student loans, and he wants to use my inheritance to pay off his.

On top of all that, the cigarettes. Bet he thinks I'm going to pay for those, too.

"Sounds great," I say.

We cut through the trees on our left, to another small clearing next to the water.

Felix has a small bag with him so we have fresh clothes after our bath. It's nice that he remembers things like that. Most men wouldn't, I don't think. Although how would I know?

The sun begins to appear, a brilliant orange dot on the water, and we sit and watch the final moments of its rise.

"They really believed we were fighting yesterday," I say.

He glances over at me. "Well, we kinda were."

"Why were you so mad?"

He shrugs. "I just can't believe you never told me about the camping. That's just so . . . wrong."

The anger appears again. It's so easy to see now. I had been thinking this might be a good time to bring up his smoking, to tell him that I knew, but now I won't. Not while he's angry.

I slip my free hand into his. "I was wrong. I'm sorry."

He leans over and kisses me. A dry, chaste kiss because we haven't brushed our teeth and we smell like instant coffee. It could have been a brother-sister kiss.

We haven't had sex on this trip. Not once. Maybe because Portia was in our room half the time, or maybe because the motels were so bad. Or it could be that transporting Grandpa's ashes across the country is the least sexy thing ever.

More likely, it's because we haven't had sex in months — three months and nineteen days, to be exact.

Oh well.

"Come on," I say. "Let's take a swim."

We strip down and get in the water and it's still not sexy. It's cold at first, then pleasant. If I had to describe my marriage, that's the word I would use. Pleasant. Mostly.

The water is smooth and clear, not a ripple as far as I can see. Felix follows me out beyond the shallow water, and I challenge him to a treading contest. He splashes at me. "No way."

"You think you can beat me?"

He does. Felix can be so traditionally male that way. "Okay, let's go."

I start to tread, he does the same.

My eyes stay on his, watching. Waiting. Not for anger. This time, I see the moment the sleeping pills take effect.

He doesn't feel it for another thirty seconds or so. "Wait," he says.

"What?"

"I'm just . . ."

"Just what?"

He shakes his head, turns toward the

389

shore. Felix starts to move toward it until I grab his arm. "Are you okay?" I say.

"I can't keep —"

"Sure you can."

He shakes his head, his eyes already drowsy. That's a hell of a sleeping pill. No wonder people get addicted to those things. So easy to get, too.

It's nothing at all for me to reach up and push his head underwater. He struggles, though. Even pops up for one more breath. Felix grasps at me, the horror in his eyes. The betrayal.

He knows.

I push his head under for good. He doesn't struggle for long.

Felix. Poor, sad, finicky Felix. Did I know from the beginning I would do this?

No. But I brought the sleeping pills, so I always knew that I *could.* If it came to that, which it did. Now I have to make sure he stays under the water.

If I weight him down, it will be obvious he was murdered. For this to be considered an accident, I have to get more creative. Luckily, the rocks along the side of the shore are helpful. Also luckily, bodies are easy to move in the water. It's a fairly simple thing to lodge his body halfway behind the rocks.

He stays under that way, like he got stuck and ended up drowning.

I take one last look before walking away.

Our marriage was never going to work.

When I met Felix, I had no one. My father was dead, my mother in prison, Nikki had been gone for years, and I certainly wasn't close to Eddie or Portia. If I'm being perfectly, totally, 100 percent honest, I was so lonely, anyone I met could've become my husband. It just happened to be Felix. He was the one I latched onto, clung to, stayed with, and married. And for the most part, he's been a wonderful husband — at least right up until he slammed his fist on the dashboard, reminding me that even the kind, easygoing men are capable of violence. I'm not waiting around to see if that fist hits me.

No, I don't need Felix anymore, not the way I used to. Don't even want him, because I'm going to find Nikki.

My mother would understand, because she realized the same thing about Dad. She just didn't need him anymore. Not if he was going to insist Nikki was dead.

Remember, a cheating wife is just one deal breaker. Murder is the other, which means neither my mother nor I can be the heroine of this story.

"We have to call the police."

When Nikki disappeared, that's what I said. *We have to call the police.*

Grandpa looked at me like I was the crazy one.

I turned to Eddie, who couldn't hate our sister that much. "We can't just leave her out here," I said.

"You know what the police said when she ran away," Eddie said.

Which time? There had been quite a few. The first was years earlier, and the police were pretty serious about looking for her, given that she had been fourteen, and young girls who disappeared were all over the cable news back then.

They found Nikki in less than a day. She was hiding at a friend's house.

The second time she ran away, they didn't take it as seriously. They said, "She'll be back in a few days."

The third time, they barely wrote a report. Nikki always came back whenever she stopped having fun or ran out of money. They usually happened at the same time.

"She'll call Mom and Dad when she's ready," Eddie said.

"No," I said. This wasn't like when Nikki ran away at home, where she had friends and family and a town she was familiar with. This was the wilderness.

And she was pregnant.

"We *have* to find her," I said.

"Where? How?" Eddie said. He was throwing his stuff in his bag, no longer looking for Nikki. "Just let her go. She knows how to use a phone."

I went to Grandpa, who was cleaning up our cooking stuff "Please," I said. "I bet we can find her."

He looked at me, his eyes hard. "Did you help her?"

"Of course I didn't help her! No!"

Grandpa just stared at me.

"Do you really want to go back home without Nikki?" A threat, yes. I'm not even sure I knew I was making it. The question just seemed obvious. "Do you want to explain this to Mom?"

"Nikki!" Portia yelled. She may have been tricked by Nikki, but Portia still wanted to find her. "Nikki!"

She just kept yelling. No one answered.

Grandpa sighed. He looked off into the woods, maybe thinking about what to do next.

"We really should call the police," I said.

He sighed. "Before we do that, let's try to find her first. You know she runs away a lot."

I had to agree with that.

"Do you have any idea where she would go?" Grandpa asked.

I smiled. Yes, I did know. "Ever seen *Thelma & Louise*?" I said.

"Your grandmother loved that movie," he said. "I never understood it."

"Nikki loves it, too. And there's a desert in it. She always talks about seeing that desert."

"Then let's go see the desert."

It was impossible for me to know, to visualize, just how big the desert was, or that there were so many of them. At least we were looking for her, though. That was the important thing.

No such luck for Felix. I went back to camp and gathered up his things before Eddie and Portia were awake. It wasn't even seven in the morning. Sometimes daylight savings is a good thing.

I hid his things in the bushes near where we went swimming. They were buried well, so no one would stumble across them anytime soon. Last, I went back to our camp and made more instant coffee, like I had just woken up and hadn't gone for a walk, hadn't gone swimming, hadn't killed my husband.

I make it sound easy, right? Like killing someone is an everyday thing for me. It isn't, I promise.

What I can tell you is that the killing is the easy part. It's the getting away with it that makes it so difficult. Eventually, Felix will be found. That's a different set of problems than having him here.

Portia wakes up first. She holds her head as she walks over to me, obviously hung over.

"Hey," she says.

"Hi."

She grabs a bottle of water and downs half of it. I drink my second cup of coffee. I did bring Felix's cup back with me, I even washed it out with our antibacterial spray to get rid of any residue from the sleeping pills.

"Is that coffee as bad as it smells?" Portia says.

"Yes."

"Can I have a cup?"

She doesn't move to make it herself, she asks me to do it for her. Like she's still a child, the baby.

I make her the cup. Portia takes a sip, makes a face. "Wow."

"Told you."

She glances over to Eddie's sleeping bag. "Of course the guys are still asleep."

"One is."

"Oh right. Felix gets up early." She glances around. "Is he already packed and ready?"

I take another sip of coffee. "He's gone."

"Gone?"

"Gone," I say. "He left."

She is stunned, and then she gets it. "Oh shit. I knew you guys were fighting, but . . ." She scuffs her toe in the dirt, scratching out a circle. "I'm sorry."

"Thanks."

"Did he say anything?"

I pull the note out of my pocket, the one I wrote yesterday. That's how long I've known for sure. I also knew phones wouldn't work out here. He couldn't send me a text.

I can't stay on this trip. It's not doing us any good. We'll talk at home.

"What a dick," Portia says. "Did he just

396

walk out of the woods?"

"Probably. I bet he called an Uber from the road. He can fly home from . . . I don't know, Portland or wherever."

"Dick."

I shrug. "Yeah. But you know, it's comforting in a way."

"Is it?"

"Sometimes it's good to be reminded they can all be assholes. Like a genetic thing. So I don't forget."

"Cheers," she says, holding up her coffee. We tap cups.

Do I think it's going to work? That I'll get away with it? Timing. It always comes down to timing.

I've laid the foundation, put everything in its place. The arguing everyone saw. The road trip no one wants to be on. The note. The plan to see him at home. When I get there and he's not around, I'll call the police and report him missing.

Without a body, a crime scene, or any suspicion of foul play, they'll assume he has left me. They'll have nothing to go on, no reason to suspect Felix is anything but a husband who had enough of his wife. I plan to be extra annoying to the cops to solidify that belief. I can be the woman no one wants to marry.

Maybe they'll ping his phone. They won't find it. What they will find, if they bother to get his phone records, is a bunch of calls and texts from me, from his boss, from his friends. He'll be the man who just walked away and went on a road trip of his own.

That's assuming Felix's body doesn't show up first.

One day it will. He will be a drowning victim. A husband was on his way to leaving his wife, he stopped to take a little bath in the lake before splitting.

That's when things could get tricky. Maybe I'll get away with it, or maybe I'll have to use money to buy my way out of it. Good thing I've got that inheritance coming.

Down to the three of us, the Morgan siblings. We're the only ones left.

"I knew he wouldn't make it," Eddie says. He's rolling up the sleeping bags, including Felix's. "He's not the road-trip kind of guy."

"Shut up," I say. "Stop talking about him."

We finish gathering everything up in silence. Before we leave, I head out to the woods to use the facilities. Also to check for that cell phone.

I may have been preoccupied with Felix, but I didn't forget that music. I never could.

I dig around in what I think is the same spot, wishing I had picked up the phone the night before. Stupid me.

"Lose something?"

Portia. She has followed me out here, maybe to retrieve that wallet or bury it a little better.

"I hid some toilet paper out here last night," I say. "I didn't want to leave it behind."

"Ah. Okay. Well, don't let me interrupt." She keeps walking past me carrying her own toilet paper roll.

I do not find the phone.

My nerves get to me before we leave. I keep checking and double-checking everything in my bag, in my head, around the campsite. Making sure I didn't forget anything.

This is the part not many talk about. The nerves. They feel electric, almost painful. I'm convinced it's a form of panic because really, it's fear. Fear that I'll be caught, fear that I've screwed up. Fear that everyone is in on it but me.

That last one is the worst.

But I don't throw myself on the ground and scream. I don't hyperventilate. No tantrums, just movement. I cannot be in this place for one second longer.

"Jesus Christ," Eddie says. He spits out the instant coffee. "This is like . . . mildewed water or something."

"Mildewed water?" Portia says.

"Yeah." He doesn't explain further.

Once all our things are picked up, we stop at the path and take one last look. The area is as pristine as we found it. You'd never know anyone was here.

"Come on," Portia says. She leads the way, Eddie goes next. I'm last.

"These road trips are so screwed," Eddie says. "We always lose people along the way."

Indeed.

The path out is uneventful. We don't talk until we get to the car, which is right where we left it. Nothing looks amiss, there are no flat tires, and I hear the doors unlock when Eddie hits the button. Even the chirp sounds perky.

Two more days. That's what I'm thinking. Two. More. Days.

The first time, I had no idea how many more days we'd be on the road, or how long it would take to reach the ocean. It didn't matter after Nikki ran away, because we had to go to the desert. The ocean had to wait.

I talked about the desert like it was a town. Eddie never told me I was wrong or stupid, which should have tipped me off. Geography was never my strongest subject. Maybe Eddie didn't know or maybe he just kept his mouth shut. Grandpa knew, though. He never said a word, just let me go on and on like there was a place called Desert.

We don't talk about the desert this time. We're all too busy looking at our phones.

I check up on Cooper and then scan through my e-mails, looking for any updates on the job cuts at work. I have an e-mail from Sandra, who says there are so many rumors flying around it's impossible to know who will be cut next. I starting typing an e-mail back, thanking her for trying to keep me in the loop, when Eddie's voice makes me jump.

"What the hell."

I look up. He has just opened the back of the car, and the lid to the hidden compartment is open.

Inside, the wooden box. Grandpa's ashes are back.

If you could bring someone back to life by staring hard enough, Grandpa would be with us again. That's how long and hard we stare at that box.

"Impossible," Eddie says.

No. Not for Nikki. I already know she was here last night because of the phone.

"Convenient," Portia says.

Eddie turns to me. "Felix left last night. You think he might've done it?"

This is the single worst thought Eddie has ever had. "Why the hell would Felix take the ashes and then put them back?"

402

"I don't know. Maybe you married a psycho?"

"He's not a psycho." He's just dead. He couldn't have done this.

Portia steps between us. "Has to be the guys from Alabama. They're still messing with us."

"Either that or it's one of us," Eddie says.

We all look at one another until one of us breaks. It's me, because you can't stand around and do nothing forever. Eventually you have to get on with it.

"Are we going to stare at those ashes all day?" I ask.

Eddie and Portia exchange a look that clearly says, *She's being a bitch because her husband left.*

I can work with that.

Eddie closes the back compartment and we load our bags in. We all managed to roll our bags down the path, except Eddie. As far as I can tell, none of the wheels broke, either. He shuts the back just as Portia says, "Shotgun."

Shotgun?

She climbs right into the seat next to Eddie, ignoring the fact that we now have two empty rows in the back. Plenty of room to stretch out and sleep, just as she's been doing the whole trip. Now all of a sudden she wants to be in the front.

I sit in my usual seat, right behind Eddie and now Portia. It doesn't feel right at all.

There's nothing in southeastern Oregon. I don't mean that in a sarcastic way, either. It's true. Once you hit I-95 south, there's a whole lot of nothing until you hit the Nevada border. A beautiful drive, to be sure, but at this point I've had my fill of scenery.

Last time, it was the most tedious drive in the world because all I could think about was finding Nikki. She had money to travel and stay in a motel. Nikki had stolen all the cash from Grandpa's wallet.

"She could've taken a bus," Grandpa said. "Tickets are cheap."

Nikki would do that. She was smart enough to figure out that a bus was her best option to get to the desert. Assuming she hadn't called our parents. She might have, since she had been talking about it not long ago.

But would she?

I spent a lot of time thinking about that in

the car because it distracted me — for a minute — from blaming myself. I never admitted it was my fault to anyone, certainly not Grandpa or Eddie. They might have tied me up, too.

It was when we were in the woods. That part was Grandpa's fault. He sent me with Nikki so she could pee. Would it have been inappropriate for him to go with her? Yes. Eddie, too. I bet Grandpa considered all of that, especially because of what Nikki had accused him of doing with Portia. So he sent me.

By then, we had finished eating and had just started on our cocoa. Nikki's hands were tied up again.

"Beth, don't you dare untie her," Grandpa said.

As soon as we got into the woods, Nikki told me to do exactly that. "I'm not going to run," she said. "I just want to pull down my own pants."

Made sense to me. And she didn't run. She even told me how to retie the knot exactly like Grandpa had done. "Just not so tight. Look at those marks."

True. She had red marks on both wrists from the rope digging into them. I left her enough room to wriggle around a little. I also took my time, because I wanted to talk to her alone. I had finally worked up the courage to tell her that I knew.

"You're pregnant, aren't you?" I said.

She stared at me, eyes wide, in a genuine state of shock.

"I saw the test in your bag," I said. "I wasn't snooping, I swear. I was just looking for your Discman because Portia was scared and . . ." The words came out in a rush as I tried to explain, tried to not make her mad. "I just saw it."

She took a deep breath, recovering from the shock, and she said the last words I ever heard from her.

"Don't. Fucking. Tell. Anyone."

When we came out of the woods, Grandpa looked at the knot to confirm it was the same. By then, I was starting to feel sleepy. Now I know it was from the pain pills. Back then, I just thought it was because the day had been so long. I bet the pills are what made Grandpa not check close enough. He only looked at the knot; he didn't check how tight or loose it was.

Though, to be fair, Nikki did a good job of selling it. She grimaced when she moved, like the rope hurt.

It never occurred to me that she would leave. She just disappeared and never returned with help.

I've wondered if that was her plan. Maybe she wanted to find a police officer or call our parents or even find a park ranger. But then something happened. Maybe she was hit by a car or kidnapped into a sex-trafficking ring. Maybe she fell and hit her head and ended up with amnesia.

But no, none of that happened.

She's still out here.

Back then, I didn't know that. I had no idea what happened to her. As we drove through Oregon, I was worried about her, upset she had left, and I wanted to make sure she was safe. When Grandpa pulled off the road and into a motel, I lost it.

"You can't stop," I said. "We have to go to the desert."

"I can't drive anymore," Grandpa said.

"But you have to!" I felt tears in my eyes, falling down my cheeks. They came so fast they surprised me.

"Oh God," Eddie said, shaking his head at me. I could feel his disappointment and I didn't care. "She ran away, okay? Nikki *always* runs away. She can't deal with life at all."

Grandpa had apparently decided Eddie was right, because he decided to stop.

Portia was curled up in a ball, next to me

on the seat. She had sniffled and cried her way through Oregon, still feeling bad about sprinkling that powder on our cocoa. But not bad enough to hate her sister. "I miss Nikki," she whispered.

"We should keep going," I said. "Or call the police."

"Nikki can't move any faster than us," Grandpa said. "If she took a bus, she'll move even slower. We'll probably beat her to the desert."

Normally, I'd look to Nikki for confirmation of a statement like that. Without her, I had to make my own choice. She wouldn't be able to fly to the desert, I knew that. So it made sense that she'd be on a bus. Would a bus drive through the night? I didn't know, couldn't know. And I also couldn't drive.

I almost told them right then.

Nikki is pregnant.

The words were right on the tip of my tongue, begging to be said. Would it have changed anything? Would Grandpa have called the police? And if we did find her, how angry would Nikki have been that I said something? That was the thing that scared me most. When Nikki was finally back, she would be so pissed at me.

So I said nothing.

We stop right at the border, just like last time. Technically, we're still in Oregon but we're close enough to walk into Nevada. The motel is the same. For the first time on this trip, I know for a fact we're at the same place. First, because there aren't that many in this area. Second, because of the sign.

"You remember that?" I ask Portia.

She looks up at the giant neon beaver on the sign of the Beaver Dam Inn. "Yeah. Of course."

I also remember Grandpa lecturing us about the beaver, which is the state animal of Oregon, and how crucial they are to the ecosystem. I didn't care about any of that. I liked the place because it looked like somewhere Nikki would stay. The big neon animal sign would get her attention.

"How many rooms?" Eddie says.

"One," Portia says. "We can all fit in one,

unless someone wants a room to themselves."

I looked from one to the other. "Well, is anyone planning to kill me in my sleep?"

Eddie rolls his eyes.

"Too chickenshit for me," Portia says. "If I kill you, you'll know I did it."

One room it is. "I'll pay."

Not only do I remember the sign; I remember the office because it was the only one I saw. Grandpa usually checked in, or Nikki, but never me. At the Beaver Dam, Grandpa let me come into the office with him.

It was a small, stuffy room that was too hot and smelled like smoke. The man behind the desk had long hair and a beard but no moustache. It looked weird. He was weird. His eyes were different colors and he looked right past Grandpa instead of at him.

I didn't go into the office to meet the desk clerk. I wanted to see the keys. Grandpa didn't know it, but I wanted to see which rooms had been rented for the night.

There were two: room numbers 4 and 9. We got number 6.

Over the past twenty years, the office has been redone. It's been painted white and the cigarette stench has been replaced with pine-scented deodorizers. A dark-skinned woman with almost-black hair sits behind the desk. She gives me the once-over as soon as I walk in.

"One room, please. For one night."

She looks behind me, at our car. "For three people?" she says.

"Oh yeah. That's my brother and sister. We're on a road trip." I don't know what she thought was going on, but I wanted to quash anything unseemly.

With a curt nod, she takes my cash and grabs a key off the board. Some things never get updated. A new key card system costs a lot more than a can of paint. We get room number 8.

"Thank you," I say to the woman.

She gives me a dirty look and grunts a little. I don't think she believes Eddie and Portia are my siblings.

Yes, the ashes are still in the car this time. Eddie brings them into the room.

Unlike the front office, the room hasn't been updated or painted. It's still stuck in the eighties, just like last time, and everything is floral. Everything. The walls, the curtains, even the headboards of both beds. The décor has nothing to do with beaver dams.

"I would've killed myself if I lived in the eighties," Portia says.

That's funny, because last time she loved it. She twirled around in circles and said it made her feel like she was in the middle of a bouquet.

All I had been thinking about was how to get out of that room and see who was staying in the others. I hoped so hard one was Nikki. Did I really believe she was? No. I'm not delusional, never have been. Even at twelve, I knew how unlikely it was that Nikki was here, if only because Eddie kept saying it.

"You're such an idiot," he said. "She's gone. She's not staying here."

"I just want to check."

I couldn't, though, not unless Eddie came with me. Grandpa was never going to let me out of the room by myself or with Portia, not after Nikki ran away. But Eddie was his partner, his sidekick. Grandpa trusted him.

Luckily, my family played Risk. I knew that to get someone on your side, you had to give them something. Everyone was bribable.

"What do you want?" I asked.

"I want you to leave me alone."

"No, really. What?"

He thought about it, toying with the idea while smiling and teasing and having a lot of fun being able to name his price. After some intense negotiation, we agreed that I had to do his chores and give him my allowance for a month.

Grandpa had no problem with us going down to the soda machine. It wasn't too late, and compared to other motels we had stayed in, the Beaver Dam was almost family friendly. Maybe because the rooms were so floral and they had Disney movies available for rent at the front desk.

As soon as we got out, I went straight to door number 4 and knocked.

"Do you think Nikki will just open the door?" Eddie said.

"If she's here, she will." I knocked again.

The man who answered the door wasn't Nikki. He wasn't anyone Nikki would talk to. First, because he was older than our grandfather. Second, because the woman behind him was half naked on the bed and half his age.

"Sorry," I said. "Wrong room."

I ran. Eddie wasn't far behind. Room number 9 was next and last. This time I hesitated.

Eddie stepped up and did the knocking. "Let's finish this already."

Nikki wasn't in that room. But the man who was changed everything.

The TV is on but no one watches. We're all too busy staring at our phones. Eddie sits by the window because we're back on watch for the black truck.

After checking in with Cooper, who is working late, I take out my laptop and look at my e-mails and the local news from back home. I also check the Oregon news from Hells Canyon and the news from Colorado.

No word from Krista. No news about any bodies being found, not a word about Felix. It's almost another job checking in on things.

Social media, especially. It's all fine when I have something good to share, otherwise it's just post after post of everyone else's life. Yes, yes, yes, I'm so happy for you — *Yay! Living the dream!* — but I have nothing good to post about myself. All the wrong people would be impressed that I got away with killing my husband. So far.

416

"Let's do a selfie," I say.

"No," Portia says.

"None of your friends will see it. I'll post it on my page."

"Whatever," Eddie says.

"Come on," I say.

They gather in close and we all stare into the camera, seeing our own image looking back at us. We aren't young or tan or wild-looking like last time. We look like losers trying to make themselves better for social media.

Portia frowns. "Do you really want this floral background?"

"Yeah, maybe we should go outside," Eddie says. "We can get the beaver sign in the picture."

"Even a plain background would be better," Portia says.

The placement of the selfie — of any selfie — takes a while. We test and delete a variety of backgrounds, both inside and out, by the car and by the motel sign. It's too tall and impossible to get in a selfie. Even when we angle the phone, it doesn't come out right.

"You know," Portia says. "The floral wallpaper is actually kind of funny. You could make fun of how kitsch it is."

We end up back where we started,

squished together in front of the floral wall in our room. Click, check, delete. Click, check, delete. We repeat this until we're all happy with the picture.

"You're doing this for Felix, right?" Portia says. "To show him you're having fun."

"Exactly," I say.

I post the picture, along with the tag: *Current mood: 80's wallpaper, 90's rock, & both my siblings.*

Within minutes, people start liking it. It's only been a few days since I posted but you'd think I'd been in Siberia. The people I know are the kind who pay attention to their social media all the time.

I take a shower, and when I get out, Portia is in our bed and already asleep. Eddie is about to turn off his bedside lamp. Before he does, he says, "You good?"

"I'm good."

Portia doesn't move.

I get into bed, place my phone facedown, and fall asleep in an instant. The knocking at the door wakes me up.

The pounding, I should say. Like someone is using the back of their fist against the door. Three times. The first woke me up. It woke all of us up.

Eddie is the first to get out of bed. Rather, he jumps up, walks across our bed, and lands by the door. The pounding stops as he gets there.

"Don't open it," I say.

He opens it.

I picture a giant man, maybe a logger with a thick beard and a plaid shirt, because yes, I stereotype. Instead, it's a woman. A rather petite woman with auburn hair.

"You Dylan?" she says.

"What?" Eddie says.

"Dylan. Are. You. Dylan."

Eddie's face turns from confusion to anger. "No."

"You sure?" she says.

"Very."

She walks away. Eddie slams the door just as Portia says, "You think she threw her whole body against the door to knock that hard?"

Auburn hair.

Like the woman in the back of the pickup.

I think about saying something when Eddie yelps after stubbing his toe trying to get back into his bed. No one else says a word about her, or even seems to recognize her. Maybe I'm wrong.

"Did that woman look familiar?" I ask.

"No," Eddie says.

"No," Portia says.

Just me, then. And it definitely wasn't Nikki.

Eddie rustles around in his duffel bag, Portia checks her phone, and eventually the room goes quiet. I'm already drifting off when she pounds on the door again. Three times, hard.

Portia is faster than Eddie this time. She throws off the covers and gets to the door in one big leap. She's already yelling when she opens the door.

"Goddammit, there's no Dylan —"

The auburn-haired woman is not standing in front of our door but two men are, and I recognize them immediately. The Alabama Godfather and the other guy, the younger one. Both of them are smiling.

Then I spot her. The woman stands behind them, the scout for this little operation.

Portia tries to shut the door, but the younger man steps forward, blocking the doorway.

I jump out of the bed and grab Portia, pulling her away from the door and away from these men. They're both inside now. The younger one shuts the door and the Godfather looks at Portia.

"What were you saying, honey?" His voice is as annoying as I remember, Southern ac-

420

cent and all.

"I was saying get the hell out of our room." Portia spits the words out.

The Godfather laughs, his friend joins in. I glance over at the nightstand, wishing I had grabbed my phone.

Behind me, I hear Eddie moving. *Now* he's out of bed.

"Let's all calm down," the young man says. He keeps his eyes on Portia, who looks like she's going to leap forward and attack him. "You, little hellcat, how about you don't move and then we won't have to hurt you?"

I feel Portia's body tense. I grip the back of her shirt with one hand and her arm with the other. She doesn't move, though it feels like she will.

"Good kitty," the young guy says.

"What the hell did you just call me?" She tries to take a step forward. Instead, he does.

"I called you a —"

"Stop."

Eddie. His voice cuts above everyone else's, and I'm just about to laugh when I see the gun. In Eddie's hand.

This takes my breath away.

A memory of the past hits me, as swift and hard as any punch. It stuns me and I do not move.

Portia pushes me out of the way, getting both of us out of the line of fire. Now there's an open space between Eddie and the two men. Neither is holding a gun. If they have one, they were too late on the draw, because it looks like we're in a Western now.

"Eddie," the Godfather says.

"Eddie?" Portia says.

The Godfather looks only at Eddie and the weapon in his hand. "There's no reason to bring a gun into this."

"You just broke into our room," Eddie says. "I'd say this is a perfect time for a gun."

The Godfather shrugs. "We thought we lost you when you decided to go camping. Now that we've found you again, I didn't want to make that mistake again."

Eddie snorts.

"Excuse me," Portia says. "But what the fuck is happening?"

The Godfather raises his eyebrow at Eddie and the young guy laughs. "I guess Eddie didn't tell you he knows us."

I've been listening and watching like this is a movie and not really happening, but somewhere deep in my mind, the wheels have been churning along, processing it all. Portia telling me about Eddie arguing with someone on the phone about money, then watching him yell at someone on the phone at the gas station. The answer comes all at once.

"Eddie owes you money," I say to the Godfather.

"Ding ding ding," the young guy says.

"Thank God one of you was born smart," the Godfather says. "You hit it on the nose. Eddie owes us money."

"And I'll pay it. You know I will," Eddie says.

Portia throws her hands up in the air. "I . . . I don't even know what to say right now. I can't. I just can't." With that, she stomps off into the tiny motel bathroom and slams the door.

That left the Godfather, the young guy, Eddie, and me to figure out what would come next.

Real talk.

Sometimes assumptions are wrong, as mine are in this case, because that young Alabama guy is smarter than I thought. When we were all distracted by Portia's yelling and storming off into the bathroom, he moved his hand real slow. Too slow to notice, until he already has the gun out.

Now we're in a motel room with two guns, and it really does look like a movie. There's Eddie, the preppy guy with the shiny chrome gun. Me, in my shorts and Jacksonville Jaguars shirt that used to be Felix's but is now mine. A young guy with a gun, a beard, and a Lynyrd Skynyrd T-shirt. Finally, the Godfather. He looks about sixty but may be younger, with a grey beard and deep lines around his eyes. The Godfather is the only one smiling.

"Looks like we have ourselves an old-fashioned standoff here," he says.

For the first time since killing Felix, I kind of wish he was around. He was pretty good at diffusing situations because no one thought of him as a threat.

Except me.

The old man looks at me and says, "It seems we're the only ones without a weapon."

I hesitate before answering. "Looks that way."

"I'm Nathan," he says. "And this young man is my nephew, Jonah."

"Who was the woman?" I say. "The one who knocked?"

"Oh, that's my girlfriend. She's waiting outside," Nathan says.

"Well, I'm Beth."

"I'd say it's a pleasure, but I suppose that would sound ridiculous."

I smile a tiny bit and Eddie glares at me. He can't see my heart pounding or feel my hands shaking, but they are. Before I can say another word, the bathroom door opens and Portia reappears. Her hair is pulled back tight, out of her eyes, and she's holding a can of something. It's pointed right at Nathan.

"Mace," she says. "Never leave home without it."

Nathan doesn't look surprised, nor does

he stop smiling. "Perhaps we should take this down a notch. No one needs to die today."

He's the only one making sense right now.

I clear my throat. "So our brother owes you some money," I say.

"That's right," Nathan says. "Roundabout a hundred, give or take."

"A hundred?"

"Thousand."

"Holy hell," Portia says. "Are you an addict? What is it? Oh wait, don't tell me — pain pills, right? You're on oxy."

"I'm not on oxy," Eddie says.

"I don't sell drugs," Nathan says. His voice is hard and a little bit scary. No one says anything, and we fall into a silent void.

"I made a few bets," Eddie finally says. "Football games, some horse races."

Portia sighs loud enough to wake the dead.

"This is a *gambling* debt?" I say. "Our trip has been sabotaged because of a gambling debt?" I shake my head, trying not to kill Eddie before these guys do.

Portia changes targets. She sprays the mace at Eddie.

The guns are down now. Eddie dropped his when the mace hit him, and Jonah lowers his because he's laughing too hard. All of us

426

are sitting except Eddie, who's curled up on the floor, rubbing his eyes while retching.

"Quit crying," Portia says to him. "You'll live."

Eddie chokes out a rather feeble, "Go to hell."

Jonah laughs again but one look from Nathan shuts him up. "This has been very entertaining, but I'd really like to talk about my money. As you have already seen, I'm a very reasonable man. I haven't hurt anyone, though I've had plenty of chances on this little road trip of yours."

I speak before Portia has a chance to. "Did Eddie tell you about this trip? About our grandfather?"

"He did. But considering how many times your brother has lied to me, I had no reason to believe it was true."

Eddie groans. He gets up and stumbles over to the sink. We all watch and then return to our conversation.

"Eddie didn't lie to you about this," I say. "Our grandfather passed away. Once we bring his ashes to where he wants them, we'll get our inheritance." Before he can ask how much, I say, "Eddie will then have the money to pay you back."

"Yes, that's what he said."

"It's the truth," I say. "And maybe this

sounds insensitive, but the three of us aren't here because we wanted to take a family vacation. We're here for the money."

"Three of you," he says. "You had five. You've lost a couple along the way."

"Our spouses weren't exactly enjoying this trip, given how many problems we had with the car."

"Ah yes. The car."

"The flat tire, the stolen starter? I assume that was you?" I say.

Nathan points to his nephew. "Jonah got a little bored on the trip, so we decided to have a little fun with your car. We wanted to make sure Eddie knew we were around. Just in case he forgot about his financial obligations."

"I never forgot," Eddie choked.

Jonah laughs. "I bet you didn't."

Portia rolls her eyes. "Do boys *ever* get sick of playing games?"

No one answers out loud, although Jonah shakes his head no.

"Back to the money," I say. "Eddie can pay you once we finish this trip."

Nathan stares at me for so long it makes me uncomfortable, and I want to fidget but I don't. It feels like he's sizing me up, trying to decide if he can believe me, since he can't believe Eddie.

Good thing I'm not lying.

"And if he still doesn't pay," Nathan says. "Are you going to cover his debt?"

Like I said, he is an intelligent man. I agree because I have to, and because I have no doubt one of us will die today if he decides that's how it has to be. I also agree because we need to get back on the road. This trip has to end.

"Absolutely," I say. "I'll cover it."

It's almost worse when Nathan and Jonah have left. Now we have to deal with the aftermath of what just happened, and everyone is pissed off.

"You just let them *follow* us," Portia says.

Eddie, who has recovered a bit, says, "You sprayed me with *mace.*"

"You better pay Nathan, because I sure as hell won't," I say.

It's not the money I'm angry about, though. I'm angry for the same reason Portia is.

Everyone has secrets, I get that. It doesn't matter to me that Portia steals credit cards or that Eddie has a gambling problem. I have a bigger secret — about Felix — but they don't need to know that because my secret doesn't affect them.

Eddie's secret does, though. It has altered our whole road trip, and he still didn't say anything until his problem knocked on our door. That's the difference between our secrets, and it's a big one.

I'm starting to think there's something about the Beaver Dam Motel. Both times we've been here, trouble literally came knocking. Tonight it was Nathan and Jonah. The first time it was the man from room number 9, the one who answered when I was looking for Nikki.

He was in number 9 alone, as far as we could see, and Eddie quickly said, "Sorry, wrong room."

That was it. We ran off and he shut the door. Less than ten minutes later, that same man came to our room and knocked. Eddie opened it.

He looked like someone out of a seventies movie, right down to his thick moustache, patterned shirt, and blue blazer. He looked around the room, his eyes landing on each one of us. Eddie, Grandpa, Portia, me.

"Can I help you?" Grandpa said, walking toward the man.

"I apologize. Two kids came knocking on my door and I just wanted to make sure everything was okay," he said. "Just seemed kind of strange at a place like this. Kids being alone and all."

Grandpa looked at me. Not Eddie, just

431

me. "We were just playing," I said. "Like doorbell ditch."

Grandpa glared at me but smiled at the man. "I'm on a road trip with my grand-kids. Sometimes they get restless."

The man smiled back. "Oh, I understand. I've got kids of my own back home."

"Thank for checking, though. Appreciate it."

"Not a problem. Glad everything is okay."

The man left, Eddie shut the door, and Grandpa told us we were not allowed out of the room again. That was the end of it, at least until the next morning. The same man was in the parking lot, packing up his maroon Honda.

The man waved to us. "Good morning!" he said.

Grandpa stared at him for a second before responding with a nod. "Morning."

"Hey," the man said, walking closer to us. "You mind if I ask you if you're heading into Nevada? I'm afraid I don't know this area very well and . . . well, I'm not much of a map reader. My wife is always yelling at me about asking for directions."

If we had GPS back then, this conversation wouldn't have taken place. The man would've had to come up with something else.

"Where are you trying to go?" Grandpa said.

"Reno," the man said. "Thought I'd try my luck there before heading to Vegas."

"Sorry. Can't help you with Reno." Grandpa motioned for us to get in the car. He waved goodbye to the man as we drove off.

I didn't think anything of him, or of the conversation, because I was too worried about finding Nikki. When we called our parents the night before, Mom's voice was tight and it was like that every time we called, so everything seemed normal, but it wasn't. We had to tell her Nikki was asleep.

Once we were back on the road, Grandpa started acting nervous, like something was wrong, and he kept looking behind us. A few times he even told Eddie to keep a lookout but didn't say why.

"You're such a traitor," I told him.

He smiled.

Somewhere in the middle of Nevada, otherwise known as Eureka County, Grandpa pulled over for a gas-bathroom-snack break. It would have felt a lot more normal if Nikki had been there. Or if the maroon Honda hadn't pulled in right next to us.

The same man got out of his car and

433

waved to us.

Grandpa didn't wave or smile back. "Little far from Reno, aren't you?"

The man shrugged. "Yeah. I guess I am."

"Since you're following us, maybe you should tell me your name," Grandpa said.

"Calvin. Calvin Bingham."

Grandpa stared at him, like he was trying to figure out if he knew him. "And what is it that you want, Mr. Calvin Bingham?" His voice dripped with something, not so much sarcasm as disdain.

Calvin stopped smiling. When he did, his whole demeanor changed, even the way he stood. He no longer looked like some touristy gambler looking to relive the seventies. He looked mad. "Where's the girl?" he said.

"Excuse me?"

"Did I see another girl with you? Back a ways?"

Grandpa narrowed his eyes. "What are you, some kind of pervert? Into teenage girls?"

"No. Nothing like that."

I watched them stare at each other, and I remember wondering if Calvin was a better person than Grandpa. I hoped he was, and I hoped he would find Nikki.

When we drove away, Calvin followed.

1 Day Left

NEVADA

STATE MOTTO: ALL FOR OUR COUNTRY

In the morning, Eddie's eyes are a little red but otherwise he has recovered from the mace. He and Portia aren't talking to each other, and I don't really want to talk to Eddie, much less be around him, but somehow I end up as the go-between.

It's a weird start to the day.

Within minutes, we cross the border into Nevada. We're in the desert now, and our first stop is at a dusty gas station. The wind is blowing, the grit so thick I can feel it in my teeth. It's already deep into the afternoon. We got a late start because of changing motels and sleeping later to make up for it. The heat isn't as relentless as last time, not this far north.

When I come out of the restroom at the

gas station, Portia is waiting for me. We're around the back of the gas station, where Eddie can't see us.

"That gun," Portia says, getting right to it. "Did you know Eddie brought that?"

"I had no idea."

She purses her lips. I can see a hint of the wrinkles she will have one day.

"What?" I say.

Portia pauses before spitting it out. "I don't like this. Not one bit."

"Me neither. But what can we do? We can't quit."

"We sure as hell can't. I bet that's what he's hoping, though. So he can have all the money to himself."

"Screw that," I say.

"Yeah. Screw that."

We go back to the car together, where Eddie is waiting for us. I sit in the front now and Portia goes to the far back seat, as far away from Eddie as she can get.

Nathan and Jonah may have caused all our car problems, but that doesn't explain everything else. Grandpa's ashes going missing — and reappearing. The van that drove by, playing Nikki's favorite song. The cell phone in the woods. That was all Nikki.

She's the real reason I won't quit this trip. The money is just a bonus.

■ ■ ■ ■

Eureka County. This is where we stopped
for lunch the first time, and it's where we
stop this time. Eddie might have even taken
the same exit, although it's hard to tell
because these roadside towns all look the
same. When he stops the car, Eddie tells us
— tells me — how much time we have to
eat.

Portia looks at me when she speaks. "I'm
not eating fast food again. I'm going to sit
down and eat a salad." She walks across the
parking lot, away from Burger King and
toward her only chance for a decent salad:
Bennigan's.

Eddie checks the time on his phone. I can
almost see him calculating how long this
stop will be.

"I didn't know you carried a gun," I say.

"I don't carry it every day. Just seemed
like a good idea for this trip." He looks up
from his phone. "Probably should've told
you."

"Probably?"

"Well, now you know." He walks away
from me and heads into a fast-food restaurant.

Once we're all back in the car and on the

road, no one speaks. Eddie doesn't mention the extended stop. Portia doesn't say anything about the giant non-diet soda he's drinking. I don't mention anything at all. No one speaks until Eddie takes an exit near Duckwater, Nevada.

"Looks the same," Portia says. "Doesn't it, Beth?"

It does.

"Our last night," Eddie says.

Overkill. We all know what night it is. We check into the same place, the Pine Cone Motel. We even go out to eat at the same place, a steakhouse and saloon called the Rib.

Portia orders a salad, Eddie orders a sirloin steak. I get a sandwich and a molten lava cake for dessert.

When we're done eating, Eddie leans back in his seat and puts his hands on his stomach the way Dad used to. "I think it's safe to say this is the last time we'll have to take this road trip." He side-eyes Portia, who looks at me.

"It better be," she says.

"I think we should get three rooms tonight," I say.

Eddie doesn't look surprised. "I agree."

Portia shrugs, says nothing, and Eddie offers to pay for both dinner and the rooms.

Maybe he feels a little guilty — hopefully a lot guilty — about what happened last night. Or maybe now that the trip is almost over, Eddie is starting to feel like a wealthy man.

I wish I could say the Pine Cone is like every other roadside motel, but it's worse. This isn't a place where people stop to grab a few hours of sleep before getting back on the road. This is a place where they have hourly, nightly, weekly, and monthly rates. Some of the rooms have plastic furniture outside their doors, like their long-term residents have set up outdoor patios. In the parking lot, a man is working on a car set up on blocks. Judging by the dirt on it, the car has been here awhile.

For a minute, I even wonder if they have three available rooms.

Silly me. Of course they do.

Once I'm alone, I start thinking about how this is going to end. About the secrets we buried, literally, and if they'll ever come out. If they can be blamed on anyone. More importantly, if they can be used to blackmail one another into giving up our share of the money. Why send someone to jail when you can get them to hand over their share of the inheritance? Like Eddie's night in jail.

Someone could use that against him, maybe even me. If I have to.

While pondering this, I get a text from Portia.

I can hear Eddie next door. He's screaming at someone.

Krista?

Maybe? Sounds like it's about money.

No surprise there.

She says:

He's an asshole,

Always.

I can also hear the people next door having sex. Eddie is actually preferable.

Nice.

I wonder exactly how much trouble Eddie is in, how many more debts he might have. Or how far he would go to pay them off.

Up until now, I've refused to consider he did anything to Krista. Just because she hasn't texted doesn't mean she's dead.

Although for Felix, it does mean that.

Felix. I'm not sad to think about him. Not exactly. Maybe a little melancholy, the way you think about a friend years after you've drifted apart. That's what it feels like, even though he's only been gone thirty-six hours. Give or take.

This is the first time I've been alone at night since the trip began. I can hear everything: the TV next door, some people standing outside talking in the parking lot, even my own breathing. It's distracting.

I take out Nikki's journal and flip to a page about Dr. Lang.

He was my doctor, actually. I didn't even see him until after Nikki was gone. She never knew him.

I remove the family saga book cover from the journal, running my hand across the front.

Thoughtful Questions for Thoughtful Girls

It's a ridiculous title. Absurd, even.

I thought that when I bought it. It was in a dollar store, sitting on a shelf with a bunch of others. I was there to buy a notebook. Instead, I happened across this journal. The second I looked at the cover, I knew Nikki would hate it. She would hate the questions, she would hate the format, she would make fun of all of it. I also knew exactly how she would answer the questions and it made me laugh.

It was about a month after I saw my mother in prison, a month after she told me to find Nikki. I think that's what made me buy the journal nine years ago, on the anniversary of the day Nikki ran away. It's why I've answered all the questions exactly how Nikki would have answered.

Though I did take a little creative license, like with Dr. Lang. And also about Calvin Bingham following us in his maroon Honda. Maybe Nikki noticed him and maybe she didn't; it's impossible to know, but I like to think she did. I like to think she noticed and she protected me by not saying anything.

Maybe I should have told you about this earlier. I probably should have, but I was afraid you would take it the wrong way. Think of me the wrong way. Like I was one of those loony women pretending to be sane, which I'm not.

You know that because you know me. You get me.

When I read through this journal, I can hear Nikki saying these words. It keeps her here, with me, right where she should be. Always.

After tomorrow, I won't need it anymore.

The Pine Cone Motel used to have a bank of pay phones in the parking lot. I go out to check if they're still here and — surprise surprise — they are, though in varying degrees of usability. Of the four, two have been removed, one has no receiver, and the fourth looks to be the only one in working condition. I wipe the whole thing down with an antibacterial wet wipe before testing it. The habit is left over from Felix, though I might keep it for myself.

We used one of these same phones last time, when we called Mom and Dad. No one knew it was our last call to them. To us, it was just our nightly duty. The thing that kept them from calling the police or the FBI or the National Guard.

Now that Grandpa was back in control, he dialed the number. "Don't mention Calvin Bingham. Don't mention Nikki," he said to me. Only to me. "Or else I'll tie you

444

up the way I tied up your sister."

Calvin, for the record, was staying at our motel. He followed us all the way from that gas station. If I could have found a way to get to him, I would've told him everything. Maybe even about Nikki being pregnant.

I just couldn't get away.

"Yes, yes, everything's fine," Grandpa said into the phone. He said that every night. "The kids are really enjoying this. They're seeing things they didn't know existed . . . Yes . . . Yes, yes, they're eating well." He looked at Eddie and winked. By the time Grandpa handed him the phone, Eddie was smiling and had his boyish chest all puffed out.

"Hi," he said. "Yes, everything's fine. We're fine. We'll be back soon . . . real soon . . . Of course we're having fun, why wouldn't we be? . . . Yes, we're eating pretty good . . . I promise . . . Okay, here she is."

Eddie glared at me as he handed over the phone. A threat, I knew. He had been threatening me with looks and words ever since Calvin started following us.

"Hi," I said.

"Baby," Mom said. "How are you?"

"I'm fine, I keep telling you that."

"You know I have to ask that, I'm your mother," she said, her voice hard. "I just miss you so much."

"I miss you. Dad, you there?"

"I'm here."

That's how our calls went every night, both of them on the phone, each on different extensions. Sometimes both talked at once.

"Are you getting enough sleep?" Dad said.

"Plenty. We sleep in the car all the time."

"And your sister? How's Nikki doing all cooped up like that?"

"Nikki?" I said, looking at Grandpa. He glared at me. "Oh, you know how she is. Half the time she can't stop moving and the other half she's asleep. A bomb wouldn't wake her up."

"Is she awake now?" Mom said.

"No, she's been asleep since we ate dinner."

"Oh."

"I'm sure she'll be awake tomorrow when we call," I said.

"I hope so."

I wanted to blurt out everything, to tell them what had happened. To tell them about Nikki being pregnant. And I almost did, except Grandpa grabbed the phone out of my hand. "You know how teenagers are — they sleep like the dead. Portia really wants to talk to you, though." He held the

446

phone against Portia's ear, always ready to grab it away.

"Mommy!" Portia yelled. She did this every night.

Grandpa continued to glare at me, and it was a lot scarier now that Nikki was gone. More like a monster than a man.

My fault, my fault, my fault.

Every time I found myself getting mad at Nikki for running away, I remembered it was me who helped her. I also couldn't blame her. If someone were keeping me tied up, I'd run, too.

"Everything's fun," Portia said into the phone, just as she was coached to do. Grandpa took the phone as she yelled, "Bye-bye!"

"See, everything's fine," Grandpa said. "The kids are safe and sound and having the time of their lives . . . Well, of course not. I wouldn't do anything to hurt these kids. You know how much I love my grandchildren . . . Have some faith in your old dad, for goodness' sake . . . All right, yes, I will call tomorrow. As always."

He hung up the phone gently, like he was handling a kitten. He gave me one final glare before walking back across the parking lot to our room.

"Go," Eddie said, pushing me in the same

direction. He had become Grandpa's little guard.

No one is pushing me around now, though.

I'm out here by myself, standing by this old bank of phones, and they're covered in so much graffiti I can't see the original paint. The phones make me want to call someone, but I have no idea who. There's no one left.

Last Day

Everyone is alive in the morning, including me, and we still have Grandpa's ashes. An auspicious start to our final day. On the downside, Portia overslept and looks hung over.

Breakfast is at Starbucks, which really does exist everywhere. As we sit down at a table in the corner, Eddie brings up today like he's not afraid to jinx it.

"You think Grandpa planned something for the end?" he says.

Portia adds a single raw sugar to her almond milk latte and turns up her nose at Eddie's artificial sweetener, which is funny, given how much soda she drank on this trip. Portia doesn't look at Eddie when she speaks, even though she's sort of answering his question. "There better be a good reason we had to do this all over again. Because all other things aside, who wants their ashes

449

scattered in the desert? And why couldn't we just fly them out here?"

I take a bite of my chocolate croissant, because who starts a day like this with bran? "Nikki," I say.

"Nikki?" Eddie says. "You really think Nikki is waiting for us in the desert?"

Absolutely.

"Nikki would never be that subtle," Portia says. "It's not her."

"I agree," Eddie says.

I say nothing.

"Maybe the lawyer will be there with stacks of cash," Portia says.

I try to imagine this. I've never met Morton J. Barrie, but I see him as a short man with thick glasses and a bow tie. A younger, dumber-looking version of the Monopoly man. He's surrounded by stacks of cash, bound together and all shiny and new, looking so clean against all the sand and dirt.

Behind the lawyer is a large hill of dirt no one would look at twice. We made sure of that before we left.

"Final guesses?" Eddie says. He crumples up the wax paper from his breakfast sandwich and tosses it into the garbage. "Before we head out, make your prediction."

"We end up rich and happy," Portia says.

450

"Or at least rich."

I don't disagree. They'll see soon enough. "Sounds good," I say.

"All right, then. Let's go get some money," Eddie says.

Portia and I walk out behind him. She rolls her eyes at his back.

Three hours. That's the approximate length of this final drive. Who knows how long it would have been if Calvin hadn't followed us. He didn't even try to hide it.

Eddie sat in the middle seat with me, keeping watch to make sure I didn't do anything wrong. He had become my permanent guard, and an annoying one. No sister wanted that much attention from her older brother.

Portia was in the way back, either sleeping or playing by herself, and that left Grandpa alone in the front with an empty passenger's seat. He kept talking, though it was mostly mumbling and mostly to himself.

"Is that asshole still following us? He is, isn't he? . . . Yes, yes . . . There he is . . . I'm going to slow down and see what he does, then I'll know for sure . . . I'll just ease off the gas and bring my speed down by . . . Oh look, there it is. He's slowing down, too."

Every once in a while, Grandpa would

451

turn and speak to us. "You see that? He's still following us."

He always glared at me as he said it, like it was my fault, but I didn't even know who the man was. Grandpa just blamed me because I had sided with Nikki, because everything was about Nikki. As it should be.

Grandpa looked back to the road and started mumbling to himself again. This went on for an hour, then another, and we were deep into hour three when Grandpa saw the sign.

ALAMO

No, not *the* Alamo in Texas. The tiny town of Alamo in Nevada, right off I-93 South.

"We'll end all this right here," Grandpa said, taking the exit. I didn't appreciate his flair for the dramatic until I became an adult.

"End what?" I said. He didn't hear me, he just kept talking.

"This asshole," he said. "The private investigator."

"What?" I said. Louder this time.

"*Private investigator.* Haven't you been paying attention?"

I shook my head, partly out of confusion,

452

and partly to answer him. No, I obviously hadn't been paying attention because no one told me Calvin was a private investigator.

"Why do you think he's following us?" Grandpa said. "And looking for Nikki?"

"Yeah, why?" Eddie said.

I was still shaking my head, trying to put the pieces together. "But who hired —"

"Your parents, obviously," Grandpa said. "I bet he's been following us the whole damn trip."

Relief swept over me like it had been dumped on my head. I should've known our parents were looking out for us. They had been the whole time.

And I bet Eddie was just as relieved as I was. He looked as surprised as I was to learn Calvin was a private investigator, but that didn't stop him from throwing a jab at me.

"Duh," he said. "I can't believe you didn't see him."

Grandpa didn't stop for another thirty minutes or so — long enough for us to get far away from any interstate, business, or even another human being. Calvin was right behind us, not even trying to hide that he was following us. By the time Grandpa pulled over, it felt like we were at the end of the earth.

I don't remember who got out first; I just remember Grandpa and Calvin facing each other between the cars. Eddie and Portia and I were pressed up against the back window. The van had those windows with a latch and they pushed out a few inches. Eddie opened one a little so we could hear.

"Are you just going to keep following us?" Grandpa said.

Calvin smiled. His teeth looked so white beneath that big moustache. "No. I'm going to call the police if you don't tell me where Nikki is."

Grandpa held out his hands, palms facing forward. "I have no idea what you're talking about. I'm just on a road trip with my grandkids."

"Sure you are."

"It's the truth," Grandpa said.

"That's not what their mother said."

Mom. I wanted to talk to her so badly right then, and I wouldn't have lied, either. I leaned forward to look in the driver's seat, trying to find Grandpa's cell phone.

"No," Eddie said, pulling me back to my seat. "Don't even think about it."

Outside, the conversation continued. Grandpa laughed.

"Okay, okay," he said. "You got me. Nikki

ran off to meet up with a friend of hers. That's the truth. She runs off a lot and you're welcome to ask my daughter about it. Ask her how many times Nikki has run away."

Calvin says nothing.

"We're going to pick Nikki up right now. That's why we're in this godforsaken place." Grandpa looked around, his nose scrunched up like it smelled bad. "Go ahead and follow us. You'll see Nikki is just fine."

I should've jumped out of the car right that second and told Calvin that Grandpa was lying. Nikki hadn't run off to meet a friend; she had run off because Grandpa and Eddie had tied her up.

I was about to do it — I swear I was — when Portia yelled, "Nikki! We're going to see Nikki!"

Grandpa heard her and smiled. "That's right. We're going to see Nikki."

Calvin got back into his car, ready to follow us.

The road to Alamo looks the same, which means there's still a whole lot of nothing. Side note about driving across the country: It's impossible to understand how big it is unless you see how much nothing there is.

Halfway into the drive, Portia texts me from the front seat.

I'm a little nervous.

Is she really nervous or is she just pretending? At this point, anything is possible. The endgame is when all the secrets come out.

Not a question, I say:

You think something bad is going to happen.

Bad? Given. Tragic and horrifying is what I'm afraid of.

I say:

Like last time.

Yeah, I'd say that was pretty tragic and horrifying.

"Hey," Eddie says. "Are you guys seriously texting each other while I'm sitting right here?"

"Yes," I say.

"I was talking about last time we were out here," Portia says.

Eddie's jaw tightens. "What about it?"

"Ummm . . ." Portia says. "It sucked? A lot?"

Yes. Yes, it did.

"Oh," Eddie says. "That."

It's hard to know how much Portia understood during the trip, or if she knew why she was the center of everything in the desert. Later, she did get it.

When we finally got back home, Grandpa went into seclusion, and he stayed that way for the rest of his life. Our parents went into overdrive looking for Nikki, and we all told them the truth. Mostly. Nikki ran away in the middle of the night and no one had seen her since.

True.

Next came the lie.

We said we had never seen Calvin Bingham, never spoke to him. Didn't even know there was a private investigator following us. Grandpa said it, Eddie said it, and so did I. Even Portia lied. Grandpa said we had to or we'd all go to jail. Forever and ever, he said.

For all our parents knew, Calvin had walked off the job and gone to Vegas instead. The last report they received had come from somewhere in the desert, when he was still following us in the van. The only person who asked questions about him was his secretary.

She could still be looking for him, even now, twenty years later. Oh, along with his ex-wife. Calvin Bingham had an ex-wife who called the police about six months after the trip ended. She hadn't received her alimony.

None of that mattered to our parents. They didn't care about Calvin Bingham. The only one they cared about was Nikki, and they looked for her until my father suggested they stop. You already know how much my mother hated that idea.

For years, the family closed in on itself, grieving over the still-missing Nikki — not to mention dealing with everything our parents didn't know. No one told our parents how Nikki took control, how she gave Grandpa the pills, or how she black-mailed him with that camera. Not even Eddie.

We also didn't tell them that Nikki had been tied up right before she ran.

And you know I didn't say a word about her condition.

I could tell you how upset my parents were, how many times they called the police, how their lives revolved around finding her, how often I heard my mom screaming and yelling at someone for nothing. That period of time was horrible, and I don't have a single good memory of it. Not one.

You get the idea.

But no one can stay like that forever. Either you die or you move on, because life does. Eddie finished high school and went off to Duke, while I went to the University of Miami to be close to Cooper. Portia was still at home and starting her teenage years. When I came home for the summer after my freshman year, she looked like a different person.

Portia had gone full goth, from the steel-toed boots to the black lipstick. The first time I saw her, I didn't know what to say. She looked awful.

"That's dramatic," I finally said.

She walked away.

Her music was horrible: rock bands with drawn-out voices and guitar riffs, the kind made for wallowing teenagers. She carried a notebook everywhere. It had a black cover and she drew on the cover with a silver pen. Anarchy signs, skulls and crossbones, that sort of thing.

Still, I didn't worry too much about her. Everyone has phases. I was in my own first-year-of-college phase and didn't even recognize it. I thought I was the smartest person on the planet and everyone was too stupid to see it.

That summer, when I was living back home, I heard Portia on the phone with one of her friends. We still talked on landlines back then. Texting was starting to become popular, but Portia didn't have her own cell phone. Not in 2006.

She was in her room and I was in the bathroom. We shared one; it was between our bedrooms and not accessible from the hall.

"I swear," Portia said. "If my grandpa hadn't done that, my life would be totally different. Totally."

Pause.

"That's what I'm saying. It's, like, a huge thing, right? It changes *everything*."

Yes, I stayed to listen. You bet I did, because I thought she was talking about the road trip and Grandpa tying Nikki up. A few sentences later, I realized she wasn't.

"You understand," she said. "Because you've been molested, too."

Too.

Portia had not been molested by her grandfather. She *knew* that. She understood what it meant to be touched in her private places, and no, Grandpa had never done that.

I walked into her room.

She was sprawled out on her black bedspread, phone to her ear, staring at the ceiling. It was plastered with rock band posters.

"Um, hello?" she said.

"Hang up," I said.

"Excuse —"

"Hang. Up."

She did. Portia sat up, crossed her arms over her chest, and stared at me in a very pissed-off way.

"Why are you telling people Grandpa molested you?" I said.

"Were you *listening*?" She got off the bed, moving around quick, all full of fire and brimstone. "Oh my God, I can't get a *sec-*

ond to myself in this house. *Not one second.*"

"Stop." I grabbed her by the wrist, making her face me. "Why are you saying he did it?"

Portia said something that, to this day, makes me think she understood a lot more on the road trip than I thought she did.

She smiled, her black lips parting to reveal her still-young, still-white teeth. "Because I can."

It's not difficult to get to our middle-of-the-desert location. If you remember enough from before, that is. I do. I took note of everything because I was looking so hard for Nikki.

Grandpa drove straight, just straight, until the road forked. He sat for a second, no blinker on, staring at Calvin in his rearview mirror. The investigator also didn't have a blinker on. Grandpa went left and Calvin followed.

Grandpa drove until he hit the dirt, which wasn't far. Instead of turning left and staying on the road, he kept going straight. We were surrounded by huge rock mountains, each one crazier-looking than the last. Just like in *Thelma & Louise.* Years passed before I learned those desert scenes had been filmed in Utah, not Nevada.

Grandpa continued winding his way through the dirt, around the hills, and after maneuvering around one particularly large hill, he pulled over and stopped. I know right where that spot is.

You think that sounds convenient, and I have to admit, if I were hearing this story, I would think the same thing. But it's not convenient. Not if you could see the rocks.

They're all different in the desert. From a distance maybe they aren't, but up close they are. Grandpa pulled over next to one big round rock and two taller ones behind it. As soon as I saw them, I knew what they looked like.

Portia was sitting behind me, and I turned to her and pointed.

"Look. It's a bunny," I said.

That's what the rocks looked like: two rabbit ears and a round nose. Portia started wiggling around, all excited. "Nikki's here? Nikki's by the bunny?"

I didn't answer.

The rocks are what made it so easy to find the same place. One turn left, keep straight until the road turns to dirt, go around the hills, and after getting around the largest one, stop at the bunny. It's not like this area had changed a lot.

It still feels like the end of the civilized world.

■ ■ ■ ■

Eddie takes the Alamo exit, pausing to pull into a gas station convenience store.

"Last stop." Before what, he doesn't say. He's just taken it upon himself to narrate the end of our trip.

Portia heads to the restroom while Eddie and I go into the store. I get a large coffee with too much sugar. Might as well. My guess is this day will end very quickly or it won't end for a long, long time.

Eddie analyzes the ingredients in a protein shake. Portia comes inside and grabs a Smartwater — no alcohol today, I guess. We all need to fuel up somehow.

Once we get back on the road, I give orders to Eddie. It's a nice change.

"Straight down that road," I say. "Left at the fork, then keep straight off the road and go around the largest rocks. Stop at the rabbit-shaped ones."

"I got it," Eddie says.

It takes longer than I thought it did, maybe because I know what's coming. Last time, every turn was a new sight, but now, as soon as the bunny ears come into view, my stomach jumps.

"There," I say.

"I *got it,*" Eddie says.

"You remember those?" I say to Portia.

She gives me a dirty look, albeit a mild one. "I wasn't a *baby* the first time."

No, she wasn't that. She was old enough to drug our cocoa, even if she didn't realize it.

When Eddie pulls over, it's almost a letdown. Nothing is here — no marching band, no welcome banner, nothing to mark our arrival. And no one is waiting for us, least of all Nikki. Just the big rocks and a sandy hill protected from the wind by the bunny ears.

A grave.

Calvin Bingham has still never been found.

"Looks the same," Eddie says.

Exactly the same.

I can still see it all, like it happened just a few minutes ago. Calvin and Grandpa, facing off between the cars, and we had ringside seats. We were in the van, looking out the back windows. Eddie had opened one of the side windows, the kind that used to have a little crank on it, so we could hear everything.

"So where is she?" Calvin said.

"Oh, Nikki will be here," Grandpa said.

466

"Anytime now."

"Really? Somehow she let you know she would be right here, in the middle of the desert?"

"Yep. She sure did." Grandpa sounded like he was about to laugh.

Portia leaned over and whispered in my ear. "Where is she?"

"She's not coming, stupid," Eddie said.

"Yes she is!"

Grandpa and Calvin heard that. They both looked up at us. They both saw Portia's little face contort into that expression kids make when they're about to cry.

"Where's Nikki?" she yelled.

"That's what I want to know," Calvin said, looking back at Grandpa. "You don't know where she is, do you?"

"Go to hell. I know where my grand-daughter is."

Calvin rubbed his forehead like he was tired. And done. "Yeah, this has been great, and thanks for the tour of the desert." He moved toward his car, then turned back one last time. "Your daughter just wanted to make sure her kids were okay. She didn't want to call the police on you. You know, she even told me about your wife dying and —"

467

"You shut up about my wife," Grandpa said.

"Look, I'm not even supposed to be talking to you. My orders were to follow and make sure the kids were okay, and you didn't get into any trouble," Calvin said. "I don't care what happens to you, and I've got no problem calling the police. You can tell them all about Nikki." He threw his hands up and turned away, back to his car.

"Stop."

It wasn't Grandpa.

I was so busy with Portia, I never heard Eddie get out of the van. Now I saw him, down below us, and he had Grandpa's gun.

Calvin saw the gun and froze. "Now, wait a minute —"

"Eddie!" Grandpa said. "Give that to me."

Eddie did not move, other than to glance at Grandpa. "He's going to call the police."

"No, I'm not," Calvin said. "I'm just going to leave. I'm quitting this job."

"You *said* you were going to call the police," Eddie said.

"No, I meant I'd call your mother and she would call the police. Who knows, maybe she won't?"

Eddie did not waver. "That's not what you said."

"Eddie," Grandpa said, taking a step

468

closer to him. Closer to that gun. "This guy is just a hired investigator. He doesn't care who Nikki is, let alone where she ran off to. He's doesn't care if the police are called or not."

I didn't move. Couldn't move, couldn't blink, couldn't turn away from the scene in front of me, which felt more like a movie than real life.

Except the only one with a gun was my brother.

"Lie," he said to Calvin, who now had both his hands up and they were both empty. "You're going to call them. You're going to turn Grandpa in."

"No, I won't."

"They're going to lock him up and look for Nikki."

"Hey," Calvin said. "I promise you I won't —"

Eddie pulled the trigger.

Not once. Three times.

This, apparently, is what we do in our family when we feel threatened. We get violent. Or at least some of us do.

We're back in the same place, and we're all staring at that sandy hill. I try to imagine what's left of that Honda. It was just a hunk of metal when we left it.

But I can still feel the heat of the fire.

Eddie gets out of the car first, claps his hands together. "This is it."

We all stand in the clearing, looking up at the bunny ears. This should be our selfie, right here, out in the middle of nowhere. Eddie in his polo shirt and khakis, his Top-Siders so worn out they're embarrassing. Portia in her short shorts and child-sized shirt, her black hair knotted up into a mess. Me in my khakis, tank top, and baseball cap. Felix's baseball cap.

"Seems smaller now," Portia says.

Indeed.

Eddie walks away from us and toward the rabbit rocks. He gets right up close to them and stands in the open space between the ears. He kneels down.

"What are you . . ." I stop because I can see what he's doing.

Portia turns around and watches him for a second. "Why are you digging?" she says.

He doesn't answer, doesn't look up. I have no idea what he's looking for or why he is digging. He's using his hands, pulling up the dirt like someone's buried alive.

The only thing I remember burying is Calvin's car, with Calvin's body burned up inside of it. We all pitched in, heaving dirt on it to stop the fire and the smoke. That's what Grandpa was worried about — the smoke. He didn't want anyone to find us before we were done.

Eddie keeps digging, using his hands the way a child does at the beach. Finally, he hits something. There's a crinkling sound as he brushes away the dirt and lifts it out.

A plastic bag. The kind you used to get at every grocery store and drugstore before they started getting banned.

"What the hell," Portia says.

Eddie continues to ignore us as he rips open the bag and pulls out what's inside.

It's my old T-shirt, the one I used to wrap up those ashtrays from the motel rooms. The one Nikki took when she ran. Only now the shirt has blood on it. Old, dried blood, a deep brownish-red color.

Eddie unwraps the shirt and I hear the clink of the glass as the ashtrays shift. He pulls out one last thing.

The other disposable camera.

"Are you kidding me?" Portia says.

Eddie looks like a kid on Christmas morning. "I wasn't sure these would burn in the fire," he says, pointing to the ashtrays. "So I buried it all instead."

"Whose blood is that?" I say.

He ignores me and looks only at the camera, inspecting it from every angle. For twenty years, it's been protected from the sun, water, and dirt. It looks brand new.

"You know there's no pictures on it, right?" Portia says. "Nikki never took any pictures of me."

"That doesn't mean there aren't *any* pictures on it," Eddie says.

My eyes keep shifting back and forth, from the camera to the bloody shirt.

Nikki took a few pictures with that camera, but not of Portia. They were nothing important, just trees and street signs and our weird motels. Just so the camera had been used, so Grandpa believed the story. They were nothing worth burying, let alone preserving.

"I've been waiting twenty years to get

ahold of this," Eddie says. "I swear, I've had nightmares about someone finding this."

"If that's true," Portia says, "why didn't you just come out here and get it?"

He doesn't answer. A list of options runs through my mind, like I'm playing a mental game of Risk and I have a secret mission to choose the likeliest course of action. I think about the drive and all the directions I gave him. All the times he said *I got it.*

"You didn't know how to get here," I say. "You just pretended."

Eddie smiles. "Thanks for leading the way. Grandpa and I both came out here so many times, but we just couldn't find it."

"Grandpa?" I say.

"Hell yes, Grandpa. You think Grandpa planned this second trip all on his own?" He scoffs. "Who do you think planted the idea in his head?"

"Jesus Christ," Portia says, spitting the words out.

Of course Eddie was in on it. He always knew this trip was coming. How did I not see that? How did I not figure it out? That's what happens when you aren't the sharpest knife in the drawer.

"It was the animal that tripped me up," Eddie says, pointing up to the bunny-ear rocks. He laughs. "We kept looking for coyote ears. Passed right by these big rabbit ears at least a dozen times."

That's how natural these dirt hills look against all these rocks. No wonder the burnt-up car is still here, still untouched.

Eddie has been on a secret mission all this time; I just missed it entirely. We're all haunted by something, and for Eddie it was old ashtrays, a camera, and that bloody shirt.

"Whose blood is that?" I say again.

He stares at that T-shirt, shaking his head at it. "Here's your Nikki," he says, nodding to it. "She's been out here this whole time." He wraps everything back up, walks to the car, and puts it in the back. The box of ashes is waiting.

I turn to Portia, who looks as confused as I do. "I have no idea what's happening here," she says.

"I found her," Eddie says. "She ran into the woods and I found her."

He turns around, but he isn't holding the wooden box. Eddie is holding the gun.

In a split second, I decide my best strategy is to ignore the gun and pretend he doesn't have it. Or maybe I'm too preoccupied by what he just said.

"What do you mean, you found her?" I say.

He leans against the bumper of the car like he's settling in to tell a long story. "When I ran into the woods that morning, I found her. Well, actually she found me."

"What the —"

"She attacked me," he says. "Nikki came out from behind a tree and swung those fucking ashtrays at me."

I shook my head. This wasn't right, couldn't be right. "You said you didn't find her."

Eddie sighs.

"Is everything you say a lie?" Portia asks.

"Eddie," I say. "What did you do?"

"That's the thing. Sometimes you don't

have a choice," he says. "When someone tries to hit you, you have to hit back. It was a reflex . . . I mean, it's not like I had an option."

I take a deep breath. "So you hit her."

He nods.

"And then what?"

"She fell on the ground. Hard." Eddie looks away from me, toward the rocks. I want to crawl into his mind and see what he sees. "But she wasn't unconscious. She kicked me."

I wait.

"So I picked up those ashtrays and I hit her." His eyes refocus, they turn back to me. "On the head."

Nikki on the ground, hurt, fighting, kicking. And my brother hits her on the head with glass ashtrays.

Imagining this makes me want to vomit.

"She's dead," he says.

"No." I shake my head. "No, no, no."

Eddie straightens up, squares his shoulders. "Don't worry, it was quick."

The world spins. It already does, I know, and now I feel it. Just like I can feel those ashtrays hitting my head.

"Grandpa knew she was dead?" Portia says.

"Of course he did! Why do you think he

refused to call the police?" Eddie stops and shakes his head. "I know you guys think he was a monster, but he wasn't. He was protecting us. Nikki was going to ruin everything. We were all going to get blamed for her death, and for what she did to Grandpa. For drugging him, stealing his money . . . all of it."

I feel tears on my face. "No."

"That's why you killed Calvin," Portia says. "You didn't want him calling the police, because you killed Nikki."

"Because she was attacking me. Don't forget that part."

"So that's why we're here? So you could get this stuff?" Portia says.

Eddie nods. "It was a loose end. I had to get it. If not for this, Grandpa would've just given me all the money and we wouldn't be here."

No road trip. No answers. And I never would've known what happened to Nikki.

"What did you do with her?" I say. "Did you bury her?"

"I dragged her into the lake," Eddie says.

Now Felix is with her. Not that anything would be left of her body after twenty years.

I look at him, my mind on that camera. "Eddie," I say.

"I had to do it," he says.

"Eddie."

"What?"

"Did you take a picture of our dead sister?"

He doesn't answer. Doesn't have to.

"You're a monster," I say.

"Stop it," Eddie says. "She was a bitch. That's all Nikki ever was. A selfish, lying, scheming bitch."

He's wrong. We're the selfish, lying, scheming bitches. Not Nikki.

Once again, I consider revealing Nikki's secret and telling Eddie that he didn't just kill Nikki; he killed her baby. But I can't, I just can't. And there's no point in revealing Nikki's secret now. Eddie wouldn't even care.

I take a step closer to him. "If she was a selfish, lying, scheming bitch, what does that make you?"

"Alive."

Asshole.

"So is this your plan, psycho?" Portia says. "Come out here, gather up the evidence of your murders, and then kill us?"

It sounds ridiculous, but for a moment, I'm surprised to find that I don't care. My mission was Nikki, first, last, always.

The money distracted me, yes, because it's a hell of a lot of money. After I heard about the job cuts at work, it became even more important. My husband distracted me, yes, but at least I learned it was never going to work out. However, since the beginning, before the trip even started, it was about Nikki.

It's been a month since Grandpa died and was cremated. That's how long it took for all of us to rearrange our schedules and get time off work for a two-week road trip. During that time, I prepared. I bought one of those poster maps of the United States, and I hung it up in the closet of our extra bedroom. The one Felix never used. I plotted out the whole trip, double-checking to make sure I hadn't missed anything, hadn't forgotten anywhere we stopped.

I called each one of the museums and attractions we had visited, making sure they were still in business and would be available during the trip. I even called some of the motels I remembered, just in case we ended up staying in the same places.

Something in me knew this would be the end of my search. I'd find Nikki, I knew I would. I could feel it like it was a living thing inside me. Maybe that's what it's like to be pregnant. I liked thinking of it that way. It was one more connection to her.

Have you ever wanted something so much,

you go ahead and pretend you have it?

Like maybe your house isn't perfect, but you tell people it's your dream home so many times you start to believe it. Or perhaps you hate your job but you won't give it up, because maybe the next one will be worse, so you convince yourself it's not that bad. It is. You're just pretending it's not.

This is how I've convinced myself Nikki is still alive, because I can't face a world without her. And I can't face what I did. Moving to Florida, following Cooper, writing the journals — it was all because I wanted to find her. Had to find her.

My fault, my fault, my fault.

One time, I thought about telling Felix everything. It was when we were engaged. He knew nothing about Nikki and he thought my parents had died in a car crash. It sounded so commonplace that he didn't question it.

We had just been to the movies, one of those Oscar-nominated dramas that's all about family secrets and regrets and no one ends up happy. I guess that's what made me want to say something — the fear of ending up like that. During the drive home, I thought I should tell him everything. Well, most of it. Not the part where Eddie shot the private investigator.

As fate would have it, Felix's favorite song came on the radio. It probably won't surprise you to know Felix was a big fan of eighties music. There he was, belting out Def Leppard's "Pour Some Sugar on Me," and I knew the moment was gone.

I never tried again, but that doesn't mean the guilt has gone away. If anything, it has grown over the years — multiplied by a billion after I saw my mother. It was just like one of those melodramatic movies.

But, finally, the second road trip would let me fix what I had done.

That's what I believed, as much as I believed Nikki was out there. Watching. Waiting. Knowing she would one day get her chance at revenge, maybe against me, but definitely against Eddie. It's why I've never stopped looking, why I moved to Florida, why I wrote that diary in her words.

It's why I've done everything.

I fall to my knees on the ground, in front of Eddie.

A lie, all of it. The worst kind of lie, because I made up an entire story about Nikki being out there, still alive, and then I convinced myself it was true.

I look up at Eddie, that shiny gun in his hand, and I know I'm ready. It doesn't matter if I die now. I don't even care now that I know Nikki is dead.

Except for one thing. Eddie would win.

"You can't shoot us," I say, standing back up. "You'd never get away with it."

He smiles a little.

"We're the only ones here," I say. "You think the police won't figure out who did it? Because I don't think self-defense is going to work against two unarmed women."

Eddie continues to smile.

Portia's voice rings out over the desert. "Button, button, who's got the button?" She singsongs the word to that old children's game.

I turn to see her holding that gold button, flicking it up in the air, and catching it like it's a coin.

That button came from Calvin Bingham's

jacket. She kept it all these years.

"This isn't over yet," she says. "We're just getting started."

The shift in focus is tangible, like the wind has changed directions. All the energy directed toward Eddie now flows to Portia. So does Eddie's gun. He now points it at her instead of at me. "Where did you get that?" he says.

Portia stops tossing the button long enough to look insulted. "I've always had it. Of course, I know it doesn't mean anything now. It's not like it could be used as evidence or anything."

"Then why keep it?" he says.

"So I never forget what an asshole you are."

"Me? What about Nikki?"

"You're asking the wrong question," she says. "The right question is, how long have I been waiting for this moment?"

Her eyes twinkle and it isn't from the sun.

"No guesses?" she says. "Well, then I'll just tell you. I've been waiting for this moment since I was six years old."

Eddie backs up a step and I do the same, which is saying something considering her only weapon is a button.

"You assholes," she says. "Both of you. All

you did was use me. *I* was abused by Grandpa, but it was a lie. *I* was the ally you needed depending on who was in charge, and *I* was the one who put pills in the cocoa but didn't even know it —"

"That was Nikki," Eddie says.

"Shut. Up." Portia takes a deep breath. "And you're going to want to hold up on shooting anyone until you hear what I have to say."

Eddie hesitates, thinking about it, trying to figure out what she's talking about. "About what?" he finally says.

Portia smiles. Grins, really. "Your financial situation."

Eddie shifts his weight a little, says nothing.

"You see," Portia says. "Given my current line of work, I've learned how to do a few things. Other than take my clothes off, of course."

"Take your clothes off? You're a waitress," Eddie says.

"She's a stripper," I say. "Keep up."

"That's right, I am," she says. "And one of the many things I've learned in my profession is that people aren't very good at keeping their secrets." She reaches into her pocket and pulls out her phone. "Most of them are kept right in here."

484

"Are you drunk?" Eddie says.

"Not today, no. But even if I was, I could still see your phone code and get into it whenever I want."

The phone.

I remember my own turned-over phone back in one of our first motels. I remember all the nights she stayed with us, or with Eddie, with plenty of time to search our phones while we slept. I remember all the things she stole on the first trip, without my noticing, even when I was sitting in the same van.

Always the sneaky one.

"What I know about you," she says to Eddie, "is that your financial situation is fucked. Your bank account is basically empty, your house is mortgaged well beyond what it's worth, and" — she pauses here to tilt her head and smile; I imagine that works well at her job — "you've got gambling problems that are a lot bigger than that man in the black truck."

"You bitch," Eddie says.

Portia smiles. "But what I found most interesting are those offshore accounts. Avoiding taxes, are we?"

"Oh please. Everybody does it," Eddie says.

"That doesn't make it legal. And it doesn't

mean you can't get arrested for it," she says, taking a step closer to Eddie. "Who do you think they're going to suspect when we turn up dead? Some random stranger in the desert, or the guy that inherits all the money and has a gambling problem?"

Eddie doesn't answer.

"So here's the deal," she says. "I've set up a transfer from your main account. Once we get back to civilization and get the cash part of our inheritance, you're going to give all your money to me."

"Like hell I am," he says.

"Like hell you are. If you cancel or otherwise screw with that transfer, an e-mail will automatically go to the IRS, detailing all your bullshit," she says with a shrug. "Because you can't have the money if you're in jail."

Eddie clenches his jaw. "That fucking rule. I told Grandpa not to put that rule about jail in there. He was still so pissed at Mom."

"Sucks for you," Portia says.

Honestly, I bet Grandpa would be proud if he could see us now. His grandchildren have found themselves wrapped inside a devil's knot. No way out unless someone dies or gets arrested.

"Well done," I say to Portia.

"Well done?" Eddie yells at me. "Well

fucking done? Jesus Christ, you really are pathetic."

That's me, the pathetic one. The sad runner-up to Nikki. Finally, I've come to accept my role. "Did you set me up, too?" I ask Portia.

"You bet I did. All of your money is coming my way, too. Your phone was even easier to get into." Portia gives me a look that makes me feel worse than I did a second ago. "Otherwise you're headed straight to a psych ward. Really, Beth. That journal? You need help. You really do."

She's right about that. She's right about everything. We did use her. Portia was just a pawn in the game back then, too young to play or fight back.

"Screw this," Eddie says. He takes a step toward Portia, I can practically see the anger swelling up inside of him. He looks just like he did back at the UFO Watchtower, when he got into a fight with Clemson. Anger always gets the best of him.

"What if I just shoot you?" he says. "I might end up in jail, but you'll be dead."

Portia walks toward him and stops just a couple feet away. "Go ahead. Kill me."

His arm tightens and his face is red with anger, because Eddie knows he has lost this game. You always know when you've lost, even if the game isn't over yet. Risk taught us that, and we still played it out to the bitter end. You have to.

Eddie points at Portia's chest. A heart shot, then. Not the head.

When I see his finger twitch, I close my eyes.

Click.

Click.

Click.

I open my eyes to see Eddie looking at the gun. "What the hell?" he says.

Portia laughs. "You idiot," she says. "I didn't just steal your phone code. I stole all your bullets."

Eddie lowers the gun and takes a deep breath, and his face slowly returns to its normal color.

Now *he* starts to laugh.

Not a small laugh, but a huge belly laugh that makes him double over. Portia and I exchange a look, like we're both thinking the same thing. Eddie has finally lost whatever is left of his mind.

When he finally stops and wipes the tears from his eyes, he says, "Doesn't matter."

"It doesn't matter?" I repeat.

"Nope. Not one bit."

We're interrupted by the music.

"I Think I'm Paranoid" blasts through the

air. Everyone freezes for a second, and we all turn, looking for the source. The music grows louder.

It drowns out the sound of the engine, so we see the van before we hear it. The greyish-green van jerks to a stop right in front of us, music pouring out of it like a physical presence.

Behind the wheel, a woman with flaxen hair. She gets out of the car, all that wild hair flying, and she walks straight toward the three of us.

Nikki.

I knew it, I always knew it. I felt it in my heart, just like Mom did.

Portia takes a step back. I take a step forward because she must be coming to me, to see me, to hug me.

Instead she goes straight to Eddie. He welcomes her into his arms and I watch, with horror, as he kisses her on the mouth. Not a sister kiss. A deep, passionate kiss. At the same time, Eddie reaches up and pulls off her flaxen hair.

A wig.

Dark hair tumbles down, settling around her shoulders.

Krista.

It feels like my knees are about to buckle all over again, that's how strong the disappointment is. The heartbreak.

"Surprise," Eddie says.

"What. The. Fuck." Portia's voice is loud. Angry.

"You know, I'm glad you took those bullets," Eddie says. "You just saved me from a big complication."

Krista looks at him. "Complication?"

Her voice sounds different, harder than it was before. Not bubbly at all.

"No worries, baby. I'll explain later," Eddie says. Then he turns to us. "I was never going to kill either one of you. But if necessary, our long-lost sister will."

"That makes zero sense," Portia says.

Eddie smiles down at Krista, who beams back at him. "You ever watch those crime documentaries? Like on Netflix or Hulu?"

As the conversation takes a turn for the

weird, Portia and I exchange a look.

"If you haven't, you should," Eddie says. "I'm talking about Ruby Ridge, Waco, Columbine, the Central Park Five . . . All of them have one thing in common. In every single one of those cases, the media got it wrong. Completely wrong. The story you think you know isn't the story at all." He turns to Krista and says, "Isn't that right, baby?"

"That's right," she says.

"Take Richard Jewell. The bombing at the Atlanta Olympics. Remember that?"

We all remember that, except maybe Portia. It happened a few years before the road trip, when we lived in Atlanta, just a few miles from the Olympic Park. The bombing and what happened afterward was the first big news story of my life. Day in and day out, we watched coverage of the bombing and the summer Olympics together, like they were the same thing.

"First he was a hero, then he was a suspect," Eddie says. "And it was all because of the media. They decided he had to be guilty because he was the one who *discovered the bomb.* They said he made himself into being the hero. Lies, all lies. He didn't do a single thing wrong, but the whole country thought he was guilty."

True. Richard Jewell was the guy, without a doubt. Even Tom Brokaw said it, and our parents loved Tom Brokaw.

"So just imagine," Eddie continues. "What the media would do if they thought some long-lost psychotic girl returned to kill her siblings in the desert? Obviously someone has to survive to tell that story, am I right?" Using the gun, he points to himself. "And since I'm the only man — much bigger and stronger than either of you — it only makes sense that I'm the sole survivor."

I shake my head, still trying to clear it from the meltdown Krista almost gave me. And their plan starts to make sense.

Who better to seek revenge than the sister we left in the woods? A demented, angry, and now homicidal sister. Everyone will be looking for the girl with the flaxen hair. No doubt she's been caught on traffic cameras around the country. The media is going to love it.

"You've been setting us up the whole time," Portia says.

"Got that right," Krista says. "Who do you think stole the ashes? Carved on the tree?" Her eyes land on me. "Or put that cell phone in the woods?"

"I have to admit," Eddie says to me. "We tried to mess with you so much, I wasn't sure you'd make it. You're so delusional about Nikki, I was pretty sure you'd have a breakdown. The fact that you're still here and still standing is pretty impressive."

Eddie and Krista look so happy, so proud of themselves. She has her arms wrapped around him, and I get a glimpse of the gun tucked in the waistband of her shorts.

Of course. That's the gun for us, not Eddie's. If it comes to that.

"But you won't kill us," I say, working out their plan in my head. "If we agree to give you all the money."

Eddie points at me with his empty gun. "Well, well, well. Look who grew a brain."

"Dick," Portia says. "I can put you in jail. Then you get nothing anyway."

"You'll die first. No way that's going to happen," Eddie says. "You must know that if you can get into my phone, I can get into yours. That e-mail to the IRS is going nowhere."

She shuts her mouth because it's true. The devil's rope just got tighter, and it doesn't feel good.

For the second time today, I find myself saying, "Well done."

"Thank you," Eddie says. "Although, I thought it might be a little poetic if you did die. Then your name would be linked to

Nikki's forever."

Krista laughs.

"That's cruel," I say.

"So is life, but what can you do?" Eddie says with a shrug. "Are we good here? You're both going to give me your inheritance, am I right?" He points to the car, toward the bloody shirt and the ashtrays. "And remember, if either of you get out of line, just know I can always blame her death on you. Maybe it won't stick, but it'll make your lives a lot more difficult." He looks at me. "Especially since it was your T-shirt."

Either way this goes, we're screwed and Eddie wins. If he kills us, Nikki gets the blame. If we try to screw him, he'll use that evidence to claim one of us killed her. Turns out he's the smart one.

Portia crosses her arms and sticks her chin out, just like Nikki used to do. "Fine. You fucker."

We're at end of the trip, and I won't get any money. My husband is dead and so is Nikki. Nothing left to do but shrug. "Take the money," I say.

"Phone," Eddie says to Portia. "Now."

Portia tosses her phone. It skims across the dirt and lands near his feet. Eddie picks it up and says, "Code."

She hesitates.

"Code," he says again. He no longer sounds like Dad, he sounds like Grandpa.

She gives it to him and he swipes through the phone, deleting the e-mail she had set up to go to the IRS. He hands it to Krista, who smiles and puts it in her pocket without asking what it's all about.

Interesting.

"Perfect, perfect. See how easy that was? No one has to die today," Eddie says.

"Oh baby," Krista says, looking up at him with those big brown eyes. "You're wrong about that."

Eddie tries to answer but doesn't get the chance. Krista is too quick. She reaches behind her, pulling the gun out of the waistband of her shorts. It happens so fast I almost miss it.

Krista shoots Eddie in the head.

His body drops with a thump. It feels like the ground shakes beneath my feet, making me queasy.

Krista turns to us. Her face is splattered with blood.

Eddie's body is right here, still warm, and I can't help but think he deserved it.

"Oh my God, oh my God," Portia says. She covers her face with her hands and keeps saying that like a mantra. "Oh my God, oh my God, oh my God."

We're going to die. Krista is going to shoot both of us.

I can't speak, but if I could, I would tell Krista to shoot me first. For selfish reasons. I don't want to see Portia die.

"Sorry, ladies," Krista says, walking closer to us. "Well, actually I'm not sorry, because you're both horrible. You really shouldn't have been so mean to me on the trip. Although it wouldn't have saved you, and

I'd have to kill you anyway because you both just saw what I did, and damned if I'm going to trust you to keep your mouth shut."

"Wait," Portia says.

"But if you had been nicer," Krista says. "The last words you hear wouldn't be *fuck you.*"

Krista shoots Portia in the head.

Executed. We're being executed.

I step back out of instinct, out of some base-level desire to live. I step back because that's what you do when someone points a gun at your head.

I make myself stop. No running, no trying to talk her out of it, no attempt to grab the gun. Instead, I stare at her, this woman I don't even recognize. The one with blood on her face and dirt brown eyes. There are no gold flecks in them now.

The real Krista.

This was her plan. All along, this is what she was going to do. "You were going to kill us no matter what we agreed to," I say. "Even Eddie. He was always going to die."

Krista smiles.

"The money," I say. "You just want the money."

"Damn straight I want it. Do you have any idea what it's like to grow up so poor that people laugh when you walk by?"

497

I shake my head no.

"I do. I know what it's like to wear clothes that don't fit because everything came from a charity box. Or to be so hungry, a piece of bread is practically a meal." She stops for a second, taking a deep breath. "As soon as I realized your asshole of a brother would gamble everything away, I had to kill him. To kill all of you. Opportunities like this don't come around more than once."

She's right, they don't. I almost hope she gets away with it. She would do more with the money than any of us would have.

I just don't think she'll get the chance.

"One thing," I say. "Just do one last thing."

Krista stares at me, waiting.

What I should tell her is that although she may get away with blaming Nikki for a while, it won't last forever. Richard Jewell was exonerated for everything. Even NBC News had to pay him for what Tom Brokaw said.

The same thing will happen to her.

It may have seemed like a brilliant plan at first, but it won't work for long. If I were a gambler like my brother, I'd bet the police would figure it out in less than a week. All it will take is one slip, one camera that caught Krista without her wig on — better yet, putting the wig on — and she'll be done.

498

Maybe Netflix will even make a show about it.

I don't tell her any of this. One way or the other, she'll know soon enough.

But I do have something to say.

"Tell my mother I never stopped looking," I say. "Please." It sounds like I'm begging because I am.

Krista says nothing, not one word. Her finger tightens on the trigger.

I close my eyes and wait for the silence. I'm ready for it.

Here we are, at the end, and we still don't know who the heroine is. You'll have to figure that one out for yourself.

AUTHOR'S NOTE

He Started It is, in many ways, a journey. Not just a journey for the family of characters but also a journey through much of the United States. For me, that meant doing a lot of research about where to go and what to see.

First, I have to note that with the exception of national chains like the Holiday Inn and Applebee's, all of the motels and restaurants are fictional.

Second, all of the attractions, tourist sites, and museums in this book are real. From Helen Keller's house in Alabama to the Codger Pole in Washington, every one of these places is open to the public. And they are amazing! There are so many fun, unusual things to see in this country that it would be impossible to visit them all. The ones in *He Started It* are just a small selection of what is out there.

Much of my research was done online, so

I must give a very big thanks to *Roadside America, Only in Your State, Trip Advisor,* and *Wikipedia* for providing all the facts about so many attractions across the country.

Because this is a work of fiction, I did take a bit of creative license with one particular location. The UFO Watchtower in Center, Colorado, first opened for business in May of 2000. The first road trip in *He Started It* took place nine months earlier, in August of 1999. I wanted to include this attraction enough to fudge the date just a little in order to use it.

I highly recommend everyone stop and see all of these wonderful places if you have a chance!

ACKNOWLEDGMENTS

They said the second book is the hardest. They said it would be so much worse than the first. I heard all of this before beginning to work on *He Started It* and I didn't believe them. After all, I wrote several books before *My Lovely Wife* was published. This wasn't my first rodeo.

Now that I've been through the second book, I can say without a shadow of a doubt:

They were right.

That means I have an extraordinary number of people to thank for making this book a reality.

Beginning with my incredible agent, Barbara Poelle, who listened to me vent an untold number of times throughout the process of getting this book completed — and somehow she is *still* my agent. I couldn't ask for anyone better.

My editor, Jen Monroe. With a never-ending amount of patience and skill, she

503

managed to guide this book from what was basically a first draft into a finished novel (and she dragged me kicking and screaming the whole way).

Lauren Burnstein, my publicist at Berkley, who I swear gets more done in a day then I get done in a week. She manages to get the most amazing coverage for my books.

Fareeda Bullert and Jessica Mangicaro, the marketing wizards of Berkley who perform miracles. I don't know how they do what they do, but I am grateful for it.

My copyeditor, Scott Jones, who not only checks my grammar but fact-checked every single thing in the book and I am so happy he did!

Emily Osborne and Anthony Ramondo, who are the most incredible cover designers on the planet.

A big thanks to Joel Richardson and the whole Michael Joseph team in the UK, who have done such a fantastic job promoting both *My Lovely Wife* and *He Started It*.

Over the past couple of years, I have met so many talented and amazing authors. Several have been kind enough to read early copies of this book and provide wonderful blurbs for it. Thank you to Mary Kubica, Christina McDonald, Kaira Rouda, Wendy

Walker, Hannah Mary McKinnon, Samantha Bailey, Michele Campbell, Mark Edwards, and Maureen Connelly. Your words are invaluable!

I also have to thank all of the amazing booksellers I was able to meet this year, and I was so lucky to visit some of your amazing bookstores. A special thanks to Garden District Books in New Orleans; Murder by the Book in Houston; Anderson's in LaGrange, Illinois; Book Passage in Corte Madera, Calfornia; and Boswell Book Company in Milwaukee. Many, many thanks to Pamela Klinger-Horn, Britton Trice, Mary O'Malley, Daniel Goldin, the Petrocelli family, and McKenna Jordan for being such wonderful supporters.

To the book bloggers, bookstagrammers, online reviewers, and podcasters: No author would be where they are without all of you!

To the readers, the wonderful people who have this book in their hands: Thank you for coming on this journey with me. I cannot express how grateful I am.

I would never have been published without the help and support of my two main writing besties, Rebecca Vonier and Marti Dumas, who always tell me the truth. I can't ask for more than that.

My day job "work family" has been incredibly supportive of my new career, and for this I am so thankful.

Last but never least, my family. I would not be here at all without your love and support!

ABOUT THE AUTHOR

Samantha Downing currently lives in New Orleans, where she is furiously typing away on her next thrilling book.